Frontier: The Untold Clark Expedition

Nicholas Kane

Copyright © Nicholas Kane 2025.

The right of Nicholas Kane to be identified as the author of this work has been asserted by him in accordance with the Copyright, Designs and Patents Act, 1988.

First published in 2025 by Holand Press.

To the explorers of the Corps of Discovery, whose courage and resilience charted the uncharted and expanded the boundaries of a young nation.

FACTS

In 1803, President Thomas Jefferson purchased over 828,000 square miles of land from Napoleon's France.

Known as the Louisiana Purchase, the transaction drastically increased the size of the United States. But the general public had mixed emotions about the deal.

To help win support, Jefferson ordered an expedition through the territory, all the way to the Pacific Ocean. Known as the Corps of Discovery, the expedition was led by Captain Meriweather Lewis and Second-Lieutenant William Clark.

During this time, there were stories among mountain men describing a creature that lurked within the forests. This creature was described as a large, hairy humanoid and was said to inhabit the remote mountainous regions of the Pacific Northwest. The stories often involved eerie encounters and sightings by trappers and explorers, and occasionally, attacks.

While many dismissed these stories as nothing more than wild tales spun by men who had spent too much time alone in an unforgiving wilderness, others swore by the truth of their experiences and warned others not to encroach upon the lands where these beasts roamed, waiting to be discovered—or to discover those who dared seek them out.

"In the end, we are all left to ponder the inexplicable mysteries that haunt the edges of our understanding."

-Unknown

"We came across the slaughtered men in the early evening. The gruesome sight left images in my mind I will never forget. The mutilated bodies of the Spanish soldiers strewn across the grasslands; their uniforms stained red with blood. Evident signs of a savage attack marred the scene, with claw marks etched deep into the earth. Only the beasts could have wrought such devastation, and their presence left a lingering sense of fear among us all."

-Excerpt from Meriwether Lewis's Secret Journal

FRONTIER

PRELUDE

October 1809
Charlottesville, Virginia

Under the cold light of the moon, William Clark drove his horse up a winding dirt path toward the top of the mountain. The stillness of the forest was unnerving, broken only by the rhythmic thudding of hooves against the rocky ground. At the summit, a sprawling mansion came into view, its shadow stretching long over the hillside. Clark pulled on the reins, his breath visible in the cool night air. He paused as a small gaggle of slaves meandered by on their way to one of the smaller outbuildings on the periphery of the grounds. One of them glanced over their shoulder, his eyes meeting Clark's for a fleeting moment, before turning back toward the small path that led to the slave quarters in the distance.

He turned his attention back to the mansion. A faint glow flickered in one of the home's windows—a sign the man he had come to see was still awake. Thunder rumbled in the distance, a storm brewing on the horizon. He urged his horse toward the barn at the edge of the estate and dismounted, tying the reins before walking briskly toward the front door. The creak of the door swinging open startled him, and a figure stepped into view, silhouetted against the dim light within. Both men paused for a moment, taking in the sight of one another. Tall and lean, the man's presence was imposing despite his age, and his hazel eyes, though sullen, held an enigmatic depth that looked as if they had witnessed a century's worth of secrets. He wore a rich, cherry-colored robe with blue trim, his hand gripping a steaming mug. Despite the lateness of the hour, he exuded calm.

"General Clark," the man said, a small smile tugging at his lips. "I knew you'd come. It's been too long."

"A few years, sir," Clark replied, ascending the porch steps. Thomas Jefferson stepped aside, allowing him to enter.

Upon stepping into the grand foyer of the mansion, Clark found himself in awe of the refined elegance and classical beauty of the home. The walls were adorned with intricate moldings and delicate frescoes, depicting scenes from ancient mythology and the natural world. Tall windows draped with rich velvet curtains allowed glimpses of the moon-painted landscape outside, casting soft beams of light across the polished marble floors. The air was redolent with the scent of beeswax and lavender, mingling with the faint aroma of old books and fine tobacco. A crackling fire burned in the hearth of a nearby room, casting dancing shadows upon the walls and bathing the room in a soft, welcoming glow.

"Let's talk in my study," Jefferson said, leading Clark into a room lined with bookshelves, relics, and maps.

As they entered, Clark's eyes landed on an intricate device atop the desk. "I've never seen a desk like this," he muttered.

"A polygraph desk," Jefferson explained, "for making copies of all my correspondence." But Clark's attention had already drifted. His gaze locked on a model keelboat in the corner of the room—a replica of the one he had captained up the Missouri River years before. His fingers grazed its smooth surface, memories flooding back.

"It's an exact likeness," Jefferson noted. "You remember those days well, I'm sure."

Clark chuckled softly, though his heart felt heavy. "Too well." His eyes shifted to the maps hanging on the wall—sketches he had drawn of the Louisiana Territory years earlier during the expedition. "You kept them."

"Of course. I made sure they came here after I left Washington City," Jefferson replied, strolling over to meet Clark in front of the maps. "The Corps of Discovery lives on through those maps and the other items scattered about this old house. I've made sure of that."

Clark stole himself, trying to fight back the wave of emotions he felt at seeing the replica of the boat he had once rode on up the Missouri River into the vast unknown wilderness of Western America. He peered around at the glass cases positioned around the study, each housing a treasure trove of specimens he and others had collected during the expedition—pressed flowers, animal pelts, and Native artifacts—all preserved as a reminder of the incredible journey he had undertaken years before.

He allowed himself another few moments of reflection before turning around to face Jefferson. The president's gaze met his, causing him to pause momentarily, unsure of how to begin.

"I received your letter," Clark announced quietly, "...about Meri."

Now it was Jefferson's turn to pause. He motioned for Clark to follow him back to his desk where the two men sat down across from another. Jefferson quickly brushed aside a letter he had been working on and placed it inside one of the desk's drawers. He then lifted another letter up out of the drawer and placed it down atop the desk for Clark to see.

"I received this from a friend in Tennessee three weeks ago. It details what was found in Captain Lewis' hotel room and the manner of death in which he died. I left those details out of the letter I sent to you in case the letter was intercepted."

Clark frowned. "Intercepted? By whom?"

"To be honest, General, I do not know."

Clark sighed and reached down to examine the letter. His hands trembled slightly as he read. "A gunshot wound...to the head." His voice was strained. "Was it suicide?"

"That's the consensus," Jefferson said, though his eyes betrayed doubt.

"And what do you believe?"

Jefferson hesitated, then smiled faintly. "I don't know. He was troubled—haunted, even. It was certainly no secret Captain Lewis' drinking had worsened over the years. And his debts were significant. But I can't help but wonder if there was more to it. A man like Meriwether Lewis doesn't simply unravel."

Clark paused as memories of the expedition flooded his mind. "You didn't see the things we saw..." He noticed a grave look flash across Jefferson's face. He let out a sigh, frustration mingling with grief. "Or maybe it was simpler. A robbery. He was traveling a dangerous route."

"Perhaps," Jefferson agreed, "but there are...complications." He handed Clark another letter, this one from President Madison.

"President Madison informed me months ago that Captain Lewis had been soliciting the War Department for payments he felt were owed to him by the government."

Clark's pulse quickened as he read. "He'd never do that."

"Desperation changes a man," Jefferson said gravely. "And if his threats were serious, if he was truly ready to reveal the secret of the expedition…that changes everything."

Clark leaned back, his mind reeling. The memories, long buried, resurfaced—images of the creatures they had encountered in the dark forests, the unspoken terror they had shared. "The Federalists would have never believed him. It's madness."

Jefferson gave a slight nod as he snatched up the letter and put it back in the drawer. He then picked up another and handed it to Clark. "I would tend to agree with that assessment, if not for this letter I received from President Madison in June." Clark snatched the letter and began reading through it. His eyes widened as he neared the end. When he was finished, he handed it back over to Jefferson, who waited for him to respond.

"Meri threatened to go to the Federalists if he wasn't paid?"

"He threatened to tell them everything that transpired on your journey." Jefferson sighed and leaned back in his chair. "The president and I had been working with a few men inside the Treasury Department to find a way to quietly get Captain Lewis his money. We had collected nearly the amount he had demanded, and he was on his way to Washington to collect it when he was killed."

Clark soaked in the troubling news about his friend. The two men had grown estranged over the years and he knew Lewis had been having problems. The excessive drinking had become worse in the years since their return and had cost Lewis his friends and family. He had certainly felt pity for his friend, but there had been little he could do. He felt especially guilty knowing the cause of Lewis's pain and why he had turned to the bottle to make the images in his mind go away—it was a terrible secret they were cursed to keep for the rest of their lives. But the fact Lewis would threaten to expose that secret to settle his increasing debts angered him.

FRONTIER

"I can't believe Meri would threaten to go to the Federalists and expose the secret."

Jefferson exhaled and stared quietly back at him. "The President believed he would, which is why he tried to get him the money."

"Even if he did expose the secret, he has no proof. No one would believe him."

"Perhaps not. But the very mention of what happened and the allegations of a cover-up by me and everyone else involved at the time would have been enough for the Federalists to open an investigation. And who knows what would have come from it. After the election last year, the Federalists are more determined than ever to unseat Mr. Madison in three years. Captain Lewis' stories about Republican cover-ups and secret expeditions into the West could have been enough to achieve that objective." Jefferson's face wore a grave expression as he peered back at Clark through the candlelight. "There was even some speculation that Captain Lewis was ready to turn over a secret journal to Senator Pickering when he got to Washington."

He eyed Jefferson with a degree of skepticism. "A secret journal?

Jefferson nodded.

"That's nonsense. If he had kept such a journal, I would have seen it."

Jefferson grinned, and then slowly, reached down into the same desk drawer as before and raised up an old, beaten, brown leather-bound journal, which he placed softly on the desk in front of him. Clark tried to hide his astonishment as leaned in and picked it up. He quickly began scanning through the pages.

"That was delivered to me two days ago by a man claiming to be an acquaintance of Captain Lewis. He told me the captain had instructed him to deliver the journal should anything happen to him on his way to Washington. When I asked his name, he refused. All he said was keep the journal safe, nothing more."

Clark set the journal back on the desk. He exhaled slowly, the weight of Jefferson's words settling in. The story was unbelievable, almost absurd. But then again, so were the things they had encountered in the wilderness. Things the world would never believe. "I don't want to believe it," he muttered, shaking his head. "But Meri...he wasn't himself. The drinking, the debt..."

Jefferson's gaze was steady. "I believe Captain Lewis might have been willing to trade that journal—secrets and all—if he thought it would clear his debts."

He flinched at the thought. The journal, filled with accounts of the unimaginable, was more generous than any map or artifact from their journey. It held the truth of what they had witnessed—a truth that was never meant to leave the shadowy forests of the Upper Louisiana Territory. He forced a small nod as he glanced over at a glass case containing a pair of pressed flowers he had retrieved during the expedition somewhere along the Great Plains. He smiled, trying to hold onto one of the few bright memories from those times.

"I'm afraid I have one more piece of information to share with you," Jefferson announced.

Clark turned his head. "There's more to all of this?!"

"Captain Lewis wrote to me a few days before he died. He said he was in New Orleans and was on his way to Washington to collect his payment. But he also wrote that he thought he was being followed, but he couldn't be sure. When I read it, I thought nothing of it. Just the fantasies of a broken, drunken man. But considering what's happened...I worry Captain Lewis was not being paranoid. Perhaps, men *were* following him, and that is why he is dead."

Clark let out an exasperated sigh. "I'm sorry, sir, that's just...hard to believe."

Jefferson returned a grim nod.

"I mean, are we to believe there is some kind of conspiracy at play amongst Meri and the Federalists?" He scoffed and glanced back down at the battered journal in front of him. "The Federalists would have nothing to gain by murdering Meri. He was a beaten down man. I am more ready to believe the bottle finally did him in than some covert Federalist scheme to expose the truth of what happened during the expedition."

"I agree with you, General. It could very well be that Captain Lewis simply could not continue living with his demons and finally succumbed to the thoughts that live in the darkest recesses of a man's mind. If so, he is at peace and his journal is secure with us. But if there was a conspiracy to steal his journal and force the secrets he bore out into the light, then we must prepare ourselves against it."

"You believe they will come for it?"

Jefferson took a deep breath and exhaled slowly. "It's possible."

Clark let out a nervous laugh as he tried to mask the feeling of apprehension and fear that was slowly taking hold of him. He had fought monsters in the shadows before, he did not relish having to do so again.

"I want you to take the journal," Jefferson said, eyeing the beaten journal still laying atop the desk in front of Clark.

"Me? Why should I take it?"

"Captain Lewis was your friend. I think he would have wanted you to have it."

Clark eyed the journal for a moment, letting his memories of Lewis creep toward the forefront of his brain. "It should be destroyed. We can burn it in the fire right now. Relegate whatever's written inside to the ash heap. It's horrible enough the events of what happened still live in the mind of me and the other men who survived. Why curse someone else with that knowledge?"

"You may do with it as you wish."

"If what's written in these pages were to ever be revealed to the public…" He stopped for a moment, studying the worn leather of the journal. "No one would ever set foot in Louisiana again. We should turn it over to President Madison. Or Minister Monroe."

Jefferson waved him off. "I will not give it to either man, especially Mr. Monroe."

"Then give it to President Madison, he can keep it safe in the President's House in Washington." He glanced up at Jefferson and could tell he was having none of it. With a reticent hand he reached forward and grabbed the journal and stuffed it inside his coat. "Now it is I who will wear the target on my back."

"Keep it safe. You know the implications should it fall into the wrong hands."

Clark nodded, a look of solemn understanding washing across his face. He had spent years trying to preserve the secret of what they had discovered during their journey into the Western wilderness—a secret that still kept him up most nights tossing and turning in his bed.

Later that evening, he retreated to the small guest room assigned to him on the second floor of the mansion. The room, though modest in size, exuded an air of quiet elegance and comfort.

As he entered, the warm glow of candlelight flickered across the walls. The furnishings were simple yet refined, with a sturdy oak bed adorned with crisp white linens standing against one wall. A woven rug covered the polished wood floor, muffling the sound of his footsteps as he crossed the room. A small writing desk sat nestled in a corner, its surface cluttered with papers and quill pens. A small oil lamp provided a soft, steady light, giving the room a warm, inviting glow. On the opposite wall, a tall, narrow window looked out onto the moonlit landscape beyond. He reached up and pulled the curtains closed, shutting out the darkness of the night. He took off his coat and settled into the plush armchair by the window. He felt a sense of solace wash over him. Despite the uncertainty he felt after his evening with Jefferson, there was still a quiet serenity to be found within the walls of the mansion.

He reached over to where his coat hung loosely over the back of the chair and removed the journal. He let it rest on his lap as his mind raced with thoughts about everything he had just learned. He thought of Meri, his friend, and all they had gone through together. He closed his eyes and breathed a silent prayer for guidance and strength. He could almost feel the weight of the moment pressing down upon his shoulders. It seemed to him that with each passing moment, the secrets of the past were drawing nearer, and he feared there would soon be no way to hold them back. But despite whatever challenges and dangers were ahead, he quietly resolved to face them head on and do what he could to protect the dark secret held within him. For the truth of their expedition, and the legacy of his dear friend Meriwether Lewis, depended on it.

Slowly, he opened the journal, took in a deep breath, and began to read…

FRONTIER

ONE

Spring 1804

Camp Wood, located within the sparse Illinois Territory, stood as a modest yet bustling outpost on the edge of the American frontier. Situated amidst rolling hills and evergreen forests, the camp exuded an air of rugged simplicity. The camp's buildings, constructed from rough-hewn timber and sturdy logs, sat within a wooden palisade encircling the perimeter. Guard towers manned by soldiers overlooked the surrounding landscape scanning the horizon for any signs of danger. Near the center of the camp stood a large log cabin, which served as the camp's headquarters, and next to that, a mess hall bustled with activity as cooks prepared the morning's meals for the men, their savory aromas wafting through the crisp morning air.

As the early morning sun rose higher above the horizon, Second-Lieutenant William Clark stood quietly at the end of a long line of canvas tents erected in neat rows along the outer edge of the camp, the sun's rays casting a halo around his tall, lean frame. With piercing blue eyes, the lieutenant possessed a gaze that conveyed both intelligence and determination. His hair was a vibrant shade of chestnut, though gray streaks had begun to appear at the temples, and his skin appeared weather-beaten, a result of spending years living along the frontier. He wore buckskin trousers and a simple cotton shirt, covered by a weather-beaten coat to ward off the early morning chill. A wide-brimmed hat shaded his face from the harsh glare of the sun as he turned to look back at the neat row of tents behind him.

As he turned, he noticed his slave, York, approaching from the center of the camp, his dark skin contrasting sharply with the uniforms of the soldiers around him. He had inherited York from his father's estate in Virginia many years ago, and he had accompanied him on many expeditions across the Mississippi River over the years and proven a dependable and capable servant. Despite his status as a slave, there was a quiet dignity in his bearing Clark had come to admire, and it commanded respect from all who knew him.

"The men are awake, sir," York announced when he got closer. Clark simply nodded and began walking forward to meet him.

"I want to be loaded up and ready to go by midday. Make sure no one's slacking in their duties. Captain Lewis is waiting for us in St. Louis."

York smiled. "The Captain couldn't wait to get his hands on that city, could he?"

Clark nodded with a grin. They had been prepared to make camp outside of St. Louis the previous autumn, but the overzealous Spanish authorities, still smarting over the recent sale of the territory to the United States, had refused them access, stating pointedly that the city and land surrounding it, was Spanish territory until the following spring. Clark had laughed at the pettiness of the Spanish and their quibbling over trivial matters concerning the recent Louisiana treaty, but there had been little they could do. And so, they had set-up their winter quarters on the American side of the Mississippi, along a long stretch of flat land that gave them an unobstructed view of St. Louis on the other side. In March, Lewis and a handful of others had crossed the river and set-up a new camp in the city once the Spanish officials officially retired from the territory. Now, as Clark took a moment to gaze across the river's sparkling waters to the land along the river's western edge, he couldn't help but smile knowing it now belonged to the United States.

He looked back toward York, who was also peering out across the river. "Will we have enough supplies to get us to the Rockies before winter?"

York asked, still peering across the river.

"We'll hunt for food once we make it up the Missouri," Clark reassured him. "We can trade with the Sioux for whatever we'll need. The President provided me with an assortment of items to trade with any natives we encounter in the region. He wants to cultivate warm and friendly relations with all the western tribes."

"That's assuming the tribes we encounter are friendly," York replied with a tinge of sarcasm in his voice. "I've heard stories about the Sioux and their lack of friendliness toward white folks."

FRONTIER

Clark smiled. "Then we'll just have to have you lead in any negotiations."

Together, they made their way down to the riverbank. As they approached, the expanse of the Mississippi River stretched out before them, its waters shimmering in the golden light of the morning sun. Along the muddy banks, a cluster of boats bobbed gently in the current. Clark could see the largest boat, a sturdy keelboat he had nicknamed *The Western Explorer*. The boat's hull stretched out like a long serpent, its sails furled and its oars at the ready. His eyes scanned its length, noting the supplies and provisions neatly stacked on deck, ready for the journey ahead. Beside it, several small pirogues floated in the water, their compact frames offering a stark contrast to the imposing presence of the keelboat.

As they drew closer, the sound of men's voices echoed across the water, mingling with the creaking wood and the flap of canvas in the breeze. Men bustled about, securing lines, and loading cargo, their movements precise and efficient as they prepared each boat for departure. Clark couldn't help but smile at the scene before him, men going about their work, their faces weary yet determined. His chest swelled with pride as he stepped down onto the muddy banks of the river and approached the cluster of men, each eyeing him nervously as he and York inspected the boats. He knew most of them. Many had come from the enlisted ranks of the Army when offered the opportunity to not only earn more money and receive large land tracts, but to explore the vast, uncharted interior of the continent. Together with Lewis, he had traveled down the Ohio River from Pittsburgh, offering the men living in the small towns and hamlets along the river the chance of a lifetime and the promise of the greatest adventure they would ever have. Now, as he stood in the bright spring sunlight watching the men of the Corps of Discovery ready their boats for their journey across the river to St. Louis, he felt a new surge of pride and anticipation grip him. He looked at York with a smile, and then hopped up onto the deck of *The Western Explorer* where he called out for the men to gather around him.

"Huddle up, men," he commanded, his voice carrying across the river. "We have a great adventure awaiting us up this river—one that will shape the destiny of our young nation. The prayers of your countrymen are with you on this endeavor, and I for one do not intend to disappoint them." The men listened with varying degrees of interest. A few vague nods answered his words, while the rest simply watched with quiet focus waiting for him to conclude his remarks. He expected as much. He knew of the thirty men standing before him, most were there for the promise of pay and glory, not the noble ideals espoused by him or President Jefferson, who had a personal interest in their expedition.

He let out a small sigh and offered the men a brief smile, as if telling them he understood they would rather finish their work than listen to him speak. "That is all." He watched as the men dispersed to resume their tasks. When they had all left, he hopped back down onto the riverbank, where York awaited him with a knowing grin.

"That went well," he teased, a twinkle in his eye. "I think you really endeared yourself to the men with that speech."

Clark laughed softly. "It doesn't matter. We'll have plenty of time to get to know each other over the next two years. I'm just looking forward to getting underway."

Glancing out at the river, he felt a surge of anticipation stir within him. "It's already May. We need to reach the Sioux lands by July if we are going to make it across the plains by autumn."

"We'll make it," York reassured him. "But either way, we're likely in for one devil of a winter in the Rockies."

Clark nodded in agreement. He felt a flicker of apprehension tempered by a genuine sense of excitement. He was well aware of the dangers that awaited them on their journey into the vast unknown, but despite that, he was determined to lead his men westward and reach the Pacific, no matter what perils lay ahead. For him, the journey was a test of endurance, but also an opportunity for discovery and adventure unlike any he had ever experienced before.

FRONTIER

TWO

As the keelboat glided gracefully along the surface of the Mississippi, Clark's eyes beheld the spectacle unfolding before him. St. Louis, with its muddy, dock-lined waterfront, was a mosaic of commerce, culture, and opportunity. Wooden structures lined the riverbank, consisting of trading posts, warehouses, and various merchant exchanges. The streets, though narrow, pulsed with life as merchants haggled over goods and traders from across the Mississippi Valley bartered furs, pelts, and other items brought back from beyond the edge of civilization. To the north and south and throughout the commercial district, wooden walls stood to guard against Indian attacks, a daily reminder to those who lived there of the dangers living on the frontier posed.

When the boat docked, Clark's eyes scanned the riverbank. Near the water's edge, roughly thirty yards down river, he spotted the familiar figure of Captain Meriweather Lewis. Dressed in a finely tailored uniform of the United States Army, Lewis stood with an air of authority as he moved about the mass of men and supplies slowly being loaded onto the expedition's boats tied up along the long wooden wharf that straddled the edge of the river. At his feet sat a large black and white Newfoundland dog with a mat of thick fur that glistened in the sunlight.

As Clark hopped down off the boat onto the dock, Lewis's gaze met his, and a smile spread quickly across his face. It took Clark only a few minutes to make his way toward Lewis and when the two men were finally face to face, each extended his arm toward the other.

"Will, it's good to see you. How was the journey down river?"

"Uneventful," Clark replied quickly, "but after six days on the river, I'm ready for some time on land."

Lewis chuckled. "You are aware we will be traveling up the Missouri for the next several months?"

"Yes," Clark replied with a grin, "but I try to put it out of my mind as much as I can." He knelt beside the dog and began scratching behind its large ears. "Hello there, Seaman," he said warmly. Seaman responded with a friendly woof, nuzzling his head against Clark's hand. "He seems ready to get underway."

Lewis nodded, his gaze turning toward the pirogues anchored nearby. "If we can ever get these boats loaded up."

Clark stood and began surveying the riverbank as the men continued loading supplies onto the expedition's boats. He was surprised to see their party had grown as large as it had. With the thirty men he had brought from across the river and what looked to be at least twenty men comprising Lewis' team, the Corps of Discovery would now consist of roughly fifty men. He had expected half that number. He looked back and saw the group of men he had come down river with from Camp Wood already starting to load more supplies onto *The Western Explorer*.

"If the weather holds, we should be able to depart by Monday, the fourteenth," Clark said as he turned back to face Lewis.

"The sooner we make it to the Sioux lands in the north the better. We don't want to get caught on the plains when winter sets in," Lewis replied in a distracted tone. His gaze returned to the wharf where a pile of oars was being loaded onto one of the pirogues. As he observed the men begin loading the oars, he furrowed his brow and shouted, "You there! This is hardly the time for drinking! We've work to do!"

Clark turned to see who Lewis was shouting at. He noticed a sturdy-built man with the weathered appearance of a seasoned traveler. But what caught Clark's attention immediately was the long scar etched across the right side of the man's face. The scarred man turned slowly; a small flask clasped in his right hand.

"Work, eh? I've worked these rivers more than you've breathed, Captain. A small sip won't hurt no one."

Lewis hurried down the small embankment they had been standing on and made his way toward the scarred man with a sense of purpose. Clark let out a long sigh and hurried after him.

"I don't care about your river tales," Lewis blurted out when he reached where the man was standing. "We have a serious expedition ahead, and I need every man under my command sober. What's your name, man?"

The scarred man straightened, a hint of defiance in his gaze.

"Name's Silas Thornfield. And I've seen more of this godforsaken country than you ever will."

FRONTIER

Clark, attempting to diffuse the situation, stepped between them. "Silas, is it? We appreciate your experience, but we also expect for you to show proper respect for both the captain and I, as well as the other men of rank in this expedition."

Thornfield let out a gruff laugh, taking another sip from his flask. "I've been beyond the Badlands, to the Rockies, and straight through to the Oregon Country. Ain't nothing I haven't seen. But mark my words, this journey of yours is foolishness."

"Foolishness, you say?" Lewis retorted. "We are well-prepared, Mr. Thornfield. We don't need the counsel of a man who can't keep his vices in check. And if you believe this expedition to be foolish, then why are you here?"

Thornfield scoffed. "A man needs money, don't he?" He took another long swig from the flask and then flashed them a wide grin. With slow deliberation, he traced one of his long fingers along the length of his scar. "You'll learn soon enough, Cap'n. Those forests beyond the plains ain't empty. They're filled with things you can't even imagine, not even in your worst nightmares."

Lewis raised an eyebrow. "Creatures in the woods? I assure you we can handle bears and the like. We have muskets, swords, pistols, and plenty of gunpowder."

Thornfield grinned cryptically. He exchanged a quick glance with Clark before stuffing the flask back inside his dusty brown jacket. "I've said my piece." They watched as Thornfield ambled away. Lewis turned to Clark. "Forget about him, Will. We have preparations to attend to."

Clark nodded, his eyes lingering on the scarred man as he moved farther away. The man's warning echoed through his mind, casting a shadow on the excitement he had been feeling only minutes earlier. He had heard such tales of creatures in the woods before from the traders and fur trappers who traversed the Rockies, but he had always dismissed such stories as the fanciful imaginations of men who had nothing but time alone in the vast wilderness of the West. He expected Silas Thornfield to be no different. But for some perplexing reason, he couldn't shake off what the man had said. And what worried him even more was that he didn't completely disbelieve him, either.

THREE

As twilight descended upon the city, the people of St. Louis gradually made their way down to the river's edge to join in the grand celebration that was taking place for the Corps of Discovery as they prepared to embark into the unknown. The riverfront, normally a bustling hub of activity, had been transformed into a vibrant spectacle of color and sound. Lanterns and torches cast a warm glow over the gathering crowd, illuminating the eager faces of the men, women, and children who had gathered to join in the festivities. Banners fluttered proudly in the evening breeze, emblazoned with the American eagle and the image of President Thomas Jefferson. Booths and stalls had been erected along the water, offering an array of provisions and supplies for the men of the expedition. Merchants hawked their items with enthusiastic cries, tempting each passerby with everything from jerky and hardtack to buffalo grease and cast-iron pans.

Clark leaned against the rough bark of a towering tree at the edge of the festivities, his arms crossed as his gaze lingered on the dark expanse of the Mississippi River. Beside him, Lewis stood with his hands clasped behind his back, his expression thoughtful as he recounted his meeting with President Jefferson the previous summer.

"You know, Will," Lewis began, his voice laced with both excitement and reverence, "the President made it abundantly clear that he views our mission as the most important endeavor in the history of the country. It's exhilarating, isn't it? To be part of something to grand!"

Clark nodded absently, his attention still fixed on the faint ripples of the river, their movements barely visible under the soft glow of the moon.

"The President wants us to find a northwest passage to the Pacific," Lewis continued, his voice growing more animated. "He stressed that it's our primary objective. That, and establishing friendly relations with the Indian tribes along the way." A faint smile tugged at his lips. "He even mentioned the possibility of discovering woolly mammoths. Can you imagine that? Woolly mammoths still roaming the earth."

"That would certainly be a sight," Clark said with a smile. He turned his gaze back toward Lewis. "But my thoughts keep drifting to the Indians. Most of these men—they're soldiers, yes—but they've never seen real combat. And as much as I hope for peace, we have no way of knowing how the tribes will react to our presence or the news that their lands now fall under the United States." He paused, his gaze turning to the bright lights of the campfires along the river. "If they turn hostile..." His voice trailed off, the weight of unspoken fears hanging in the cool night air. "God help us."

Lewis sighed, his eyes following Clark's toward the fires. "We'll take it one tribe at a time. We just have to hope for the best but be prepared for the worst."

Clark nodded faintly but didn't look reassured. After a moment, he spoke again, his voice quieter. "I keep thinking about what Silas said earlier."

Lewis raised an eyebrow and let out a scoff. "About the bears? As I told him then, we've got plenty of guns and ammunition to handle bears—or anything else lurking in those woods."

Clark gave a small nod, though his thoughts were far from settled. He had known men like Silas for years—grizzled frontiersmen with stories meant to unnerve green recruits for their own amusement. But there had been something different about Silas's warning—something in his tone and the way he looked at them. It wasn't the exaggerated jest of a seasoned man toying with the inexperienced. It had been serious, deliberate, as though he had spoken not to frighten but to prepare.

"Maybe," Clark said finally. "But Silas doesn't seem like a man who scares easily. And the way he said it...It didn't sound like a joke." His gaze returned to the river, its endless, unknowable depths mirroring the vast wilderness ahead of them. "It felt more like a warning."

A sudden eruption of cannon fire echoed across the river, drawing the attention of the gathered crowd. Laughter and cheers filled the night air as the men from the Corps of Discovery, caught up in the spirit of the evening's revelry, fired off more rounds from their rifles into the black waters of the Mississippi. Lewis chuckled. "Seems our men are in high spirits."

Clark grinned in agreement. "Aye, and rightly so. Tomorrow, we set out into the unknown, bound for lands uncharted. Let them have tonight. God knows it may be the last night like this we have for quite some time."

As the men continued to fire off rounds, Clark noticed a young man emerge from the throng of people, his figure illuminated by the flickering light of the campfires. He moved with purpose, his strides confident and eager as his eyes scanned the crowd as if searching for something—or someone. He wore a white linen shirt with the sleeves rolled up to reveal a pair of tanned, muscular forearms, while behind his back was slung a rifle, its polished wooden stock gleaming softly in the firelight. Clark raised his hand in greeting as the man approached.

"Meri," Clark said, nodding toward the young man as he drew near. "Looks like we have a visitor."

Lewis turned to follow Clark's gaze, his curiosity piqued. His eyes met those of the young man, who approached with a mixture of determination and nervousness evident in his demeanor. Clark motioned for the man to join them. "Come lad," he said warmly, "What brings you to us on this fine evening?"

The man hesitated for a moment, his gaze flickering between Lewis and Clark. "I've heard about your expedition," he began, his voice filled with a mixture of excitement and reverence. "I—I want to be part of it. To explore the unknown, to chart new lands…it's my dream."

Clark regarded the young man with interest as he exchanged glances with Lewis. "Well, son, we could always use another brave soul eager to venture into the wild unknown. Tell me, what's your name?"

"Peter. Peter Harrington."

"And what do you do, Peter?"

"I'm a blacksmith's apprentice, sir. Here in St. Louis."

Lewis looked the boy up and down before settling his gaze on the rifle. "Do you hunt as well?"

FRONTIER

The boy nodded eagerly. "Yes, sir, I do. Rabbits, mostly."

Lewis nodded, a smile growing across his lips. "Let's prove your marksmanship." He eyed Clark with a sly grin before straightening his back and gazing out toward a clump of trees fifty yards away. "You see that bent tree just over to the right?"

The boy squinted into the darkness for a moment, and then nodded.

"Shoot it from here."

The boy hesitated, and then slowly began loading his rifle. Lewis watched silently while Clark motioned for the other men to come over and watch the demonstration about to take place. The boy, with a nervous sigh, raised his rifle and took aim. Behind Clark, York stepped forward from the darkness and edged his way up to where Clark was standing and slowly leaned in.

"I've seen more skilled men in the Army miss shots from this distance," he whispered into Clark's ear. Clark nodded and glanced back over toward Lewis, who stood quietly waiting for the boy to fire. A few more seconds passed as a hushed silence gripped the group of spectators. There was a loud *crack* as the boy squeezed the trigger and fired. Clark's eyes darted toward the bent tree off in the distance. In a flash, splinters erupted, sending shards of wood flying in different directions. The boy lowered his rifle and flashed a wide grin as he turned to look back at Lewis, who offered his own smile back at the boy in return. The crowd erupted into applause as Clark stepped forward and patted the boy approvingly on the shoulder.

"Good job, lad," he said, looking back at Lewis.

Lewis nodded approvingly. "Not bad, young man, not bad at all. Tell me, how old are you?"

"Seventeen, sir."

"Married?"

"No, sir."

"Military experience?"

"No, sir."

Lewis nodded and stared quietly at the boy for a few more seconds. Peter shifted nervously as he re-slung his rifle behind his shoulder. Around them, the men of the expedition had returned to the festivities as more shots began to ring out across the darkened water of the Mississippi. Finally, Lewis let out a long sigh and stretched forth his hand toward Peter.

"Welcome to the Corps of Discovery, Private Harrington."

FRONTIER

FOUR

Excerpt from Lewis's Secret Journal

The Missouri River winds tirelessly through the heart of this vast wilderness, each bend revealing new wonders and challenges. As I sit to record our progress, the sun is already dipping below the horizon, casting the riverbanks in hues of orange and gold. The sight is breathtaking to behold.

We have traversed the expanse from St. Louis to the lands north of the Platte River, a journey fraught with both the expected and the unexpected. The landscape is constantly changing, and it commands a sense of reverence. Towering bluffs stand as sentinels, their shadows playing on the surface of the Missouri as our keelboat glides upstream. The air carries the scent of the untamed, and the symphony of unfamiliar birdcalls and rustling leaves is our constant companion. Our encounters with wildlife have been plentiful—deer, elk, and a myriad of avian species populate the riverbanks. Lieutenant Clark has bagged two deer already and rewarded the men with a feast two Friday's past.

The Indian tribes of these lands, thus far, have remained elusive to us. Our interactions on the river have been solely with fur trappers traveling south to St. Louis. One man was of great interest to us. His name is Pierre Dorian, and he has informed us he lived for a time with the Yankton Sioux in the northern lands of the Louisiana Territory and can speak their language. We have hired the man on as an interpreter and hope he will be of some use to us in the coming weeks and months. I can only pray the Sioux in the north will be hospitable to us when the time comes.

Our journey into the heart of the continent continues, guided by the promise of discovery and the unwavering spirit of exploration. It swells me with joy to rest tonight beneath the sprawling canopy of stars, contemplating the vastness of the unknown that stretches before us, waiting to be discovered and explored. What fortunate souls we are.

-Meriwether Lewis
July 31st, 1804

FIVE

Clark let out a groan of frustration as he watched the group of men in front of him scramble from one side of *The Western Star* to the other, trying to shift the weight on board enough to allow the large boat to turn and avoid a tree that had fallen across the river's eastern edge. The boat seemed to protest the sudden change in direction, its timbers groaning and creaking as it lurched hard to the left. Clark gazed down at the water as the boat's hull narrowly avoided colliding with the tree's sprawling branches. He let out a sigh as the boat straightened out safely in the middle of the river. The Missouri had seemed determined to force them back since their departure from St. Louis two months earlier, and as the expedition had pushed further upstream, it had become increasingly evident that the mighty waterway harbored a fierce determination to thwart their progress. Clark leaned back against the edge of the hull, his gaze sweeping over the weathered, sun-beaten faces of the crew around him. He felt their pain. Their journey up the river had been relentless, back breaking work. On days when the wind was at their back, they could at least raise the sail and travel close to twenty miles in a single day. But on windless, sun-soaked days such as this, they could expect to travel little more than five miles by late afternoon. And each day had brought with it new challenges. There were rapids to navigate, sandbars to evade, and shallows that crept up seemingly out of nowhere that threatened to ground their boats. Making matters worse were the mosquitos, which plagued them daily and seemed to thrive in the damp, marshy environments along the riverbank. Swarms of the relentless insects descended upon the crew every morning and remained with them throughout the day, their incessant buzzing filling the air and their sharp stings leaving behind welts on the exposed skin of the men. Despite the crew's best efforts to ward off the pests with smoky fires and makeshift mosquito nets, the insects remained a constant nuisance, their persistent presence a reminder of the unforgiving nature of the wilderness they were traversing.

FRONTIER

Clark glanced over at York who was approaching him from the bow, his figure cutting a striking contrast against the backdrop of the river. "Private Bratton still has some buffalo grease left for the mosquitos," he announced as he leaned slightly against the edge of the boat.

Clark nodded in appreciation. "Tell Private Bratton I appreciate the offer, but the stuff never works for me. I would just as rather not afflict my nostrils with the stench in addition to swatting away the pests."

York nodded understandingly, his gaze sweeping out across the water before returning to Clark. "We're past the mouth of the Platte now," he stated matter-of-factly. "This land is beautiful, shocking, and intimidating all at once. I've never seen anything like it."

Clark furrowed his brow, his expression thoughtful as he considered York's observation. "It's the lack of trees that worries me," he replied. "Without the cover of the forest, we're more exposed to the elements and any threats that may lurk nearby."

"You mean the Indians?" York asked, though he already knew the answer. Clark gave him a knowing nod and turned to glance out at the vast expanse of open prairie stretching out before them, the grasslands rolling in gentle undulations as far as the eye could see. It was a landscape unlike any he had ever encountered thus far—a seemingly endless sea of grass, teeming with life, but also fraught with uncertainty.

He turned back to York. "We've heard enough stories about the tribes of these lands and their encounters with white settlers to proceed with caution. Some are friendly, but others, like the Sioux, not so much."

Up ahead, one of the pirogues lurched suddenly to the right. Clark and York exchanged worried glances as they both shielded their eyes from the afternoon sun trying to get a better look at what was happening in front of them.

"What's happening?" Clark called out, his voice cutting through the commotion as he scanned the water ahead for any signs of danger.

"It's a sandbar!" came a reply from one of the crew members in the front of the keelboat. "They've run aground!"

Clark's jaw tightened as he surveyed the scene before him. The pirogue ahead of them, its hull grinding against the submerged obstacle, was in danger of becoming stranded if they didn't act quickly. "Get the poles!" he shouted as he ran toward the bow. "We need to help them push off before they're completely stuck!"

With a flurry of activity, the crew sprang into action, grabbing long poles and maneuvering them into position against the riverbed as *The Western Star* came up behind the nearly stranded pirogue. With each powerful thrust, they worked together to dislodge the pirogue from its precarious position, their muscles straining against the resistance of the water. Finally, with a collective heave, the pirogue broke free from the grip of the sandbar, its hull gliding smoothly back into the deeper waters. A chorus of cheers erupted from the crew as they celebrated their success, their faces flushed with exertion but also jubilation at their collective accomplishment. Clark gazed out across the watery expanse separating *The Western Star* with the pirogue. He spotted Lewis standing near the boat's stern, his face alight with a mixture of relief and pride. He waved at him with a smile. "I think that's enough excitement for one day, don't you, Captain?"

Lewis laughed in response and nodded. "I wholeheartedly agree, Lieutenant."

FRONTIER

SIX

Lewis watched as the last rays of sunlight dipped below the horizon, casting a golden farewell across the endless expanse of the plains. He stood at the edge of the camp, his gaze fixed on the distant horizon where the fiery orb of the sun sank lower and lower, painting the sky with hues of crimson and amber. In that fleeting moment, as day surrendered to night, he felt a deep connection to the land and the sky. He was but a transient visitor in this vast wilderness, yet in that moment of quiet contemplation, he felt a sense of belonging.

With a silent nod of reverence, he turned away from the fading light and made his way back to the warmth of the campfire. Around him, the camp was a hive of activity, illuminated by the warm glow of the many campfires and lanterns that emitted pockets of light in the gathering darkness. Near the river's edge, he spotted Clark and York, their figures silhouetted against the darkening waters as they cast their lines out in search of fish. The two men worked in tandem, their movements fluid and practiced. Off to the side, a group of men had gathered around a makeshift game of dice, their laughter ringing out into the night as they indulged in a moment of camaraderie and relaxation. Nearby, John Colter sat hunched over a journal, his quill scratching across the pages as he meticulously recorded the day's events. Lewis glanced over to his left and noticed George Drouillard motioning for him to join his group by the fire.

"Come, Captain, join us," Drouillard said as he gestured with his hands. Lewis smiled and approached the group. In the flickering light of the fire, he noticed the faces of Pierre Dorian, Peter Harrington, and Sergeant's Floyd and Ordway staring back at him.

"Peter here was just asking us when we would encounter some Indians," Drouillard said with a grin, his eyes twinkling with amusement. Harrington sheepishly glanced over at Lewis with an embarrassed expression.

"I thought we would have seen them by now, is all."

"I'm sure we will see them soon enough," Lewis replied calmly as he settled down on the ground next to Harrington.

"We crossed into Otoe lands days ago," Dorian interjected. "They know we are here. They're probably watching us at this very moment." He gazed out around him into the darkness. He turned back and grinned slyly at Harrington who shifted uncomfortably.

Drouillard let out a laugh. "Don't worry, lad, no harm will come to you. Not with Lieutenant Clark around."

Harrington gazed over at Drouillard with curiosity. "Has Lieutenant Clark fought Indians before?"

Drouillard glanced over at Lewis, his expression thoughtful, before turning back to Harrington with a knowing smile. "He's been in his fair share of scraps, hasn't he, Captain?"

Harrington turned to look at Lewis, awaiting a response.

Lewis smiled. "I met Lieutenant Clark in ninety-five. We served together under General Wayne fighting the Shawnee and Miami in Indiana Territory. There isn't a man alive I'd trust more in a battle."

"He was *Captain* Clark back then, wasn't he?" Drouillard asked with a sarcastic grin.

"Yes, he was a Captain then. He was demoted for drunkenly challenging the commanding officer of the regiment to a duel."

Drouillard and the others began to laugh while Harrington looked back at Lewis with a confused stare. "He actually did that?"

Lewis smiled. "Unfortunately, yes. It wasn't Will's finest hour."

"Still no better man at navigating this wilderness," Floyd offered as he leaned back slightly and began rubbing at his sides.

"The pain still there, Sergeant?" Lewis inquired, his voice laced with concern as he watched Floyd struggle to sit back up.

"Yes," he replied with a strained groan. "I tried that willow bark John Colter gave me yesterday and it's had no effect."

"Perhaps you need something stronger," Dorian said, holding out a flask. Floyd smiled and snatched the flask from his hand and took a swig. "Better," he said with a relieved sigh as he passed it back to Dorian.

As Lewis observed Floyd's discomfort, a sense of responsibility settled over him. He knew that in the coming days and weeks, he would have to keep a vigilant watch over the sergeant's condition. He prayed in his mind that whatever ailed the man would soon

FRONTIER

pass, but a part of him also recognized the dangers inherent in such afflictions, particularly when so far removed from the comforts of civilization. The wilderness held both peril and promise in equal measure.

SEVEN

The sun hung low in the sky as Clark and his companions traversed the sweeping plains, their boots kicking up clouds of dust that danced in the golden afternoon light. He tugged hard at the sling of his rifle as his eyes continued to stare down toward the horizon where the land seemed to stretch on endlessly.

"Keep your eyes peeled, boys," he called out, his voice carrying across the open expanse. "I'd like to bag an elk before nightfall."

A few yards away, Colter and York nodded in agreement as they scanned the horizon, their eyes searching the grassland for any sign of movement. Suddenly, a sharp *crack* shattered the silence, followed by the startled cry of an elk as it darted away toward.

"Dammit!" Clark cursed with frustration. "That's our dinner running off, Samuel!" From about thirty yards away the figure of Samuel Treadway rose from behind a clump of rocks and brush. He gave Clark an apologetic shrug. Clark shook his head in resignation, his gaze fixed in the direction the startled animal had run off in. But as he went to look back at Treadway, a sight caught his attention. He held his hand up over his forehead to block out the sun's rays and quickly realized what he was seeing and smiled. A vast herd of buffalo were thundering across the plains in the distance, their massive forms moving in perfect harmony with the rhythm of the earth.

"Look at that!" Colter shouted in awe as he stopped his horse and watched the buffalo herd thunder across the empty plains. Clark nodded and took a moment to take in the majestic sight before him. He had seen buffalo before but never a herd of this size all galloping together toward a destination only they knew. The image was enough to make man pause in awe. But as he stood there transfixed by what he was seeing, he noticed something else moving alongside the massive herd. Intrigued, he reached down and pulled a telescope out of his pack, pressing it against his right eye. Though the figures were still far off, he could make out two of them, each riding atop a horse and each with painted faces and feathered headdresses. He removed the telescope and motioned for the men to rally to his position.

"Boys, stay close. That herd's got Indians with it."

Colter and the others quickly hurried over to where Clark stood and watched as a pair of Indians broke off from the herd and began galloping toward them. Instinctively, Clark began to reach for his rifle, but stopped himself. He didn't want to make any sort of provocative action that could instigate the approaching men.

"Those must be the Otoe," Colter remarked, his eyes narrowing as the two Indians moved closer.

"I suspect you are correct," Clark replied as the warriors drew closer. "Mr. Dorian told me this morning that we were approaching their hunting grounds." He peered forward, assessing the situation, then motioned for the men to follow behind him. "Let's go introduce ourselves."

As the two Indians approached, they eyed Clark and the others with suspicion, their own rifles held at the ready.

"I don't like this, sir," York said in a hushed tone beside him. "Why don't they react?"

"Steady, York," Clark replied calmly, his eyes remaining fixed on the two Indians.

When they were within earshot, Clark held up both of his hands in a friendly gesture. "We come in peace," he announced, his tone measured but firm. "We seek to trade and establish friendly relations with your people."

The two Indians exchanged curious glances, their expressions cautious but not hostile as far as Clark could surmise. As they continued watching Clark and the others, Clark slowly reached down for his bag. One of the Indians noticed and began yelling at him, his voice sharp and urgent. Clark froze, his heart pounding in his chest as he braced himself for whatever came next. But as the seconds passed, nothing happened. The Indian stopped yelling and simply stared back at him with a fixed gaze. With bated breath, Clark waited, uncertain of what to do next. He glanced over at York, who simply shrugged back at him. With a measured sigh, Clark slowly reached back down for his bag, his eyes remaining fixed on the Indians high atop their horses. Slowly, he reached inside and began rummaging around for the item he was looking for. Finally, he felt his fingers clasp onto the item he was seeking. He smiled and removed a long strand of beads, which he held up so the two Indians could see. The colorful beads glinted in the late afternoon sun as he dangled them loosely in front of him.

"We come seeking peaceful relations with your people," Clark repeated in a steady voice. The two Indians looked at each other in silent deliberation, and then turned back to face Clark and the others. After a few more seconds of silence, each of them nodded and slowly, one of them reached down and removed a small knife he had sheathed to his thigh. He held the knife out toward Clark, who stepped forward slowly with the beads and exchanged them for the knife. The Indian let out a loud *whoop* as he placed the beads around his neck and galloped off. The second Indian remained for a moment, continuing to eye Clark and the others with a look that could only be described as curiosity before turning his own horse and galloping off after his companion.

Clark watched them go, a mixture of relief and apprehension flooding his senses.

"Where are they going?" Colter asked as the two figures disappeared over a grassy hill.

"Back to their village to tell the others about us," Clark replied knowingly.

"I thought we wanted to trade with them. Why aren't they taking us with them?"

"Don't worry, they'll find us. We need to get back to the camp and tell the others. I expect we will have a lot to discuss before the Indians return." He grabbed his rifle and slung it back behind his shoulders as he began heading back toward the camp. His emotions became a blend of nerves and excitement at having finally had the opportunity to make contact with one of the plains' tribes. He knew they could not pass up an opportunity to reach out and establish diplomatic ties with these natives. And more importantly, acquire whatever knowledge they had of the lands west of the Missouri River. He knew the success of the expedition hinged on it.

EIGHT

It would be another two days before the Indians returned, this time accompanied by over a dozen other warriors. As they approached the Corps camp early in the morning, Clark waited impatiently for Lewis to arrive with the gifts they had prepared to hand over to the Indians upon their arrival.

"Hurry up, will you," Clark shouted as Lewis jogged up the bluff to meet him. "Do you have the coins? And the buckles?"

"Yes, yes, I have those and the silver trays," he replied, motioning to the leather bag slung beside him. "Sergeant Ordway provided me with some Virginia tobacco as well that I think they'll enjoy." When the Indians arrived, the two sides exchanged gifts, with the Natives providing them with blankets, necklaces, and buffalo hides. To Clark's relief, one of the Indians spoke French, and through the translation of Pierre Dorian, a meeting was set for the following day at a small bluff a half a mile north of the camp. When the appointed meeting time arrived, Clark let Lewis take charge, dressed in his full military dress uniform. He ordered the men to conduct a dress parade for their Indian guests as a display of the Corps' military precision and discipline. The men paraded by the assembled Indians, their movements synchronized and purposeful, the barrels of their rifles glinting in the mid-morning sunlight. When the parade was over, the men retreated to the edge of the bluff while Lewis addressed the assembled Indian delegation. Clark stood next to Dorian, who waited to translate Lewis's words into French for the Indians.

"This land," Lewis bellowed out in a loud voice, his words echoing out across the grassy bluff, "now belongs to the United States and your new great chief, Thomas Jefferson." He paused to let Dorian translate his proclamation back to the Indians. As the message was conveyed, the Indians exchanged puzzled glances. "America is your friend," Lewis continued, "and wishes to foster friendly relations with all the tribes of the West. America will open trading posts across the plains and will construct forts to protect you. We will send agents to assist you and you may send your chiefs to the great city of Washington to meet the great white chief, Jefferson." He paused to let Dorian finish. He took a deep breath and said, "Chief Jefferson wishes for all tribes to be at peace with one another. He will not tolerate endless warfare along the plains. If you disobey his commands and displease him, the armies of the United States will consume you as the great fire consumes the grass of the plains. America will cease all trade with you and leave you no guns, powder, or other goods. Therefore, you must not displease him."

As Lewis's words hung in the air, the Indians exchanged uneasy glances among themselves, their expressions a mixture of confusion and concern. After a few tense minutes of deliberation, the Otoe chief rose from his seat and stepped forward, his face a mask of solemn resolve. Clark eyed him as he strode toward Lewis and the hushed murmurs among his people fell silent as their eyes turned to him. The chief began to speak, his words quickly translated to English by Dorian.

"We hear your words, emissary of the great white chief," he began, "But know this: our ancestors have walked these plains for many generations, and their spirits remain woven into the fabric of this land. We will honor your chief's words and trade goods and other medicines with all white men who come to our lands. We will strike treaties with your great chief of Washington and live in harmony with all the tribes of these lands. But we will not relinquish our lands." When he was finished speaking, the chief bowed his head in respect to Lewis and stepped back. Lewis glanced over at Clark who offered a simple shrug in reply.

With a heavy sigh, Lewis looked over at Dorian and whispered, "Tell the chief I thank him for meeting with us today and that we look forward to future friendly interactions with his people." Dorian nodded and began translating Lewis' words to French as Lewis sauntered over to where Clark stood watching the Otoe.

"At least they met with us and didn't put our heads on spikes," he said reassuringly to Lewis. Lewis simply sighed and looked back at the Indians all gazing around at the members of the Corps standing nearby.

"Establishing friendly relations with these tribes was one of the President's top priorities, Will," Lewis replied gravely. "Getting them to agree to trade with us is certainly a step in the right direction, but we need more than that. We need them to understand these lands belong to the United States now and they must allow settlers to pass through without molestation."

"They will," Clark replied assuredly. "They know our intentions are peaceful. And they know what the consequences will be if they don't cooperate."

Lewis returned the nod, his eyes still fixed on the departing Otoe chief and his entourage. As they left, he couldn't shake the feeling of the weighty responsibility resting on his shoulders. The success of their expedition depended not only on navigating the physical challenges of the frontier, but the diplomatic challenges as well. He hoped, as the Otoe departed, that their encounter had sown the seeds of understanding and cooperation and had at least laid the groundwork for future interactions with not only the Otoe, but all the natives that inhabited the vast western frontier. But he knew only the future would determine if he had succeeded.

NICHOLAS KANE

NINE

A somber atmosphere gripped the expedition as they gathered atop a small bluff overlooking the Missouri River. Clark stood at the head of a long wooden coffin, inside of which laid the remains of the expedition's Quartermaster, Sergeant Charles Floyd. He offered a brief glance to Lewis, who had concluded his speech to the men. It was now his turn. Slowly, and with a tinge of sadness in his voice, he began.

"Sergeant Floyd was a valued member of this expedition, and his loss weighs heavily upon us all. Though we may never fully understand why the Lord chose to take him from us so soon, we honor his memory and mourn his loss." He straightened, offering a crisp salute toward the coffin. When he stepped back, he motioned to the four men assigned grave detail. They moved forward, their boots crunching on the dry dirt as their shovels clanked in the stillness of the morning air. Each man bent down, gripping a corner of the coffin, their movements deliberate and careful as they lowered it into the freshly dug grave. A faint creak of the wood echoed as the casket settled into the earth. Then, in silent unison, they reached for their shovels, the metallic scrape of spades biting into the dark soil breaking the quiet. One by one, they tossed the earth over the coffin, the thud of dirt marking the finality of the moment.

Clark watched as the men lingered briefly, heads bowed, before turning to trudge back down the bluff toward the camp along the riverbank. His gaze lingered on the grave, his thoughts heavy with the loss of Floyd. He had only recently begun to know Floyd well, but the man's quiet demeanor, sharp mind, and role as Quartermaster had quickly proven invaluable to the Corps. Losing him so early in the journey was a blow—not just to morale but to the expedition's delicate logistics.

Clark sighed deeply and crouched down near the grave. Beside him lay a small wooden stake he had brought from the camp. He picked it up, running his fingers over the black lettering he had carefully etched onto its surface: *Sergeant Charles Floyd,*

FRONTIER

Quartermaster. August 20, 1804. It wasn't much, but it was all he could offer. After a moment of reflection, he drove the stake firmly into the ground at the head of the grave.

"We'll name this Floyd's Bluff in his honor," he said, standing and brushing the dirt from his hands. He gazed out across the flat, desolate plains stretching beyond the bluff. "I'll mark it on the map tonight."

York, standing silently beside him, nodded in quiet agreement. "A good idea, sir. But if we aim to reach the Sioux lands by the end of summer, we can't afford any more delays."

Clark nodded as his eyes scanned the horizon. "I know. Captain Lewis knows it too. We'll have to pick up our pace from here." He paused and took one last glance down at the grave. "I pray this is the last grave we have to dig on this journey."

York nodded but cast a sidelong glance at Clark, the doubt in his eyes betraying his agreement. "I reckon this expedition is bound for great things, sir. You and Capt'n Lewis will surely bring back discoveries that'll shape the future of this country. But as far as I'm concerned, I've got one job on this journey."

Clark looked at him, his eyebrows raised. "And what job is that?"

York's lips curved into a faint smile. "To keep you alive."

Clark chuckled softly, the sound brief but genuine. "Then I'll count on you to do just that."

The two men began their descent down the large bluff, the distant hum of the camp growing louder with each step, the memory of Floyd quietly etched into both their hearts and the unforgiving soil of the plains behind them.

NICHOLAS KANE

TEN

Excerpt from Lewis's Secret Journal

Each step forward carried with it the weight of our grief, yet also the promise of discovery and adventure that beckoned from beyond the horizon. The wind, gentle yet insistent, stirred the grasses at our feet, as if urging us onward in our quest to uncover the mysteries of the untamed wilderness.

As we journey up the Missouri, the unending plains sprawl before us in every direction. Towering skies stretch overhead, vast, and unyielding, while each dip of the oars sends cascading crystalline droplets dancing into the summer air, many times catching the light of the sun and scattering it in a dazzling display of color.

And so, with each passing mile, we press on, our spirits buoyed by the knowledge that we carried with us the legacy of those who had come before. For in the vast and unforgiving landscape of these Great Plains, we find not only the echoes of the past, but also the promise of a future filled with possibility and a nature teeming with unseen wonders waiting to be discovered.

-Meriwether Lewis
September 1st, 1804

FRONTIER

ELEVEN

The Yankton Sioux village stood just a mile north of the confluence of the Missouri and Bad Rivers. Nestled amidst the sprawling plains with the majestic Missouri flowing nearby, the village was comprised mostly of circular earth lodges that dotted the landscape, their sturdy frames adorned with intricate designs and vibrant colors. The aroma of burning wood wafted from the central hearths of the earth lodges, mingling with the savory scent of cooking meat and the sweet tang of dying herbs and wildflowers.

Above Lewis's head, the sun beat down relentlessly. The intensity of its glare seemed to sear through the air, creating a shimmering haze that danced upon the horizon toward the west. Sitting across from Lewis was the Sioux chief, War Eagle, his piercing dark eyes fixed squarely on Lewis as he watched the American present gifts he had brought for the tribe. Upon his head rested a magnificent headdress adorned with feathers, while around his neck hung necklaces of bones, shells, and beads. Lewis paused, his eyes resting on the necklace of beads that gleamed in the sunlight.

"Finally, I present to you this flag, a symbol of our nation, which I hope you will fly proudly above your village to acknowledge your obedient support to the United States and the great white chief, Jefferson." Lewis glanced quickly at Dorian sitting beside him, who began translating his words to the chief. War Eagle, his expression grave, listened intently as his eyes remained fixed on Lewis.

After a brief pause, the chief replied, his words filtered from his native tongue to English by Dorian as he spoke. "These gifts offer hope that our two peoples can live harmoniously, Captain Lewis." He took a breath before continuing. "While we acknowledge the power your people possess and the power of your Chief Jefferson, we must also ensure that the rights of the Sioux are respected and honored. Our lands are sacred to us, and if treaties are to be struck between our people, we must approach them with careful consideration."

Lewis nodded, knowing the council had reached its conclusion. There was little more to be done in the way of cultivating diplomatic relations. For now, their gifts and their pledge of support to War Eagle as the leader of the Yankton Sioux would have to be enough. He stood up and brushed the dirt from his pants as War Eagle and his warriors looked on. Clark approached from the edge of the council ring, his face earnest as he gazed over toward the onlooking Sioux.

Lewis flashed an appreciative smile and bowed slowly toward War Eagle. "Many blessings to you and your people, Chief War Eagle." He turned and began walking toward the village, Clark following closely behind him. When they were out of earshot of the council, Lewis turned to face him. "Did you garner any news about the Sioux to the north?"

"Pierre says we should not expect the same welcoming as we received here," Clark replied in a cautious tone. "The Teton Sioux are more aggressive toward newcomers. We're going to have to approach them with caution."

Lewis nodded thoughtfully. "Did you glean anything else from your conversation with Pierre?"

"Apparently, the Sioux are not happy with our gifts. They want gunpowder and muskets, not flags and coins. And many are unhappy with our acknowledgement of War Eagle as the supreme chief. We'll probably get a backlash from the supporters of the rival chiefs Standing Bear and Winoveya."

"I don't want to get caught up in the political machinations of these tribes. Have Pierre apologize for the slight and tell the men to prepare the boats. I don't want to linger here any longer than we must."

Clark nodded and hurried off to find Dorian and the others. Lewis gazed around the village, letting the faint whiffs of freshly tanned hides and cooked meat fill his nostrils. The faint hint of cedar and sagebrush lingered in the air as well, carried on the breeze that rustled through the trees and stirred the grasses of the nearby prairie. He tried to enjoy the brief respite from the inhospitableness of the wilderness, but his senses told him they had to get moving before things began to sour with the Indians. But he also worried about what lay ahead. They were in Sioux territory now and based on Dorian's warning, they were moving into potentially dangerous lands filled with an enemy that would not hesitate to destroy them.

TWELVE

The cool September breeze brushed gently across Clark's face as the pirogue glided gracefully toward the western shore of the Missouri. He repositioned his rifle against his right shoulder, feeling the weight of both the weapon and the uncertain tension that hung in the air around him. He glanced over at York, who stood near the bow of the boat, flanked by three Sioux chiefs. Each of them regarded Clark with suspicious stares, their expressions revealing a mix of curiosity and guarded trust. He let out a long sigh as he turned his attention back to the blue waters of the river. He understood their frustrations. They had spent hours trying to clumsily translate their intentions to the chiefs, but Dorian had struggled to interpret their dialect, and eventually, he had given up entirely. Adding to the awkwardness was the chief's lack of interest in their gifts. Like the Yankton Sioux to the south, they continually demanded gunpowder and rifles to help them in their war against the Omaha. The entire morning had been a complete waste of time in his mind, and he blamed the Indians for it. He turned to his right and motioned for Sergeant Ordway to come over to him. As the sergeant slid across the thwart, he flashed another frustrated stare in the direction of the Sioux.

"When we get to shore, thank them, and get them off the boat. I don't want to linger here any longer than we must."

"Captain Lewis wishes to perform a final parade for the chiefs before sundown," Ordway replied in a hushed tone. Clark flashed him an angry stare.

"I don't care what Captain Lewis wants, I'm tired of dealing with these savages. Bid them a good day and have the men row us away from here as quickly as possible."

"Very well, sir," Ordway said as the boat began to drift closer to shore.

Clark peered toward the shore and noticed dozens of warriors standing near the water, their eyes fixed on the approaching pirogue as it glided quickly toward them. He also saw Lewis and a dozen other men from the Corps standing nearby, their gazes

FRONTIER

fixed nervously on the warriors waiting for the return of their chief.

As the boat reached the water's edge, Clark, Ordway, and two other men leapt out into the shallows, their boots splashing as they grabbed hold of the towlines. Together, they hauled the boat onto the muddy shore, their muscles straining as the heavy vessel scaped against the riverbank. When the task was done, Clark straightened and watched as the three Sioux chiefs disembarked, their imposing forms rejoining the cluster of warriors waiting on the shore. The chiefs exchanged brief words with their men, their expressions unreadable.

To Clark's left, the sound of approaching footsteps drew his attention. He turned to see Lewis standing a few feet away, his brow furrowed with concern. "How did it go?" he asked.

Clark let out a heavy sigh. "How do you think? He muttered, yanking one of the towlines loose before wading ashore. Water streamed from his buckskin trousers as he stomped onto the muddy ground.

"What about the gifts?" Lewis pressed. "Did they like them?"

Clark let out a dry laugh, his exhaustion evident. "Meri, I'm not sure flags, bicorn hats, and coins with the President's face on them are going to cut it anymore. These tribes aren't dazzled by trinkets like that. They expect more, and frankly, they demand it."

Lewis crossed his arms, a worried expression washing over his face. "We'll have to find a way to appease them. The President made it clear that cultivating friendly relations with the tribes, especially the Sioux, is critical to our mission."

Clark spun around, his frustration flaring. "I know that. But how am I supposed to accomplish that when we can't even communicate properly? Pierre can only translate so much, and half the time it feels like we're guessing at their intentions." He paused, shaking his head. "It's like trying to negotiate blindfolded."

Before Lewis could respond, a commotion erupted nearby. Both men turned to see four Sioux warriors grabbing one of the boat's towlines, shoving Drouillard and York into the water. The two men splashed as they scrambled back, water soaking their clothing as the Sioux warriors held onto the line with defiant expressions.

"Hey! Stop that!" Clark bellowed, rushing over to confront the warriors. He reached for the towline, but the Sioux screamed back at him in their own language, yanking the line out of his reach.

Dorian hurried over, his hands raised in a placating gesture as he tried to mediate. The chiefs shouted furiously, their voices rising over the clamor of the riverbank.

"What the hell are they saying?!" Clark demanded as he eyed one of the Sioux with a harsh gaze.

Dorian hesitated, his brow furrowed as he strained to catch the meaning of the chiefs' rapid words. "They say…we can't leave."

Clark's frustration boiled over. "And why the hell not?" he snapped, his glare on the warriors holding the towline.

Dorian listened intently as one of the chiefs shouted at him, then turned back to face Lewis and Clark. "They say our gifts are insufficient," he explained, his voice tight. "We've…insulted the Sioux people. They demand proper tribute. A boat filled with guns and ammunition." Behind Lewis, Ordway, Thornfield, and four others were readying their rifles.

Clark's eyes burned with fury as they locked onto the chiefs. "Tell them no."

"They say this river belongs to the Sioux and we can't proceed."

Clark's blood began to boil. "That's an outrage!" In one brisk movement he reached down to his waist and snatched his pistol. He raised it and pointed it toward the closest Sioux chief, who returned a look of both shock and anger in Clark's direction. "All men to arms!" he shouted. On the boats, the men immediately unslung their rifles and aimed them toward the Sioux standing on the shoreline. In response, the Sioux raised their bows and aimed them directly at Lewis and Clark. Lewis tried to stammer something, but the entire situation had unfolded so quickly he was still in a state of shock and unable to form any words.

For a few tense moments, no one moved. On the shoreline, the Sioux warriors stood with their bows drawn, arrows poised to fly, while on the water, the Americans aimed their rifles, each man's finger hovering near the trigger. The air was thick with tension, the only sounds coming from the gentle lapping of the river against the boats. Clark's eyes locked onto the Sioux chief standing closest to him, his breathing slow and steady despite his racing heart. He studied the chief's face, searching for a flicker of intent, some indication of what might happen next. He inhaled deeply, his jaw set. With a subtle nod, he turned to Dorian and spoke in a calm but deliberate voice. "Translate this message. This expedition must continue. We will defend ourselves if necessary, and we have enough firepower to kill every one of your warriors in a single day. If you do not let us go, you will feel our power."

Dorian hesitated for the briefest moment before nodding. He stepped forward and relayed Clark's words in the Sioux language. The Sioux chiefs stood unmoving, their eyes narrowing as they listened, their stoic expressions betraying nothing. On the boats, the Americans grew restless. The tension was unbearable as each man gripped his rifle with sweaty palms, their nerves stretched thin. Clark remained steady, his focus still fixed squarely on the Sioux chiefs.

"Will, what the hell are you doing?!" Lewis hissed beside him.

"What I have to."

The standoff dragged on, the silence pressing down like a physical weight. Clark could feel the beads of sweat trickling down his back, his every sense heightened. His peripheral vision caught the glint of an arrowhead aimed directly at his head by a nearby warrior. He knew that in the span of a single breath, this confrontation could end in bloodshed—or a chance to move forward.

Suddenly, one of the Sioux chiefs stepped forward. The movement was swift and deliberate. With a sharp motion, he grabbed the towline from the hands of the warriors, yanking it free. The warriors hesitated, glancing at one another before slowly lowering their bows. Clark exhaled silently, lowering his pistol with measured precision. He turned back toward the pirogue and motioned for Dorian and the others. "Get on the boat. Now," he said.

As the Sioux began stepping back from the water's edge, Clark didn't waste a moment. He splashed into the river, the cold water soaking him to the knees as he gripped the side of the boat and hauled himself aboard. He glanced back at the shore, his eyes scanning for any sign of treachery. The Sioux stood watching, their expressions focused on the boats as they quickly moved away from shore. Clark glanced back at Lewis, who immediately began issuing orders to begin rowing hard down river. Within a few seconds, the pirogue was pushing farther away from shore and gliding out into the middle of the river. Clark holstered his pistol and let out a relieved sigh as he watched the Sioux along the shoreline fade away behind them. He let himself sink down between the thwarts, happy to be off Sioux soil. *Perhaps we'll find a different route home,* he thought to himself as the boat drifted away from shore, away from the scented air of the trees, away from the Sioux.

FRONTIER

THIRTEEN

The pirogue veered jarringly to the left as Clark grabbed hold of the bow railing to keep from being lurched overboard. He glanced to his right and watched as the other pirogue, flanked by *The Western Star,* made landfall along the Missouri's western shore. Clark watched as Drouillard directed the crew on his pirogue to glide the vessel forward onto the sand, at which point, he eagerly hopped off and quickly made his way over to Lewis.

"Well, this is it," he said excitedly, gazing around at the vast empty grasslands to the west.

"This is what?" Lewis replied, puzzled.

"The last point on our map. We are now truly sailing into the unknown."

Lewis let out a chuckle as the rest of the Corps leapt from the boats and began exploring the shoreline. Together, he and Clark made their way up a small grassy knoll where they stopped and surveyed the surrounding landscape using Clark's telescope. As Lewis peered toward the northwest, something caught his attention. He pulled the telescope down from his eye and handed it to Clark.

"Look, there toward the northwest." He gestured with his hand, pointing in the direction he had just been aiming the telescope in. Clark held the instrument up to his eye and peered through. At first, he saw nothing except an endless expanse of grass and bluffs. But as he focused his attention on the shoreline of the Missouri River to the northwest, he suddenly spotted what Lewis had seen. In the distance, there appeared to be a small cluster of huts pressed up against the edge of the river.

Clark let out a sigh as he handed the telescope back to Lewis. "The Mandan?"

"Has to be. We're in their lands."

"We should probably head north, make contact with them."

Lewis nodded. "Agreed. Let's gather the men."

A short time later, the Corps was back on the Missouri rowing as fast as they could toward the Mandan village. Clark gazed quietly out across the river as the pirogue he was on glided swiftly down the center of the fast-moving river. Within an hour, they were upon the village, but to everyone's bewilderment, it appeared deserted.

"Where are they?" Ordway asked as he walked beside Clark into the small, deserted village. Around them, the bones of people and animals littered the ground. The village seemed to have the stench of death clinging to it.

"Are they all dead?" asked Peter Harrington, who gazed out from within one of the abandoned mud huts of the village.

"I don't know," Clark replied as he knelt to examine one of the human bones near his feet. A few yards away, Seaman began to bark, causing Lewis, Ordway, and a few others to dart over to where he stood. Clark rose and began making his way toward where the dog was near the edge of the village. When he arrived at the spot Seaman was at, his mouth dropped in shock at the grim sight before him. A stack of bodies, their forms contorted and charred by fire, lay before him and the others. He held his hand up to his face as he examined the grisly scene before turning to glance at Lewis, who looked back at him with a mixture of shock and confusion.

"The pox," came a voice from behind them. Clark turned and noticed Thornfield approaching, his eyes fixed squarely on the pile of dead Mandan's. "They burn their dead like this when there's an outbreak of the pox. I've seen it before."

"It killed all of them?" Harrington asked, his mouth still agape.

"Most, I'd reckon. The few who survived likely fled west to their winter hunting grounds. They'll return in the spring."

"If they went west, then that's where we'll find them," Lewis said, turning to leave. He glanced at Clark, his eyes reflecting a mixture of determination and concern. "Let's get back to the boats. I don't want to linger in this place any longer."

Clark nodded and watched as Lewis and the others trudged slowly back toward the river. He took one last look at the pile of charred bodies before finally tearing himself away to follow Lewis and the others back toward the river. His mind buzzed with questions, haunted by the grim scene before him. How long had the Mandan suffered before succumbing to their terrible fate? How many more villages in the region had been ravaged by the deadly smallpox outbreak that had devastated this one? As he glanced toward the western horizon, he couldn't shake the sense of foreboding that settled over him. They had expected challenges on their journey, but the magnitude of the hardships they had already faced left him wondering what other horrors awaited them as they pushed westward.

FOURTEEN

The bitter bite of January had taken a firm hold of Fort Mandan, its icy grip wrapping around the fort's wooden walls like a vise. Snow blanketed the ground, muffling the sounds of the wilderness and casting a serene aura over the small outpost. Within the fort's walls, the men of the Corps of Discovery bustled about their daily routines, their breath hanging in the frigid air as they went about their tasks. Small cabins had been constructed in a semi-circle at the center of the fort to house the men and their supplies for the winter. A handful of teepees also dotted the courtyard, sheltering the numerous Mandan, Hidatsa, and Lakota Sioux who had journeyed to the region for the winter months with the hope of trading with the Corps' members. The Corps had encountered the Mandan a few days after discovering the abandoned village. They had learned that the smallpox outbreak that summer had virtually wiped out the Mandan living along the Missouri River in that part of the territory. The remaining Mandan had fled west, fleeing not only the disease, but the Arikara, who had been raiding their villages since the spring. To the Corps' amazement, the Mandan had quickly set up a prosperous trading post along the Missouri near a small tributary called Turtle Creek. In early October, thousands of Indians began flocking to the site. From the west came the Crow and Cheyenne; from the south, the Arapaho and Kiowa; and from the north, the Cree, along with dozens of French and British fur traders from Canada. By November, the site resembled a large city, rivaling St. Louis, and swelled to a population of well over 3,000 Indians and traders. Lewis, wanting to learn more about what lay west of their location, decided to make Winter Quarters north of the Mandan city, and by December, the small fort had been erected, ready to house the Corps over the long and bitterly cold winter.

From inside one of the small wooden rooms of the fort, Clark stared out at the small courtyard filled with men and Indians, his hands pressed against his lips as he tried to warm his fingertips with his breath.

FRONTIER

"I don't think I've ever known such cold," he said through clenched teeth.

Lewis, huddled over a table a few feet away, looked up. "You mean to tell me those Kentucky winters of your youth weren't like this?"

Clark smiled and walked back over to the table where Lewis was studying a large map that was illuminated only by the dim light of a flickering lantern. Clark leaned in and traced his cold finger along one of the winding rivers depicted on the map. "Two hundred miles, you reckon? To the divide?"

Lewis nodded. "That's probably an accurate estimation. Of course, none of it will matter if we can't secure a guide to get us across the mountains."

Clark sighed as he brought his hands back up to his mouth. "Do you think that French fur trader and his wife will help us?"

"For the right price, yes. We just need to determine what that price will be."

"You really think the man is going to help us cross the Rockies with a pregnant Indian wife in tow?"

Lewis shrugged. "I don't know. But I hope so. His wife's Shoshone, her tribe lives west of the mountains. We'll need her as a translator. I'm afraid Pierre's skills end at the divide."

"I just pray our interactions with the tribes on the other side of the divide are better than our interactions with the Sioux."

Lewis let out a chuckle as he rolled up the map and placed it back into a long leather cylinder. "Perhaps, if you don't pull a gun on them, they will be friendlier toward us."

There was a soft knock on the door followed by the creaking of hinges. Standing in the doorway was Joseph Field, one of the younger members of the expedition. He and his brother, Reubin, had been hired by Lewis in St. Louis as laborers.

"Captain Lewis, Lieutenant Clark?"

"Yes, what is it, Joseph?" Clark replied briskly.

"That French trapper and his wife have arrived. They're waiting for you in the tavern."

Lewis glanced over at Clark with a look of surprise. "Tavern? Since when do we have a tavern?"

"It's what Lieutenant Clark named the common area, sir," Joseph replied excitedly. Lewis just shook his head and gathered up the rest of his papers. Clark glanced down and noticed a small leather-bound notebook near one of the legs of the table and reached down to grab it.

"Don't forget this," he said, handing the journal to Lewis. Lewis smiled and grabbed the journal out of his hand and stuffed it into his leather satchel. Together, the two men walked over to one of the smaller cabins constructed near the north wall of the fort, the frosted ground crunching beneath their feet as they walked. When they arrived, Clark paused for a moment to stare up at the long stone chimney soaring above the cabin's roof where billowing clouds of dark gray smoke wafted gently into the frigid afternoon air.

The two men stepped into the dimly lit cabin where they were immediately met with the scent of burning candles and damp earth. The room was small and cramped, its rough-hewn walls lined with shelves stacked high with supplies and equipment. A dozen or so men, along with a few Mandan and Cheyenne Indians, were scattered about the room, their voices murmuring in hushed tones as they talked amongst one another. In the center of the cabin sat the man they were looking for, Toussaint Charbonneau, a tall, lean man with weathered features that portrayed someone who had spent much of his life in the rugged wilderness. His dark hair was streaked with gray, and his deep-set eyes seemed to flicker in the light of the candles. He wore a leather jacket over a frayed shirt, the sleeves rolled up to reveal muscular forearms weathered by years of outdoor labor. His wife, by contrast, was petite and slender, her delicate features softened by the flickering light of the candles. Her dark hair was pulled back in a loose braid, and her almond shaped eyes sparkled as they settled upon Lewis and Clark entering the cabin. Despite her young age, she still gave the appearance of a woman who possessed a quiet confidence and inner strength far beyond her years.

The two men approached the table. Charbonneau looked up and gave them a brief nod and motioned for them to sit down opposite him and his wife.

FRONTIER

Lewis cleared his throat, his voice steady but filled with urgency. "Mr. Charbonneau, thank-you for meeting with us."

Charbonneau nodded, his weathered face betraying no emotion as he listened intently to Lewis's words. His wife said nothing, her gaze steady and unwavering as it went from Lewis to Clark, and back to Lewis.

"As you are aware from our last conversation," Lewis continued, "we intend to disembark from here sometime in early April and continue our west across the Rockies into the Oregon Country. And we will need experienced guides to lead us safely through the wilderness."

"And a translator to help us with the local Indians," Clark interjected, his gaze settling on Charbonneau's wife.

Charbonneau's brow furrowed slightly as he considered the offer, his gaze shifting between Lewis and Clark. "And what would be in it for us?"

Lewis exchanged a glance with Clark before responding. "We are prepared to offer you a salary for your services."

"And Sacagawea?" He glanced over at his wife.

"We would provide compensation to your wife as well, sir. She is Shoshone, is she not?"

"I am, Captain," Sacagawea replied in a soft but firm voice, "and I can answer for myself."

Lewis gave her an apologetic look. "Yes, of course. My apologies."

"And what of the risks?" Charbonneau asked, his voice laced with a tone of skepticism. "Crossing the Rockies is never easy, even if you know where you're going. If you're lucky, you'll make it to the pass by early summer when the snows have melted at the lower elevations. But then you'll have to worry about the rivers being swollen with snow melt from the higher elevations and the spring rains. And on top of that, you have the Indians." He glanced at his wife briefly and then back at Lewis. "Some of them don't take kindly to white men crossing their lands. Especially *armed* white men from a nation claiming to now own their territory. There's no guarantee of success even with my help."

"We understand the risks," Lewis replied sharply. "But we believe with your knowledge and expertise, we stand the best chance of completing our mission."

"Et il y a les bêtes qui gardent les montagnes don't il faut les avertir," said Sacagawea in a hurried voice.

"Ils n'ont pas besoin d'entendre parler des êtres mythiques qui vivent dans les bois," Charbonneau replied in frustration.

Lewis raised an eyebrow and glanced over at Clark who gave him a confused look.

"I apologize, she speaks out of line," Charbonneau snapped, still eyeing Sacagawea.

"What does she mean by *beasts in the woods*?" Lewis asked.

Charbonneau looked surprised. "You speak French, Captain?"

Lewis nodded. "I do. I was President Jefferson's private secretary in Paris during his time as minister to France."

Charbonneau sighed and leaned forward, his voice low. "There are myths among the tribes in the West of…creatures that roam the woods, beings unlike any other. They are said to be as tall as eight feet in some cases, with hair as dark as the midnight sky covering their entire bodies." He paused, letting his words sink in before continuing. "They move with silent grace, leaving no trace of their passing save the stench of rot and decay that lingers in the air where they were. Some believe they're spirits, guardians of the wilderness, while others claim they are monsters, born of the darkest depths of the earth."

Clark leaned back slowly in his chair trying to hold in a laugh. Lewis glanced at Sacagawea, who stared back at him with a solemn expression etched across her face.

"I have no doubt your people believe in such things," Lewis said, searching for the right words to respond with, "but I must admit, the notion of beasts roaming the forests is a little fanciful for me."

"I have been across the Rockies more times than I can count, Captain," Charbonneau responded quickly, "and never once have I witnessed anything close to these beasts my wife describes."

Sacagawea shifted angrily in her chair, her first show of any outward emotion since their meeting began. Charbonneau grabbed her leg and steadied her. "Enough," he said with a firm voice. She

FRONTIER

looked over at him and then back down at the table. Silence descended between them as Lewis and Clark both exchanged worried glances. Eventually, Charbonneau broke the silence.

"Four hundred dollars. For four hundred dollars we will help you make it to Oregon."

"Two hundred," Lewis countered. "One hundred now and one hundred when we reach the Pacific." He glanced over at Sacagawea. "And twenty-five dollars to your wife if she agrees to be our translator and give us introductions to her people."

"Thirty dollars for my wife."

Lewis sighed. "Agreed."

Charbonneau looked over at Sacagawea and then back at Lewis and Clark. "Very well, Captain. We accept your offer. We will join your expedition."

A sense of relief washed over Lewis' face. He reached out and shook Charbonneau's hand. Clark did as well, followed by a brief nod toward Sacagawea. She simply stared down at the table with a look of worry etched across her face.

"Joseph!" Lewis exclaimed, turning himself slightly in his chair, "Fetch us some rum! We have cause for celebration tonight."

With a swift nod, Joseph hurried off to retrieve the spirits. A few minutes later he returned carrying a glass bottle and four wooden cups which he passed around to each of them. Sacagawea politely pushed hers over to her husband.

"Don't mind her," Charbonneau said with a smile, "Liquor makes her squeamish on account of the baby and all."

Lewis raised his cup as a toast. "To new beginnings and great discoveries!" he declared. The three men raised their cups high, their laughter mingling with the shadows encroaching upon the edges of the firelight.

FIFTEEN

Clark narrowed his eyes, squinting as the brilliant sunlight reflected off the snow-covered clearing stretching out before him. The snow glistened like a sea of diamonds, the brightness almost blinding under the stark blue sky. Beside him, Lewis, York, and the rest of the Corps of Discovery stood in a semi-circle, their faces etched with a mix of anticipation and exhaustion. Across the small clearing, the Mandan and Hidatsa chiefs sat on a low hill, their imposing forms wrapped in buffalo-hide robes. The rich patterns of the hides blended with the earthy tones of their blankets, woven from bear fur, which they had spread beneath them to shield against the frozen ground.

Between the two groups, a small fire crackled weakly, its flames struggling to compete with the biting cold. The rising smoke twisted in the icy air, quickly vanishing into the wind. Clark shifted uncomfortably, tugging the collar of his fur-lined coat higher around his neck. Despite the heavy layers, each breath burned his lungs with a sharp chill while the cold air gnawed at any exposed skin. His gloved hands instinctively tightened around his rifle, more for warmth than defense. For a while, silence prevailed, broken only by the faint rustling of fur and fabric as both sides adjusted against the cold. The chiefs remained stoic, their dark eyes watching with quiet intensity. A gust of wind swept across the clearing sending loose snow spiraling into the air. Clark steadied himself, planting his feet firmly against the frozen earth to avoid being knocked back.

Finally, Lewis stepped forward, his breath visible as a puff of mist in the frigid air. He cast a quick glance at Clark, who nodded faintly in reply. He pressed his lips into a thin line as he braced against another gust of wind. The cold had settled into his bones, but he pushed it aside, focusing on the significance of the moment.

"If we're successful here," he began, his voice steady but low, "we'll hopefully learn how much farther we have to go to reach the mountains. And whether the Missouri continues into Oregon or ends at the base of the Rockies."

FRONTIER

"Why don't you ask them when winter ends in this God forsaken place," Clark shot back angrily as he tried to warm his fingers against his mouth.

Lewis sighed and turned back toward the chiefs. He stepped forward, along with Charbonneau and Dorian flanking him on either side.

"Wise ones," Lewis began, his voice tinged with excitement, "the Corps of Discovery, as well as the people of the United States, extend our deepest gratitude for your generosity during these trying months. Your supplies of corn and furs have been invaluable. Without them, these winter months would have been even harsher to endure." He paused, allowing Dorian and Charbonneau to translate his words into French and Mandan. The chiefs listened in silence, their eyes reflecting the light of the fire. "We seek your wisdom," he continued, his gaze sweeping across the group of chiefs. "Do you know how far the great river extends? And does it connect to other great rivers that flow westward, across the mountains, to the vast waters of the Pacific?" Again, he waited as Dorian and Charbonneau translated. Clark, standing just behind Lewis, took a deep breath, his eyes flashing back and forth between Ordway and York, who stood to his left. The fire crackled softly, the only sound as the chiefs exchanged hushed murmurs among themselves.

After a minute, one of the chiefs, his buffalo-hide robe dusted with frost, turned back to face Lewis and began speaking in Mandan. Lewis's eyes darted to Charbonneau, his body leaning slightly forward in anticipation.

Charbonneau hesitated briefly, his breath clouding the air as he began to translate. "He says there is another great river that runs parallel to the Missouri."

A flicker of excitement lit up Lewis's eyes as he turned toward Clark. "That must be the Columbia," he whispered, his voice barely audible over the wind.

Charbonneau continued. "The other river flows westward, toward the peaks of the ragged mountains. He warns, though, that the river is guarded by towering cliffs on either side. To reach the great waters of the West, you must first cross the mountains."

Lewis's excitement dimmed slightly as Charbonneau's tone grew more solemn. "He says we will need to trade with the Shoshone for horses to cross the mountains. Without them, we will not make it."

"Tell the chief we have anticipated that need and have hired a Shoshone woman to translate our needs with the Shoshone," Lewis replied briskly.

Charbonneau translated the words in Mandan, speaking carefully to ensure accuracy. The Mandan chief listened intently, his expression growing more serious as he nodded solemnly in acknowledgement. He replied in a firm tone. Charbonneau hesitated for a moment before relaying the message.

"He say's the Wahatoka guard the passes through the mountains," Charbonneau began in a low voice. "Their territory stretches from the end of the great river to the western waters. To trespass on their lands invites certain death."

Lewis's brow furrowed deeply. "The Wahatoka?" he repeated, unfamiliar with the term.

"The giant, hairy beasts I told you about," Charbonneau replied, his tone laced with a hint of skepticism, almost as if mocking the idea.

Lewis exhaled sharply and shook his head, brushing off the statement. "We don't have time for Indian superstitions," he said flatly. "Ask him if we can traverse the river to reach the great sea in the West with our boats."

Charbonneau turned back to the chief and repeated Lewis's question. The old man's expression darkened, and he responded in a firmer tone, speaking directly at Lewis. Lewis's frown deepened as he watched the exchange, his patience wearing thin.

"What did he say?"

Charbonneau sighed, glancing between Lewis and the chief. "He says the Wahatoka are not to be trifled with. Their territory is sacred, and to enter is to invite ruin."

Lewis's frustration mounted, his hands balling into fists at his sides. "This is a waste of time," he muttered under his breath. "Ask him again if the river leads to the great sea in the West?"

FRONTIER

Charbonneau reluctantly repeated the question, but the chief only stared back at Lewis, his face hard with disdain. Finally, Charbonneau turned back to Lewis with a resigned shake of his head. "He won't say. He believes you've disrespected him and the other chiefs."

Lewis let out a long, frustrated sigh and turned away, his boots crunching against the snow as he strode over to where Clark stood. He ran a hand through his hair as he quickly glanced back toward the watching chiefs. "These people and their fables," he muttered irritably. "We can't afford to alienate them. If we're going to unite the tribes of the plains against the Teton Sioux, we need the Mandan on our side."

Clark adjusted his coat collar, his lips pressed into a grim line. "Then you'll need to convince them we've done what we promised the Arikara—stopped their raids on Mandan land."

Lewis nodded distractedly, his mind clearly elsewhere. "The chief did mention a water route," he said, his tone betraying a glimmer of optimism. "Whether it's the Columbia or not, we can't be certain. But it's a lead—a hope that the passage does exist."

Clark gave him a sidelong glance. "We've gotten all we can from these people. They've shared what they're willing to, and it's clear they don't fully trust us. It's up to us now to figure out a way through the Rockies."

"As long as we find the Shoshone, we'll be fine," Lewis said confidently. "They'll know the land and can confirm whether the passage exists."

Clark gave a slow nod, though a flicker of doubt crossed his face. "Let's just pray we don't run into any of those Wahatoka first," he said, the corner of his mouth twitching into a faint grin.

Lewis let out a sharp sigh, clearly unimpressed. "Enough with the stories," he said dismissively.

Clark chuckled softly, turning away to gaze at the distant horizon where the snow-capped peaks of the Rocky Mountains loomed, jagged and imposing against the pale sky.

SIXTEEN

Excerpt from Lewis's Secret Journal

As the first rays of sun pierce the horizon, I cannot help but feel an overwhelming sense of anticipation for the journey that lies ahead. The past few months spent at Fort Mandan have been a respite from the rigors of our expedition. Our interactions with the Mandan, Hidatsa, and all the other nearby tribes of the region have been peaceful and productive and have allowed us to replenish our supplies as we prepare to embark on the most difficult part of our journey.

We are blessed to have come across a French fur trader named Charbonneau and his wife, a Shoshone woman from beyond the mountains, who have agreed to guide us and serve as translators. Lieutenant Clark is sure we will reach Lemhi Pass by August and be over the mountains by November. I am not so convinced, but I remain hopeful, barring any unforeseen barriers, we can accomplish that feat.

As we broke camp this morning, I could not help but feel a pang of sadness at leaving behind the safety of the walls and departing the place we called home for these last harsh winter months. Yet, I know our future lies farther west, and soon, I will dip my toes into the tranquil waters of the Pacific Ocean. I pray our resolve never wavers as we face the challenges that lie ahead.

-Meriwether Lewis
April 7, 1805

FRONTIER

SEVENTEEN

The Missouri flowed swiftly, its waters tumbling over hidden rocks and carving through the rugged expanse of the northernmost reaches of the Louisiana Territory. Tall, jagged cliffs flanked the riverbanks, their surfaces weathered by centuries of erosion. Overhead, the vast sky stretched out endlessly, a brilliant dome of blue interrupted only by the faint brushstrokes of drifting clouds. The expedition's boats bobbed and weaved, carried along by the swift-moving rapids as Lewis peered ahead from the bow of *The Western Explorer*. Beside him, Seaman laid lazily beneath one of the thwarts, his head resting comfortably atop his large paws. He glanced over his shoulder and noticed Charbonneau making his way toward him with his usual nonchalant gait. Sacagawea remained at the boat's stern gently rocking her infant back and forth in her arms.

"I can see why they refer to this region as Big Sky country," Lewis said as Charbonneau approached, "I've never seen anything quite like it."
"You haven't seen anything yet, Captain," Charbonneau replied with a smile. Lewis chuckled and turned back to face the river. The keelboat creaked softly as it rounded a bend, his eyes continuing to sweep across the rippling water for any sign of obstacles. Then, something caught his attention—a stretch of frothy whitewater churning violently against the rocks. He narrowed his gaze, leaning slightly forward for a better look. The rapids stretched across the width of the river, their foaming waves crashing and swirling in a chaotic dance. His heart began to race.
"I don't like the looks of that," he said to Charbonneau, pointing a finger toward the approaching rapids.
Charbonneau followed his gesture, his confident smile fading into a more serious expression. "That stretch looks dangerous. You might want to portage around it, Captain. The rocks alone could splinter a keelboat."

Lewis shook his head firmly. "Portaging would cost us precious time—more than a day, at least. We're already behind schedule." He glanced to his right where Clark stood at the bow of the neighboring keelboat. The two exchanged a wordless glance, Clark's furrowed brow mirroring Lewis's concerns. Lewis raised a hand, signaling for the flotilla to gather. Slowly, the boats maneuvered toward the center of the river, the oarsmen working carefully against the current. Once the boats wre close enough for all to hear, Lewis steadied himself near the middle of his own vessel. The roaring of the rapids made it difficult to speak, but he raised his voice, his words carrying across the water. "We have a decision to make!" he called out. "Do we risk the rapids, or do we take the boats overland?"

He looked over at Clark who was continuing to survey the turbulent waters ahead. "We're already behind schedule," Clark shouted back. "I say we push through. It's our best chance to make up for lost time."

The rest of the group exchanged worried glances as they weighed the risks with the rewards of their options. Inside one of the boats, Joseph Field and his brother whispered to one another in hushed tones, while inside *The Western Explorer,* Drouillard nodded at Willard and Thornfield before glancing up at Lewis.

"Captain," Drouillard called out, his voice straining to rise above the roar of the river. "These rapids pose a serious risk. The currents are strong, and the rocks are unforgiving. One wrong move could spell disaster."

Lewis nodded. He respected Drouillard's experience as a navigator, but he also knew they could not afford to lose any more time. "Thank you, George," he replied in a steady tone despite the tension gripping his chest. "But we're behind schedule as it is. We can't afford to lose another four or five days taking the long way around."

Drouillard pressed on, his tone edged with urgency. "With all due respect, sir, the safety of the men must come first. We've come too far to risk everything on a gamble. Now, we've made these decisions before as a group, I say we do the same here."

FRONTIER

"I agree with George," Clark said, eyeing Lewis. "Carelessness could cost us dearly." He paused as he turned his gaze back toward the frothing rapids ahead. "But we also can't afford to lose days walking the boats and supplies overland. I vote we push through. It's a risk, yes, but a calculated one."

Lewis scanned the faces of the men in the nearby boats, his eyes searching for input. "Does anyone else have an opinion?" he called out, his voice carrying over the relentless rush of the river. A few murmurs rippled through the group, but no one spoke up. Most stared at the churning rapids with trepidation.

Lewis exhaled sharply and turned back to Clark. "Shall we put it to a vote?"

Clark nodded and straightened to address the men. "All in favor of continuing on by river, raise your hands." Nearly every hand went up, though many rose reluctantly.

Lewis gave a stiff nod. "Very well. The majority has decided. Secure the ropes and supplies. We don't want to lose anything." He glanced at the water again and let out a deep sigh. "And may God help us."

The decision made, the crews braced themselves as the boats surged forward into the maw of the rapids. The roar of the river swallowed all other sounds as the frothy water sprayed across the decks, soaking everyone aboard. Lewis gripped the edge of the thwart tightly, his knuckles white as his eyes darted between the jagged rocks ahead. Beneath him, Seaman let out a low whimper, his soaked fur clinging to his body as he scrambled under the thwarts. The river's power was overwhelming as it bucked and heaved the boats like leaves caught in a storm. Crew members clung to their oars with desperate strength, their muscles straining as they fought to keep the vessels on course. Every second felt like an eternity, each wave threatening to capsize them or slam them into the sharp rocks that loomed like sentinels on either side.

"Steady as she goes!" Lewis shouted, his eyes scanning the turbulent water ahead for rocks. On the lead boat, Clark's hands clenched the edge of the keelboat as it narrowly avoided a massive boulder jutting from the water. The vessel lurched violently, nearly tossing a crewman overboard.

Clark barked out orders, but his voice was barely audible above the deafening roar of the rushing water.

Lewis's heart skipped a beat as he heard the ominous sound of splintering wood behind him. He whirled around, his eyes widening in horror as he watched one of the boats careen dangerously off course, its hull cracking under the force of impacting a large rock. The river seemed to swallow the boat whole, its churning waters engulfing the vessel in a violent embrace.

"Will!" Lewis shouted, his voice hoarse with panic as he looked on helplessly. As Clark turned toward him, he pointed desperately at the boat struggling to avoid the jagged rocks of the river's edge. A surge of water crashed into the side of the boat, sending it bow-first into another submerged rock with a sickening *crunch*. The impact sent all the men inside lurching forward while at the bow, Lewis watched with horror as Joseph Field's body flung violently from the vessel into the frigid waters of the Missouri and disappeared beneath the waves.

"Joseph's gone in!" Shouted Joseph's brother, Reubin. "Joseph!" he shouted again, his voice raw with desperation as he scanned the tumultuous river for any trace of his fallen comrade. But the rushing water seemed to have swallowed the man whole, leaving nothing behind but the haunting echo of his name in the wind.

A surge of adrenaline shot through Lewis as he scanned the river, his eyes darting frantically in search of Joseph's struggling form. His grip on the edge of the boat tightened while his heart continued to pound in his chest. Out of the corner of his eye, he caught a sudden blur of movement. It looked up in time to see Sacagawea darting toward the side of the boat, her dark hair tucked neatly into her deerskin dress.

"Sacagawea!" Charbonneau's voice cracked as he shouted from the stern, leaping forward to stop her. But he wasn't quick enough. Before anyone could react, she vaulted over the side of the boat and plunged into the icy water below.

"Sacagawea!" Charbonneau screamed again, his voice filled with both anger and fear. Behind him, Harrington cradled Pompey tightly, the baby's cries cutting through the chaos.

FRONTIER

Lewis felt his chest tighten as he watched her disappear beneath the dark waters. His breath caught in his throat, and time seemed to slow as he strained to catch a glimpse of her amidst the swirling rapids. Just when he feared the worst, her head broke the surface. Relief coursed through him as he saw her gripping Joseph's arm.

"Keep your feet and your head above the water!" she commanded to Joseph, who was struggling to cough the water out of his mouth. Lewis and the others watched as she fought the current, guiding Joseph alongside the boats as they surged downriver.

The river carried them relentless for another half-mile, the rapids tossing and twisting them like rag dolls. The boats rocked violently as the crew struggled to maintain control. Finally, the torrent began to subside. The frothing water gave way to calmer currents and the roar of the rapids faded into the distance. A collective sigh of relief swept through the Corps as they glided into a serene stretch of river.

"Toussaint, help her!" Clark cried out, pointing toward the figures of Joseph and Sacagawea as they swam their way back to Joseph's boat. After Joseph was pulled from the water, Sacagawea made her way back to *The Western Explorer* and was helped back on board by Charbonneau and Drouillard. Once safely on deck, Charbonneau's worry exploded into rage. He grabbed her by the shoulders, his face contorted with anger.

"What were you thinking?!" he roared, shaking her slightly as if to shake sense into her.

"I couldn't let him drown," she shouted back at him.

Sacagawea stood firm, her calm demeanor unshaken by her husband's rage. "I couldn't let him drown," she said simply.

"I told you not to go in!" Charbonneau bellowed, his face contorted with rage as his anger boiled over. "And you defied me!" His grip on her tightened as his voice rose to a fever pitch. Then, in a flash of fury, he pulled back his hand as if to strike her. His fist hovered in midair, trembling with a barely restrained anger. The boat fell deathly silent. The crew stood frozen, their eyes wide as they watched the confrontation unfold. Even Seaman, lying beneath the thwarts, let out a low growl, sensing the tension in the air.

Sacagawea remained calm, her gaze locked onto Charbonneau's with an unflinching resolve. Her voice was measured, deliberate. "I couldn't let him drown," she repeated.

Charbonneau's expression darkened further. "How dare you speak your husband in such a way. Perhaps you need reminding of—"

"Mr. Charbonneau!" Lewis's voice thundered from the bow of the boat, cutting through the scene like a crack of lightening. Charbonneau turned his head sharply to see Lewis standing tall, his usually calm demeanor replaced with a fierce, unrelenting glare. "That will be enough."

Charbonneau hesitated, his hand still poised midair. Lewis's icy stare bore into him. The boat creaked softly beneath them, the only sound in the oppressive quiet.

Slowly, Charbonneau lowered his hand and released Sacagawea's shoulders. He turned back to her, his jaw clenched but his anger now tempered by the silent judgment of the crew and the looming figure of Lewis.

"I—I apologize for my temperament," Charbonneau stammered. He turned and began walking quietly toward the stern where he picked up Pompey and cradled him until Sacagawea joined him. Lewis let out an exhausted sigh as he turned in Clark's direction. Clark simply looked back at him, his own face showing signs of exhaustion. The journey was taking its toll, and they still had unknown trials awaiting them in the shadow of the Rockies.

FRONTIER

EIGHTEEN

"Which way?"

Clark's words hung in the air as he stared ahead at the fork in the Missouri River. Beside him, Lewis consulted the map, his brow furrowed in concentration.

Clark turned to look at Sacagawea, who stood a few feet away next to Charbonneau. "Which way do we go?"

"I do not know," she replied softly, her gaze shifting between the two branches of the river. "I have never encountered this fork in the river before."

Clark frowned, feeling a pang of frustration at the uncertainty of their situation. "We need to make a decision."

"The Hidatsa never mentioned anything about a fork in the river," Lewis whispered with a sigh.

Clark leaned forward against the bow of the keelboat and gazed as far as he could in either direction. The north fork of the river appeared slower moving and muddier, while the south fork seemed shallower and wider. But he knew only one branch could be the Missouri River. He turned back to face Lewis and Sacagawea. "We need to choose wisely. We can't afford to lose days or weeks going up one branch only to find it was the wrong direction."

Lewis studied the river intently. "The northern branch seems to follow the general direction we've been traveling," he remarked, gesturing toward the wider expanse of water to their left. "But the southern branch is wider and faster moving. That could indicate the water is flowing down from the mountains." He paused for a moment before giving a slight nod in the direction of the south branch. "I think we should proceed south."

"I agree," Clark replied.

"My people say that the swifter waters can be treacherous," Sacagawea began, her gaze lingering on the northern branch as it moved along steadily through an expanse of jagged rock cliffs. "The northern branch may be slower, but it is steadier."

NICHOLAS KANE

"I agree with the Indian," Thornfield added. He had been standing behind her listening to their conversation. Beside him stood Ordway and York, each scanning the northern branch of the river.

"I agree with her as well," York said a few moments later.

"If we're wrong, we'll never make it over the mountains by winter," Clark replied, eying York and Thornfield. "We have to be sure."

"We'll split up," Lewis interjected. He turned around to face the men. "Two groups. One will head up the north branch and one will head down the south branch. Scout ahead for a few miles and then report back here with your findings." He turned to Clark. "Will, you take a group down the south branch, I'll go north. We'll make camp here and report back by nightfall."

Clark nodded and motioned for York and the others to steer the keelboat toward the shoreline. When they were ashore, he grabbed York, Drouillard, Ordway, and two other men, Elias Winchester and Samuel Treadway. Together, the men trudged their way south along the muddy banks of the river. The air was crisp, carrying with it the scent of the damp earth and the distant murmur of the flowing river. After about an hour of traveling along the edge of the water, however, the sky began to darken. Clark glanced up at the ominous clouds overhead and urged the men to quicken their pace up the rocky slopes of the shoreline. Within minutes, the clouds opened, and they were pelted by a relentless downpour. The rain fell in sheets, soaking them to the bone within minutes. Clark gritted his teeth against the deluge, his focus unwavering as he pressed on, each step growing more difficult as the muddy ground became slick and treacherous beneath their feet. Eventually, the downpours relented, giving way to a light rain that fell gently across his face as he peered ahead toward the imposing figure of York a few yards away. He seemed to be waving at him, signaling for him to come over. Clark frowned and slowly began trudging his way through the mud toward him.

"What is it?" He said as the other men gathered around.

"Take a look at these tracks," York said, directing his attention to a pair of large footprints imprinted in the soft mud.

FRONTIER

Clark knelt and studied the tracks intently. "What do you make of them?"

York shrugged. "Hard to say. I thought they were bear prints at first, but the stride is too long, and the shape is all wrong. It could be a large cat, but I've never seen a mountain lion track this big."

"Could it be some other kind of large predator?"

Drouillard, who had been examining the tracks closely, spoke up. "These prints are fresh. Whatever made them couldn't have passed through here more than a few hours ago."

"They almost look..." Ordway's voice trailed off as he stared down at the tracks.

"Look what, Sergeant?" Clark asked, his eyes darting furtively between York and Drouillard.

Ordway glanced up. "They almost look human."

"Human?" Elias Winchester let out a laugh. "Who would be out here running around the forest with no boots on?"

"I'm serious, look at the toe and heel prints." He pointed his finger at the intricate details of the footprints. Clark knelt back down beside one of them. Indeed, there was something peculiar about them- the shape of the toes and the depth of the impressions suggested a bipedal creature. But the size...

"It's far too large to be a human footprint," Clark muttered, standing back up. He wiped a bead of rain from his brow and gazed out across the rushing waters of the river beside them. "But whatever it is, it's big. We should head back to the boats."

"We've only gone two miles," Drouillard protested, his voice carrying over the sound of the rushing river. "We can't turn back now. We need to see where this branch leads, and besides, I'd like to find out what made those prints."

Clark hesitated. He knew if they pressed forward, they could discover potentially valuable information on not only the river, but whatever creature made the prints in the mud. On the other hand, the unknown dangers of such a creature lurking in the wilderness gave him pause.

"It's getting late, and this rain is making our route more treacherous. We'll head back to the boats and reassess our options from there."

The men nodded in agreement, relief evident on some of their faces at the prospect of returning to the safety of the keelboat. With one last glance at the mysterious footprints in the mud, Clark turned and began leading the men back over their steps along the riverbank. As the group made its way back through the undergrowth near the water's edge, a sense of unease settled over him. His mind lingered on the enigmatic footprints they had encountered. The thought of people wandering through the woods barefoot didn't strike him as odd. Indians roamed this wilderness and knew the lands better than he or any other member of the expedition, save Sacagawea, ever could. But the size of the person or persons that made those prints terrified him. The imprints from heel to toe had to have been at least fifteen inches, far larger than any man's. The idea of encountering a being of such size and unknown nature in the wilderness sent a chill down his spine, reminding him of the untamed wilderness that surrounded them and the unseen terrors that lurked within its shadows.

FRONTIER

NINETEEN

For the next three days the expedition camped near the fork of the Missouri River. Lewis ordered three more scouting parties up both branches trying to determine which one was the true path of the Missouri. When the final group returned from scouting the south branch late in the afternoon on the third day still unsure of whether it was the true branch of the river, Clark decided to make a judgment call.

"I say we take the south branch," he announced as the last group of men settled in beside a newly lit fire. "The rocks are smoother, and it has a faster moving current. It *has* to be the true path of the Missouri."

"But if you're wrong..." Lewis replied in a cautious tone, "we could be wasting valuable time."

"I'm aware of the risks," Clark shot back, "but I'm tired of dithering here wasting precious time. I say we head down the south branch at first light tomorrow."

Lewis wasn't quick to respond, but after a few moments of contemplation, he gave a nod. "Very well. We'll head south."

That had been five days ago.

Since then, the Corps had traveled down the narrow south branch and seen nothing but sloping hills and wide-open expanses of grassland. The rocky ledges had given way to fields and meadows that stretched on endlessly as far as the eye could see. On the fourth day, the forest returned, and the river was flanked by dense thickets or trees, their branches creating a canopy that filtered the sunlight and cast dappled shadows on the water below. The air was alive with the chirping of birds and the rustle of leaves, a welcome change from the monotonous grasslands they had traversed.

Clark stood at the bow of the *Western Star*, his gaze fixed on the winding river ahead. The current tugged at the boat, urging it forward through the thick foliage that crowded the banks. He furrowed his brow in concentration as he scanned the water for any signs of obstacles or hazards. With each bend of the river, uncertainty gnawed at him. Where was the waterfall the Hidatsa had told them about?

"I'm starting to think this wasn't the right choice, Lieutenant," said Thornfield, sitting a few feet behind him near the center of the keelboat.

Clark turned and eyed him with a hint of irritation. His patience was already wearing thin and the last thing he needed or desired was a lecture from Thornfield.

"You were very sure of yourself," Thornfield sneered. "Yet, here we are, rowing slowly up a river in the wrong direction."

"We've been moving in a southerly direction since yesterday, Silas, we are hardly going the wrong way," Ordway shot back from the stern of the keelboat. Thornfield scoffed.

"We should be moving west. Just like we should have reached the mountains by now."

A hot gust of wind blasted Clark in the face as the keelboat swerved around another bend into a straight part of the river. He held up his hand and the voices in the boat went silent.

"Take us to shore, Sergeant," he commanded firmly.

Ordway sighed and began steering the boat toward the sandy shoreline. Across the river, the pirogues followed until all the boats were pushed up onto the edge of the river. When they were beached, Clark hopped out and stared quietly down the river. Lewis slowly approached, his own eyes scanning the river ahead.

"We may have to reassess our course," he said in a soft whisper.

Clark let out a long sigh. "I know. But I still think we're going the right way."

"Perhaps. But we must be sure, Will."

"I'll scout ahead," he replied firmly. "I'll bring Sergeant Ordway, York, and the Field brothers with me. We'll find the waterfalls."

"And if they're not there?"

Clark let out another sigh and shook his head. "They have to be there."

"I hope you're right, Will. Or we're going to be in a lot of trouble."

FRONTIER

TWENTY

The small group pushed their way through the underbrush as they ventured further down the river, the thick foliage brushing against their clothes and skin. Every step was a struggle against the tangled vines and roots that seemed determined to impede their progress. Clark led the way, his eyes scanning the surroundings for any signs of a viable path. But within a few hours, the forest thinned, and the river seemed to pick up speed.

"We're close," Clark said confidently, waving a hand toward the others, urging them forward. Their steps quickened as the forest continued to recede, giving way to open terrain. The sound of rushing water grew louder as they approached a bend in the river where the water churned with a newfound intensity. Clark's heart quickened with anticipation.

"What do we do when we reach this waterfall, Lieutenant?" Ordway asked a few minutes later as the group trudged through a small clearing along the south bank of the river.

"We'll need to build canoes for the rest of our trip upriver," Clark replied. "We'll store the larger boats for the winter and retrieve them in the spring on our return trip."

"Assuming there is a return trip," York said with a smile.

Clark let out a small chuckle as he gave York an acknowledging nod.

"Shouldn't joke about such things," said Reubin Field, who was slowly trudging up beside York and his brother, Joseph. "These woods can take a man as easily as a wild animal."

Clark's expression sobered at Reubin's words. "You're right," he replied, "we shouldn't joke about such things."

"Perhaps, the thing that made those tracks downriver will be the end of us," York said, turning his head to grin at Reubin and his brother.

"I'm more worried about bears and big cats," Ordway stated as the group descended a small slope that took them closer to the river's edge.

"You're not worried about whatever it was that made those huge tracks back there, Sergeant?" Joseph exclaimed.

"Why should I be? It was probably some big toed Indian fetching water from the river."

"I've never seen an Indian with such big feet," Joseph shot back.

"You hadn't seen an Indian at all until a few months ago," Ordway replied, grinning.

Reubin frowned and looked down at the ground as he continued walking.

"Maybe they're the creatures the Hidatsa warned us about," Joseph said in a hushed tone.

"Nonsense," Ordway replied quickly. "That's just a savage superstition."

"Something made those tracks, Sergeant, and it sure as hell wasn't no Indian."

"Quiet, all of you," Clark snapped, holding his hand above him in a fist. The group stopped immediately. He began scanning the forest down to the water's edge. "Can you hear that?" They all fell silent, straining their ears to listen. Over the rustling of leaves and the distant calls of birds, a faint roar echoed through the forest—a sound that grew louder with each passing moment.

As they edged closer to the riverbank, the sound of rushing water grew louder. Clark craned his neck, trying to see ahead down the river. He quickened his pace as he hurried along the shoreline. The current picked up more and the sound of rushing water grew louder the farther he ran. A few minutes later, he stopped to take in the magnificent sight before him. A towering waterfall cascading from a sheer cliff, its waters thundering down into a frothy pool below. Mist billowed up, creating a veil of spray that caught the sunlight, casting rainbows in the air around him. He stood in awe at the power and beauty of the natural wonder standing before him. As the rest of the group caught up to him, their expressions mirrored his own sense of wonder.

"We've found it," Clark said, his voice barely above a whisper. "The great falls of the Missouri." He peered upward at a large outcrop that jetted out from the fall's left side. Quickly, he began ascending the muddy slope toward it. Behind him, Joseph Field and York hurried after him. It took only a few minutes before they arrived at the summit. Clark stood silently, his chest heaving from the exertion of the climb. In the distance rose the majestic peaks of the Rocky Mountains, their snow-capped summits glowing in the golden light of the setting sun.

He smiled as Joseph scrambled onto the summit beside him. "See? No giant beasts. Just a handsome view of the mountains."

Joseph nodded silently as he took in the grand sight before him. Clark took a deep breath and let out a loud *whoop* as York and the others began climbing onto the summit beside him. He felt a fresh sense of relief and exhilaration as he stared out across the expanse of river and forest that separated them from the mountains. He felt vindicated, not only that they had chosen the right path down the river and found the great falls, but that they were now almost to the Rockies. They would soon traverse the mountain's jagged peaks and spill out onto the other side—to Oregon Country, and eventually, the Pacific Ocean. For the first time, he felt a real sense they would accomplish their mission. They were so close now with only a stretch of mountainous terrain and a handful of Indians left standing in their way.

NICHOLAS KANE

TWENTY-ONE

Excerpt from Lewis's Secret Journal

Today we accomplished what I consider to be our greatest feat yet on this expedition—crossing the continental divide. As we ascended through the winding corridors, the air grew thin, and the landscape transformed with every step. The divide, a natural barrier that marks the separation of waters flowing to the Atlantic and Pacific Oceans, was both a physical and symbolic milestone in our journey. I cannot help but feel a profound sense of accomplishment, not only for myself, but for every member of the Corps.

Surprisingly, we have not encountered any Shoshone. Despite frequent forays into the countryside in search of any sign of the people Sacagawea assures us inhabit these lands, we have been met with silence. I grow increasingly worried the longer it takes us to make contact. Without Shoshone horses, we stand little chance of making it through the mountains by winter.

The men are still troubled by the howls at night coming from the woods. I tell them it is likely coyotes or wolves, but they insist it's something else. The tracks we've noticed near the camp each morning have only amplified the feeling we are being watched by something unseen in the evening darkness. I pray it is just my nerves getting the better of me. Lieutenant Clark has little tolerance for ghost stories and believes we were likely being stalked by a bear these last few days but are now safely through its territory. I know logic dictates he is correct. Perhaps it is the feeling of being so far from the safe bosom of civilization that makes my mind wander to strange and terrifying places. As much as I enjoy the beauty this unknown wilderness has to offer, I will be glad when it finally fades behind us...

-Meriwether Lewis
August 12, 1805

FRONTIER

TWENTY-TWO

The Shoshone did not reveal themselves, and their absence spread a sense of uncertainty throughout the camp as August gave way to September. Adding to the sense of uncertainty enveloping the camp was the sudden sickness of Clark, who was stricken with a high fever, chills, and muscle cramps during the last week of August. For a few days, he struggled to remain conscious, as Sacagawea tended to him and did all she could to help him recover. But by September first, his condition seemed to worsen, and the Corps prepared for the worst.

"He's going to die, Captain," George Shields said the morning of the second as he, Ordway, Willard, and Drouillard huddled around Lewis's morning campfire. "We should prepare for that inevitability."

"I'm not ready to give up on him," Ordway replied in a firm tone. "He's fighting it, give him time."

"We've given him two weeks, Sergeant," Shields snapped back. "How much longer are we going to let him hold us back?"

"We aren't going to just leave him behind!"

Shields let out a sigh of frustration. "Of course not. But it's almost winter, and if we don't reach the Lemhi Pass by then—."

"Then we'll try again in the spring," Ordway snapped, cutting him off.

"We won't have the rations to wait for spring," Drouillard announced in a low voice. "But the point is moot if we don't find the Shoshone. Without horses, we'll never make it through the pass."

Lewis, who had been listening in silence, finally spoke, his voice tinged with a mixture of concern and determination as he stared down at the dying embers of the fire. "We will do everything in our power to save him. We owe him that much." He looked up at Drouillard. "In the meantime, it's about time we found the Shoshone."

TWENTY-THREE

The Missouri had become nothing more than a small creek by this stage in their journey—its once-grand banks now exposed and dry. Lewis stopped to gaze out over the landscape, his eyes tracing the path of the dwindling river. A sense of foreboding settled over him as he took in the sight of the once-mighty river now reduced to a mere trickle.

Beside him, Drouillard stood looking out over the valley as well, his face etched with concern. "What are we going to do?"

"We press on," Lewis replied as he pulled tightly as the sling of his rifle.

Drouillard sighed and motioned to Willard, Harrington, and the others to continue moving. The group of men forged ahead into the arid valley, their footsteps kicking up clouds of dust as they trudged onward beneath the scorching sun. Lewis led the way, his eyes scanning the horizon for any sign of the elusive Shoshone. He began to wonder if the Indians had all left—forced to retreat south to better hunting grounds during the bitter winter months. But Sacagawea had assured them they were still there, somewhere.

An hour passed and the group arrived at a large meadow dotted with sparse patches of grass. In the distance, the rugged peaks of the mountains loomed, their jagged silhouettes cutting sharply against the bright blue sky. Drouillard halted and turned toward Lewis. "This might be a good place to rest and regroup, Captain," he suggested.

Lewis stopped and turned his head toward Drouillard and the others. He stared at the faces of the men for a moment before offering a simple nod of agreement. With a collective sigh of relief, the group settled onto the soft grass, their tired bodies grateful for the chance to finally rest.

Lewis sat down beside a small boulder that shaded him from the afternoon sun. He reached back and snatched his canteen. He brought it to his lips and took a long, refreshing drink, relishing the cool water as it quenched his parched throat. Setting the canteen aside, he leaned back against the rough surface of the

FRONTIER

boulder, allowing its shade to envelop him. He closed his eyes and allowed himself a brief moment of rest. He knew they couldn't linger in the meadow long, but a few minutes of rest wouldn't hurt. He glanced around at Drouillard and the others, each taking swigs from their canteens. He knew they were tired, but they had to press on. They had to find the Shoshone.

With a sigh, he leaned back harder against the boulder, his eyes scanning the horizon as he savored the tranquility of the moment. The meadow stretched out before him, bathed in the golden light of the afternoon sun—a peaceful oasis amidst the rugged wilderness. But suddenly, he spotted something in the distance. He sat up and pulled out his spyglass. He peered through it toward the object in the distance moving along the edge of the meadow. Drouillard, seeing him looking through the spyglass, hurried over to his side.

"What is it, Captain?"

"I'm not sure. But it appears to be a young boy."

He handed the spyglass to Drouillard who peered through it intently. "He seems to be alone, Captain."

"Yes," Lewis replied with a sigh. "We must be careful not to frighten him." He replaced the spyglass in his bag and motioned to the others to stand up. Slowly and cautiously, he began leading the group across the meadow toward the young Indian boy. As they approached, the boy looked up and noticed them. He appeared startled by their sudden presence. Lewis smiled and made a friendly gesture with his hands.

"Tab-ba-bone," he said, holding his hands up in front of him, trying to show the boy he meant him no harm.

The boy appeared scared. He took a step back, his eyes darting from one man to the next.

"Tab-ba-bone, tab-ba-bone," Lewis repeated, stepping in closer to the boy.

"Tab-ba-bone?" Shields whispered from a few away. "What does that mean?"

"It means white men, now hush-up," Lewis replied in a low voice. The boy continued to stare back at Lewis with a nervous expression.

"Tab-ba-bone. We are Americans. Do you understand us?"

The boy hesitated for a moment, until suddenly, he turned and darted off into the woods. Lewis threw up his hands in frustration. "Dammit! We scared him off."

"I don't think he knew what you were trying to say to him, Captain," Drouillard said as he stared off in the direction the boy had disappeared in.

"Sacagawea told me to use that phrase if we encountered any of her people. Now, that boy is probably going to return with a Shoshone war party to kill us all." Lewis took a deep breath and knelt in the grass as he tried to collect his thoughts. Their situation had turned more dire. If the boy relayed to the tribe that white men were trespassing on their land, they would undoubtedly send a war party out to slaughter them all. He prayed that would not be the case. In the meantime, he could be relieved about one thing—they had finally found the Shoshone.

FRONTIER

TWENTY-FOUR

It would be another two days before the expedition encountered any more Shoshone. Early on the morning of September 5, while refilling his canteen, Lewis heard Peter Harrington cry out, "There! Indians, Captain!"

Lewis capped his canteen and stood up to scan the edge of the large field where sure enough, what looked to be about sixty Shoshone warriors sat atop their horses peering back in his direction. He groaned and quickly unslung his rifle, letting it drop with a *thud* to the ground beneath him. Four of the warriors spurred their horses toward him, while another seven or so trotted off toward the other side of the field toward the camp. Lewis motioned for Harrington to hurry over to where he stood waiting for the Shoshone to arrive.

"Stay calm and throw your rifle down on the ground next to mine," Lewis instructed.

Harrington swallowed hard and nodded, his trembling hands fumbling as he tossed his rifle beside Lewis'. His wide eyes flicked toward the approaching Shoshone. "What do you think they'll do to us, Captain?"

Lewis kept his gaze on the advancing figures. "Hopefully, they'll try to communicate."

"And if they don't?"

Lewis hesitated, his lips pressing into a thin line. "Then…they'll scalp us and take our guns."

Harrington let out an audible gulp. The Shoshone were close now, their horses' hooves crunching softly against the dry earth. Behind one of the men, astride a smaller horse, sat the boy from before, his sharp, unyielding stare locking onto Lewis.

Lewis moved slowly but with deliberation as he reached into his bag. He produced two silver coins, which he placed on a flat rock in front of him before stepping back, raising his hands in a gesture of submission. His heart pounded in his chest, each beat echoing louder than the last. The lead Shoshone warrior stopped several paces away, his piercing eyes narrowing as they swept over Lewis.

Behind him, three others dismounted with quiet efficiency. The coins glinted like bait on a trap in the sunlight, and Lewis's breath hitched as one of the men darted forward, snatching them up. He held the coins aloft, catching the light as they were passed from hand to hand. The warriors studied them intently, their murmurs too low for Lewis to decipher. Finally, the lead Indian reached out, claiming the coins and tucking them into a leather pouch at his waist. His sharp gesture sent another warrior toward the discarded rifles. Lewis stiffened as the man picked up his rifle and began examining it, running his hand along the polished wood stock. His dark eyes lifted, locking with Lewis's. The warrior's gaze was unreadable—a mix of curiosity and suspicion, and something deeper, something primal.

Harrington took an unsteady step back, but Lewis held his ground, his hands still raised, his expression resolute. Every instinct in him told him to act, to speak, to bridge the divide between them. But his throat felt dry, his words caught somewhere between thought and breath. He desperately needed to find a way to communicate with the Indians and assure them that their expedition meant them no harm. But how?

Finally, after a few moments, he looked over Harrington. "We need to get them to come with us back to the camp."

"How the hell do you propose we do that, Captain?" Harrington replied in an excited tone, his eyes still lingering on the lead Indian with the menacing stare.

Lewis stared back at the lead Indian and began gesturing toward the camp with his hands. "Come," he said as he waved his hands, though he knew the Indian had no idea what that word meant. "This way." He pointed to the pouch the Indian had placed the coins into, trying to somehow make him realize that if he followed them, he would receive more gifts. The lead Indian let out a grunt of consideration, his sharp eyes glancing between the three warriors who now held the rifles. He muttered something in Shoshone, his voice low but firm. The three other Indians nodded quickly, their movements precise and obedient.

Lewis, catching the unspoken cue, gestured to Harrington. "Lead the way, Peter," he said quietly.

FRONTIER

Harrington didn't hesitate. He turned and began moving across the small field toward the camp, his steps quick but cautious. The Shoshone followed, their horses moving with a quiet grace that betrayed no sound beyond the soft thud of hooves against the earth. Lewis matched their pace, every nerve on edge as the distant shapes of tents and flickering firelight came into view.

When they reached the camp, Lewis wasted no time. He dismissed the four men standing guard with a wave of his hand. "Fetch Sacagawea and Charbonneau," he demanded. They nodded and hurried off, each casting a nervous glance back at the Shoshone warriors who lingered just outside the camp. A few moments later, Sacagawea appeared, her infant son cradled snugly in a shawl tied across her back. Charbonneau followed closely behind, a look of apprehension splashed across his face.

The atmosphere shifted the moment the Shoshone warriors saw Sacagawea. The lead Indian's stern expression faltered, replaced by a flicker of surprise. He straightened in his saddle, his lips parting as if he couldn't quite believe what he was seeing. The other warriors exchanged startled glances, their hands briefly tightening on the reins of their horses.

Sacagawea, oblivious to their astonishment at seeing her, shouted something in Shoshone. The words flowed with urgency, drawing the warriors' full attention. They stared at her, wide-eyed, their expressions now a blend of bewilderment and something deeper—recognition.

The lead Indian leaned forward slightly, his brows furrowing. He replied in their shared tongue, his voice cautious yet curious. Sacagawea took a step closer, speaking again, this time slower, her tone softer. She gestured to Lewis and Harrington, then to herself, explaining something that seemed to ease some of the tension hanging in the air.

The lead Indian's eyes widened as realization dawned. He muttered something to his men, and after a moment's hesitation, they dismounted. One by one, they stepped forward, placing the rifles they had taken on the ground in front of Lewis and Harrington. The lead Indian spoke to Sacagawea again, this time with a note of familiarity, his rigid posture softening slightly.

Lewis grasped the stock of his gun and quickly slung it back behind his shoulder. To his right, York appeared carrying an assortment of blankets and small trinkets, which he placed down in front of the Shoshone.

"This is Suyeta," Sacagawea told Lewis, pointing to the lead Indian. "He wants to know why you are trespassing on Shoshone land?"

"Tell him we wish to trade with the Shoshone for horses. And for knowledge of what lies beyond the mountains to the west."

She turned back toward Suyeta and relayed Lewis's message in her native tongue. Suyeta seemed unconvinced. He uttered a long message back to her.

"He says you look like a war party coming to attack their villages. You do not look like traders."

Lewis scoffed. "Tell him to look around. We have rifles, that is all. No cannons or horses. How could we possibly defeat any great Shoshone war party?"

Suyeta continued to eye him with suspicion as Sacagawea relayed Lewis's words. Finally, after more back and forth between him and Sacagawea, and due in large part to what appeared to be reassurances by Sacagawea, Suyeta relented. Through Sacagawea, a meeting was arranged with the Shoshone chief for the following day. He watched as Sacagawea and Suyeta exchanged some final words before the Shoshone trotted off toward the north in the direction they had appeared from. When they were out of sight, Lewis sauntered over to Sacagawea.

"That must have been strange for you," he said softly.

"He told me he remembers me from when I was a child. We used to chase frogs together along the creek."

"He will tell the chief we wish to trade for horses and any other supplies he can give us to get us across the mountains before winter?"

"Yes, he will arrange everything for tomorrow."

"Do you think his chief will help us?"

She smiled. "I believe Chief Cameahwait will favor our endeavor. After all, he is my brother."

FRONTIER

TWENTY-FIVE

The Shoshone village, nestled between rolling hills and framed by the majestic peaks of the Rocky Mountains, echoed with the crackling of campfire and the aroma of roasting meat. Tepees of various sizes, adorned with vibrant patterns and symbols, formed a circular arrangement, creating a sense of communal harmony within the natural surroundings. Within the village, Shoshone women, clad in intricately beaded garments, worked diligently on various tasks. Some tended to simmering pots over fires while others sat laughing atop wool blankets crafting baskets and beadwork. Near the center of the village, a row of logs had been arranged around a large glowing fire. At the center sat the Shoshone chief, Cameahwait. The man gave off a commanding presence, almost mirroring the rugged mountains behind him. Adorned in a ceremonial headdress embellished with feathers that danced in the evening breeze, his presence commanded attention. A cloak of richly dyed hides, adorned with symbols depicting the Shoshone way of life, hung loosely over his sturdy frame as he listened intently to Sacagawea, who sat directly beside him.

Lewis stood with his arms crossed, his gaze fixed on the circle of Shoshone gathered near the fire. The fire's flames cast long shadows over the assembly, creating an almost otherworldly atmosphere. He glanced at Drouillard and Charbonneau, who were standing a few paces away, their eyes locked on Sacagawea as she conversed animatedly with her brother, Cameahwait, the Shoshone chief. A few feet beyond them, several members of the Corps sat alone on scattered logs and stumps, their postures rigid, their eyes wary as they observed the Shoshone men sharpening tools, tending to their horses, or preparing food. Among them was York, his tall frame towering over the others, his eyes reflecting the dancing light of the fire with a quiet intensity.

Charbonneau leaned toward Lewis, his voice barely audible above the crackling fire. "Hard to tell if it's going well."

Lewis didn't reply immediately, his focus still on Sacagawea, who gestured emphatically as she spoke to Cameahwait. He finally turned his head slightly, speaking with quiet resolve. "She will get us the horses. Have faith."

Charbonneau let out a skeptical huff, his voice tinged with unease. "She better. Or this expedition is doomed."

Lewis shot him a sharp glare. "Hold your tongue, Pierre. You've been helpful, but your defeatism is becoming tiring."

"You know I'm right, Captain. Without horses, we'll never make it over the mountains before winter."

Before Lewis could reply, York approached. "Captain," he began, eyeing Charbonneau, "Lieutenant Clark is holding on, but he's still weak. Sacagawea asked some of the women here to tend to him. They've given him some Shoshone remedies, mostly herbs and roots. Let's hope they help."

Lewis nodded, a flicker of relief softening his stern features. "Good. But we can't linger here long. Once we secure the horses, we leave immediately. Time is not on our side."

"When will you speak with the chief?" York asked, glancing toward the fire where Cameahwait sat, flanked by his warriors.

Lewis inhaled deeply. "As soon as Sacagawea finishes discussing the terms."

As if summoned, Sacagawea turned, her expression serious. "My brother says the Shoshone welcome you to their land." Her voice was steady, but there was a slight tension lingering beneath her calm tone. "But the mountains are dangerous, and he wants to know what you will offer in return for his help."

Lewis squared his shoulders and stepped forward. He knew this was his moment and every word and movement he made had to be deliberate and measured. He extended his hand, a gesture he hoped conveyed goodwill. "On behalf of President Thomas Jefferson and the United States, we offer friendship, trade, and the knowledge of our people. Our journey here to these Shoshone lands is one of discovery and unity." He paused, listening as Sacagawea translated his words into Shoshone. When Cameahwait nodded slightly, he continued, motioning for Joseph Field and Winchester to bring the sack of gifts. He knelt and began removing items one by one, placing them on the ground before him. "Mirrors," he said, holding up one and tilting it so it caught

FRONTIER

the firelight, "knives, coins bearing the image of our leader, and..." He rifled through the bag, his fingers closing around the brass compass. He held it aloft, certain it would capture their attention. "This compass, crafted in Philadelphia, and a marvel of modern science."

Sacagawea took the compass and studied it briefly before handing it to Cameahwait. The chief accepted it cautiously, turning it over in his hands, his expression unreadable. His warriors murmured among themselves. For a moment, Lewis's heart raced, his pulse pounding in his ears as he waited for a reaction. When the Indian chief finally looked up, a faint smile tugged at the corners of his mouth as he handed the compass to one of his men. He spoke to Sacagawea and gestured toward Lewis and the others. After a few moments, Sacagawea turned to Lewis with a smile.

"My brother says he will provide thirty horses, tanned skins, food, and elk meat for your journey. But he warns that this will not guarantee your safe passage through the mountains. Do you agree to his terms?"

Lewis exhaled, the tension in his chest easing slightly. "Yes, we agree," he said, nodding emphatically. He turned to York and Charbonneau, a look of relief washing over his face. "We have our horses. Now we just need to reach the Pacific before winter."

"And make it through the Nez Perce lands," York replied in a grave tone.

Lewis sighed. He had heard about the Nez Perce from traders back in St. Louis. They were rumored to be fierce and proud, with a deep connection to their ancestral lands. Their reputation preceded them, and he knew that navigating their territory would pose its own set of challenges. But he would focus on one challenge at a time. First, they would have to traverse the Lemhi Pass and make it through the mountains before winter. If they failed to do so, they would be snowed-in and trapped in the unforgiving wilderness of the Rockies for the winter—a prospect that would doom any hope of them ever reaching the Pacific.

TWENTY-SIX

That evening, a massive bonfire roared in the center of the Shoshone village, its flames reaching toward the night sky like flickering tongues. The fire's warmth radiated in pulsating waves as the crackling embers danced in the air, casting a warm and vibrant glow that painted the surroundings with shades of amber and gold. Encircling the fire were men and women, each moving in unison with the rhythm of their handmade instruments. The men, adorned in vibrant, beaded attire, moved with a wild, untamed energy. Feathers adorned their hair, catching the glow of the fire as they danced in leather moccasins embellished with beads and quills, their movements transforming into a kaleidoscope of motion as they twirled and stomped, each step a rhythmic rebellion against the stillness of the night. The women's movements showed equal fervor, their dresses a blend of beaded patterns, flowed and swirled in response to the pulsating drumbeats.

Clark stood on the periphery of the vibrant Shoshone celebration, his eyes absorbing the spectacle unfolding before him. He was still very weak, but he had finally summoned enough energy to leave his tent and attempt walking around the outskirts of the village. His fever had broken overnight and the chills were gone, but his limbs still felt heavy when he walked. Still, he felt better than he had in weeks, and he hoped the worst was finally behind him.

As he stood watching the Shoshone dancing in front of him, he noticed York and a few other men from the Corps disappear into a tan colored teepee. Swirls of smoke wafted lazily out one of the open flaps in the canvas. Through the smoke he saw the silhouetted form of a woman approaching. He quickly realized it was Sacagawea, her dress flowing gracefully in the night air, each fringe and tassel swaying with each step she took adding to the fluidity of her movements. Feathers adorned her hair, intertwined with braids and beads, creating a headdress. The feathers seemed to catch the firelight, creating a subtle, ethereal glow around her.

FRONTIER

"Quite the celebration," he exclaimed as she approached him.

"It warms my heart to see everyone together like this," she replied with a smile.

"Will the Nez Perce be as warm and inviting as your people have been?"

She gazed back at the fire for a moment, her eyes lost in thought as the orange flames danced in her eyes. "The Nez Perce are known for their hospitality, but they are cautious with strangers. It will be wise for us to approach them with respect and openness."

He nodded understandingly as he peered back over toward the teepee York had disappeared into earlier. "How long do you estimate it will take us to reach the Pacific?"

"Two, maybe three moons. It is hard to know for certain."

He turned back toward her and met her gaze. "Thank you, Sacagawea, for helping us. You and your husband have been extremely invaluable to our mission, both as guides and interpreters. I honestly don't know where we would be without you."

She offered a reassuring smile. "We are a team, Lieutenant Clark."

He smiled. "Yes, we are."

Just then, a Shoshone man emerged from the flickering shadows of the teepee and approached them. He was bare-chested with white paint stretching across his upper body from shoulder to shoulder. He stopped in front of Clark and began speaking. Sacagawea waited for him to finish before translating his words.

"He is inviting you to join the Náóomiwi."

"The what?"

"It is a purification ceremony that will prepare you for the journey ahead. It is a great honor."

He smiled at the man as he tried to decide if he should accept. He looked back at Sacagawea and gave her a nod. "Tell him I am honored to join." He waited for her to translate his words to the man. When she finished, the man motioned for him to follow him back to the teepee. When they arrived, he removed his boots and was guided inside by the man. The transition from the vibrant glow of the bonfire outside to the dimmer, sacred space within was like entering a realm suspended in time. The air inside held a subtle fragrance of sacred herbs, and the soft glow of a central fire illuminated the tapestries and hide coverings that adorned the interior. Seated around the small fire were an assortment of tribal elders, each wearing regalia furnished with beads, feathers, and symbols painted across their bare chests. At the end of the circle of elders sat York and Lewis, their faces glistening with sweat.

As he took his place within the circle, one of the Shoshone elders began the ceremony. The air was filled with the sonorous chanting of prayers as the elders lowered their heads and closed their eyes. As he listened to the sounds of the chants echoing around him within the sacred confines of the teepee, he began to feel an inexplicable connection to the rhythm of the ceremony. He took a deep breath and let the heavy air embrace him. He closed his eyes, letting the rhythmic chants weave around him like a gentle current, and allowed himself to be carried into a trance-like state. As he drifted, the boundaries between the physical world and ethereal world seemed to blur. The foreign words of the Shoshone elders became a melodic undercurrent, a river of sound leading him to an uncharted realm within himself.

He opened his eyes. Sacagawea had appeared and was standing behind him. Lewis eyed him silently from across the fire with a solemn gaze. One of the elders, an aging man with a nearly toothless smile, began addressing him. After he began, Sacagawea began translating his words.

"Nawetsa speaks of the land, the spirits that guide us, and the strength we find in unity. He speaks of the journey, the challenges, and the resilience needed to overcome them. It is a prayer for guidance and protection as we embark on the final part of our journey to the great water."

Clark nodded appreciatively back at the elder.

The elder then gestured toward a small woven sack on the ground nearby. "That is sagebrush," Sacagawea explained. "It is a sacred herb—a protector. The spirits of the land have gifted it to us." The elder's expression grew solemn as he leaned back and looked up toward the canvas roof of the teepee. "In the lands of the jagged rocks that you will traverse, there are powerful creatures you will encounter. We call these creatures Nawabitsi Skanopi." He paused, as if offering silent reverence to the creatures he was describing. "Nawabitsi Skanopi possesses a wisdom as old as the mountains and a spirit as free flowing as the rivers. Its footprints, like those of a giant, bear witness to its guardianship over the vast wilderness, ensuring the delicate balance of nature remains undisturbed. The scent of the sage will be your protection against these great and majestic beings." He gestured once more to the sack filled with sage. "Carry it with you. Burn it when you sense the presence of Nawabitsi Skanopi. Let the smoke be your offering—a gesture of respect that will create harmony between your journey and the spirits that roam the jagged rocks."

Clark couldn't help but harbor a quiet sense of disbelief. In the recesses of his mind, the tales of colossal creatures and ancient spirits seemed more like folklore than fact. But he knew the tribes of the West possessed powerful beliefs in the supernatural world and those beliefs were largely woven into the fabric of their lives. Though his educated mind quickly dismissed such fantasies, he knew he had to at least acknowledge their importance to the Shoshone.

He slowly retrieved the small sack of sage from the ground. The elder had finished speaking, his aged face impassive. The man's dark eyes held a weight that seemed to carry the solemnity of generations. The air was heavy with smoke and the earthy scent of burning herbs, a strange and foreign aroma that seemed to seep into Clark's thoughts. The elder's gaze continued to linger on him. Clark straightened, feeling the unspoken weight of expectation pressing against his chest. Nervously, he turned his head toward Lewis, seeking the familiar steadiness he had come to rely on in his companion. He expected to see Lewis's usual look of quiet disbelief or detached skepticism, the expression that had become second nature whenever they encountered the unfamiliar or the inexplicable.

But we he saw instead startled him. The dancing light of the flames painted Lewis's face in sharp contrasts of light and shadow, and beneath that shifting glow, his expression betrayed something far deeper than skepticism. Unease—or even fear, seemed to grip him. His eyes were fixed on the elder with an intensity that bordered on alarm. The firelight played tricks with his eyes, casting restless, elongated shadows that flickered like ghostly apparitions against the canvas walls of the tent. It was as though the flames themselves had conspired to amplify the tension.

Clark swallowed hard, realizing for the first time that whatever was troubling Lewis might be something he couldn't reason or strategize his way out of. And if Lewis, the most logical and steadfast man Clark knew, was shaken…what did that mean for the rest of them?

FRONTIER

TWENTY-SEVEN

Clark gazed out across the rugged terrain before him and the majestic peaks of the Rocky Mountains rising high into the azure sky above. They had finally reached the Lemhi Pass, and to him, it was a scene of unparalleled natural beauty, with slopes carpeted in a patchwork of vibrant greenery, interspersed with colorful wildflowers that swayed gently in the warm mountain breeze. The pass itself was a narrow corridor carved between towering cliffs of rugged rock, its winding trail snaking its way through the mountainous landscape like a slender ribbon of earth. The air was filled with the sweet scent of pine, mingling with the earthy aroma of sun-warmed soil. Birds chirped melodiously overhead, their cheerful songs echoing through the mountainous valley below.

Beside him, Lewis took a long swig from his canteen as he surveyed the wondrous landscape around them.

"Have you ever seen such beauty?" Clark asked, his eyes scanning the field of wildflowers that beckoned them forward.

"Never before, and never again, I suspect," Lewis replied with awe, his own eyes scanning the mountains around them.

Clark smiled faintly, his eyes scanning the rocky slopes ahead for any sign of movement. The vast mountainous landscape stretched on before them, bathed in the warm glow of the late afternoon sun. Though the only creatures they had encountered since leaving the Shoshone village four days earlier were squirrels and birds, a nagging sensation gnawed at the back of his mind. It was subtle but persistent, like shadow he couldn't quite place, and it made his hand linger near the rifle slung across his saddle. He shook his head, trying to brush off the unease, and glanced over at Lewis.

Lewis, riding a few paces behind, seemed distracted. His eyes flicked toward Clark every few seconds, as though debating whether to say something. His usual air of quiet confidence was absent, replaced with a tension that Clark couldn't ignore. As they steered their horses around a narrow bend in the trail, Lewis finally broke the silence.

"Will," he began, "do you remember what the Shoshone said about creatures living within the mountain passes?"

Clark slowed his horse slightly and turned to look at his friend, raising an eyebrow. "Of course. It was quite the eerie tale," he said with a dismissive chuckle. "But there's no truth to any of it. Nothing out here but wolves, bears, and Indians."

Lewis nodded, but his agreement seemed half-hearted. "Yes, of course," he replied, though his tone carried a note of uncertainty that wasn't lost on Clark.

Clark's expression hardened slightly as he studied Lewis. "You think there's more out here than Indians and bears?" His voice carried a hint of incredulity. "You can't seriously believe in those Indian superstitions."

Lewis shrugged, his eyes shifting to the rugged peaks looming ahead. "I don't know what I believe," he admitted after a moment. "The Shoshone speak with such conviction, as though they'd seen these...things themselves. And the warnings weren't just from one or two of them. It was everyone. Even Sacagawea."

Clark sighed and adjusted his reins, his gaze sweeping the horizon again. "Meri, we've been through miles of wilderness, across rivers, and over plains. We've faced hostile tribes and survived some of the harshest conditions imaginable. Don't let a few campfire stories rattle you."

"It's not just the stories," Lewis said, his voice dropping slightly as if he didn't want the men a few yards behind them to hear. "It's the way they acted when they spoke of it. Fear like that doesn't come from nothing."

Clark frowned but didn't respond immediately. Instead, he let his horse trot a few more steps forward, his thoughts lingering on the Shoshone's words. *The Wahatoka*...Their stories had been vivid, filled with descriptions of shadowy figures lurking in the passes, watching travelers from the dark. The Shoshone had warned them to avoid certain areas entirely, calling them cursed.

"You're letting it get to you," Clark said finally, though his tone was less certain than before. "It's natural for people living in places like this to come up with tales to explain the unexplainable.

FRONTIER

Stories about monsters and curses keep their children close to the campfire at night."

Lewis smiled faintly, though it didn't reach his eyes. "Perhaps you're right," he said, though his gaze lingered on a shadow moving across the distant ridge. His fingers tightened briefly on the reins before he shook his head, forcing himself to focus. "Let's hope it's just stories."

***

The group's pace slowed as they continued into the mid-afternoon. Above them, the sun slowly arched its way high overhead as it began its slow descent toward the western horizon. At around three o'clock, Clark spotted a small meadow about a hundred yards ahead and motioned to Lewis.

"We should rest there," he suggested, pointing toward the meadow. Lewis nodded and spread word around to the others. They quickened their pace as they began making their way down the narrow path toward the meadow, the sound of a creek growing louder as they approached. When they arrived, Clark dismounted his horse next to a small birch tree and slowly trudged his way down toward the creek. When he reached the water's edge, a sense of calm washed over him. He paused and closed his eyes, letting the babbling sound of the creek's water sooth him as he stood silently beneath the warm rays of the late afternoon sun.

Within minutes, the rest of the Corps had arrived and settled into the small meadow to rest. A few men pitched a tent, underneath which, they began distributing jerky and assorted fruits to the rest of the group. On a nearby boulder, Sacagawea sat down and began nursing Pompey, while Charbonneau made his way toward the water, a pair of canteens dangling loosely from his shoulder. Clark peered down the creek a way and noticed it split off into two, with one meandering lazily toward the northwest while the main tributary continued ceaselessly westward. Quietly, he began walking along the edge of the sparkling water, the gentle rush of the stream soothing his senses. He came across a small eddy where the water danced in circles, creating a mesmerizing pattern of ripples on the surface. He knelt beside the water, the warm breeze tussling his hair as he unscrewed the cap of his canteen. He dipped it into the clear, icy stream, watching as it filled to the brim with refreshing water. He brought it to his lips and took a long swig. The cool water felt soothing inside his parched mouth. But as he rose from the water's edge, a sudden movement caught his eye. He turned his head just in time to see a flash of brown fur as a deer emerged from within a small tangle of trees. Its graceful form glided across the meadow with effortless ease, its delicate hooves barely making a sound on the soft grass. He watched in silence as the deer bounded its way across the meadow before vanishing once more into the depths of the forest beyond.

As he watched the deer disappear, he suddenly felt a heightened sense of vulnerability take hold of him. A cold shiver went down his spine as he once again felt the eerie sensation he was being watched. Slowly, he stood up, his eyes scanning the edge of the meadow and continuing up the jagged slopes of the mountains off in the distance. And then it hit him, the familiar odor from before, its foul smell assaulting his senses. His heart began to race, his breath coming in short, shallow gasps as panic began to take hold of him. With trembling hands, he reached down toward his waist and began fumbling for his pistol, his fingers closing around the familiar weight of the weapon as he fought to steady his nerves. Frantically, he scanned the tree line once more, searching for any sign of movement. But all he saw was the stillness of the forest, the branches swaying gently in the afternoon breeze. He slowly withdrew the pistol from its holster and held it steady in front of him. He could still feel the eyes of some unseen predator boring into him from somewhere beyond the trees. He felt exposed, like a lamb awaiting the slaughter. He gripped the pistol tightly, his knuckles turning white as he scanned the tree line once more. The forest seemed to close in around him, its shadows stretching like sinister fingers reaching for their prey. His mind raced with thoughts of what could be lurking in the darkness beyond, unseen and unfathomable. Was it the same presence that had haunted their camp weeks before? The air thickened with an unsettling tension, the stench of decay still hanging heavily in the breeze. As he cautiously retraced his steps, he couldn't shake the feeling of being hunted. Every rustle of leaves, every soft whisper of wind, set his nerves on edge. He chided himself for succumbing to such irrational fear, but deep down, he knew there was something out there, something waiting beyond the trees.

And then, just as suddenly as it had arrived, the sensation passed. The foul stench slowly dissipated just as it had before. With his heart still pounding in his chest, he slowly holstered his pistol and began walking back toward the men. He shook his head and cursed himself under his breath as he tried to push the irrational fear that had just taken hold of him away. But part of him knew *something* was out there, and whatever it was, it had been waiting for the perfect moment to strike.

TWENTY-EIGHT

Clark awoke with a start. He could feel the cold sweat clinging to his brow as the howls echoed louder through the still night air. In the distance he could hear Seaman barking wildly, but at what was unclear. He arose from his bedroll and donned his coat as he hurried out of his tent into the cool night. Above him, moonlight flickered down through the dense canopy of trees. He made his way toward the spot where Seaman stood barking into the trees, the dog's gaze remaining fixed on the shadows.

"Lieutenant Clark, you reckon it's wolves?" Clark recognized the voice as belonging to Private Gibson. He turned and saw the private scanning the trees, his rifle at the ready.

Clark shook his head. "Wolves, perhaps, but not like any I've heard." Another long howl pierced the night, rising above the chorus of Seaman's barks. Beside Clark, Gibson's hand tightened around his rifle. Soon, York appeared, followed by Thornfield, the Field brothers, and a handful of others, each casting furtive glances into the darkness. A rustle in the underbrush sent a chill crawling up Clark's spine. He peered intently into the forest, but he couldn't make out anything in the darkness.

"Will?" Clark looked to his left and saw the shadowy figure of Lewis approaching from the main camp, his rifle slung loosely behind him. "What's going on? Wolves?"

"I don't think so."

The howls ceased, leaving behind an oppressive silence. Then suddenly, a strong odor hit them causing them to step back involuntarily. The smell was overpowering; a potent amalgamation of sulfur and decay that made them recoil in disgust.

"My God, what is that smell?" Gibson uttered.

"Back to camp," Clark ordered, turning to face Lewis. "Whatever's in there, it's close." The men, casting one last glance toward the vacant shadows, retreated toward the tents. Seaman continued to bark intently. Gibson grabbed the dog by the neck and pulled him back with him. Seaman, still reacting to the lingering scent that hung in the air, resisted momentarily before yielding to Gibson's firm grip. Quickly, Clark rushed back to his tent and retrieved his rifle. He moved back over to the edge of the camp where Lewis still waited, his own rifle hung low at the ready. The smell had almost completely dissipated, and the night embraced an eerie calm. In the distance, an owl hooted, its haunting call slicing through the night air.

"Whatever it was, it's gone now," Clark said, his eyes still scanning the trees for any signs of movement.

Beside him, Lewis stifled a small cough as he slung his rifle back behind him. "We'll leave it behind tomorrow when we move out of the pass. I'll be glad to be over these damned mountains." He gave Clark a quick glance before turning to head back to his tent. Clark watched as he sauntered away while out of the corner of his eye, he spotted Silas knelt in front of his tent staring at him. He paused briefly as the two men's eyes locked onto one another before Silas slowly turned and retreated into his tent. Clark sighed and turned to go. As he walked, he looked up to take in the starry night above, basking in the indifferent glow of the moon's silvery radiance. When he reached his tent, he pulled off his coat and settled back down onto his bedroll. As he prepared to close his eyes and try to fall back asleep, he paused. Slowly, he reached for his rifle and moved it close to his side. *Just in case,* he thought to himself as he slowly drifted off to sleep.

TWENTY-NINE

The Corps journeyed on deeper into the pass as September wore on. Their progress was slow but steady, driven by the determination to reach their ultimate destination. However, on their sixth day in the pass, ominous clouds gathered overhead, casting a heavy pall over the landscape. By mid-afternoon, the skies opened, unleashing a relentless downpour that drenched the men to their cores. The rain quickly turned the trail into a muddy quagmire, making further travel impossible. The chilling downpour soaked their supplies and extinguished any hope of building a fire. For two long days, the Corps was pinned down by the unyielding storm. The men huddled together for warmth and set their tents up under the towering pines, hoping to receive some sort of shelter from the pelting rain and howling wind. Meals were reduced to sparse rations of dried meat and parched corn, their supplies to wet to prepare anything more substantial.

On the third day, Lewis sat quietly beneath an improvised canopy of oiled cloth, his journal open but untouched as the rain splattered across its surface. Beside him, Clark worked on sharpening his hunting knife, the rhythmic scrape of steel against stone providing a faint distraction from the relentless monotony of the storm.

"We're losing time," Clark said, breaking the silence. His tone was calm, but Lewis could tell there was a hint of frustration behind his words.

"I know," Lewis replied, nodding. "But pushing forward in this weather would be madness. The river's likely swollen, and the trails will be impassable."

Clark sighed and leaned back against a damp log. "I just hope this storm lets up soon. We're already weeks behind where we should be." He glanced at Lewis and noticed he was scribbling into his journal. "It's been a while since I've seen you write in that thing."

Lewis glanced up. "Sorry?"

FRONTIER

Clark smiled and shook his head as he returned to sharpening his knife.

***

It was late in the evening as Clark sat on a makeshift stool in the corner of his tent, the only light coming from the lantern on the ground next to his feet. In his hands, he held a worn map of the Oregon Country, its edges frayed from constant use. He hugged a wool blanket tightly around himself, trying to keep the early autumn air at bay as he peered intently down at the map. His fingers traced a long line from their current position to the Columbia River, which would take them to the coast. He let out a long sigh and brought his hand up to his forehead as he tried to rub the drowsiness away. Though the days had gotten shorter, their journey remained just as difficult and arduous as ever. But despite the fatigue that threatened to overwhelm him, he remained determined to make it through the Pass before winter completely set in.

It was when he peered back down at the map that he noticed it—the faint smell of sulfur. His eyes widened as he slowly recognized the pungent odor as the same foul smell that had assaulted him in the meadow.

In an instant, he was on his feet. He began searching for his rifle when he heard the stillness of the night broken by the desperate cries of one of the horses in the distance. Quickly, he snatched up his rifle, the cold metal pressing hard against his hands as he raced outside into the autumn night. In the distance, the horse's cries morphed into something far more gut-wrenching. The once-desperate *whinnies* now twisted into agonized screams that echoed through the stillness of the forest around him. He raced toward the pen, hoping he wasn't too late. When he got there, he noticed two horses were missing. Other men began to arrive as he desperately surveyed the surrounding area trying to ascertain where the dying screams of the missing horses were coming from.

"What in the name of all that's holy is that smell?!" Ordway shouted, waving his hand in front of his face.

"Fan out!" Clark barked. "Something's attacked the horses. I want teams of four to search in every direction. Go!" The men, armed with rifles and lanterns, began splitting off into the darkness.

He watched as Lewis and York emerged from the darkness, each holding a rifle and gazing wide-eyed at the horse pen.

"Was it a grizzly?" Lewis asked through bated breath.

"No grizzly would take two horses at once," Clark responded as he walked past them toward the tree line.

"Will!" Lewis called out after him. Clark stopped and looked back. "The smell, Will. It's like before."

Clark sighed and resumed his brisk pace into the trees. Lewis watched as York ran after him. A few yards away, Seaman was barking wildly into the dark forest. He could hear the men's shouts cut through the night as they pushed deeper into the trees.

"Where are they going?" A voice asked from behind him. Lewis turned and saw the figure of Sacagawea standing nearby, concern etched across her face.

From somewhere behind her, Charbonneau began to yell after her. "I told you to stay in the tent with Pompey!"

"They must not go into the trees!" She screamed at Lewis. "Stop them!"

With an angry snort, Charbonneau raced forward and grabbed her by the arm, throwing her toward their tent. "Get back in there and protect our child!"

Sacagawea stumbled backward, her eyes wide in defiance. Charbonneau ignored her and hurried toward Lewis's side. The men's voices from within the trees were growing more distant with each passing minute. More men soon appeared, each armed with a lantern and rifle, as Lewis directed them where to begin searching. Drouillard, armed with a hatchet and pistol, volunteered to lead a team of five back down the Pass toward the east to see if thieves had stolen their horses. Lewis agreed and dispatched the men down the Pass.

As Lewis took control of the men still in the camp, Clark proceeded deeper into the forest, the putrid smell growing stronger as he advanced. Above him, the moon's feeble light filtered

FRONTIER

through the thick canopy. He heard a shout cry out somewhere off to his right. "Here! Over here!"

He glanced back at York who stood a few feet away masked in the shadows of the trees. "Let's go." The two men raced toward the sound of the shouting. Within a few moments, they arrived at a small clearing illuminated by the silvery glow of the moon and stumbled upon a gruesome discovery. Horrified gasps escaped the lips of the expedition members as they entered the clearing and laid eyes upon the mutilated corpses of the missing horses laying in the moonlight.

"Holy Mary Mother of God," Ordway muttered, his hand over his mouth as he took in the grisly scene.

"What kind of animal could've done this?" Alexander Willard asked, his eyes wide with fright.

A few minutes later, Lewis and Charbonneau arrived. When Lewis laid eyes upon the corpses of the horses, he exchanged a troubled glance with Clark. The putrid smell still hung heavy in the air around them. Clark slowly knelt to examine the corpses more closely.

"Be careful, Lieutenant," Joseph Field cried out from the edge of the clearing. Clark nodded in acknowledgement as he studied the mutilated horses, their lifeless forms twisted into grotesque shapes. Clumps of fur and patches of skin were torn away, exposing flesh and bone. The limbs had been contorted at unnatural angles, and the ground beneath them was stained with dark, viscous fluids. His breath caught in his throat as he took in the macabre scene. He was certain of one thing— whatever had befallen the horses possessed an unearthly strength and ferocity that exceeded the laws of the natural world.

"Was it a bear, Lieutenant?" Peter Harrington asked in a nervous voice.

"What the hell kind of bear could have done *that*?" Reubin Field exclaimed.

"It was not an animal," another voice declared. He glanced up and saw Sacagawea standing defiantly in the moonlight, Pompey wrapped in a blanket and sleeping in her arms. "This was a warning. From Nawabitsi Skanopi. It wants us to leave these lands."

"Enough with that," Charbonneau replied, his voice tense. "No one here believes in that Shoshone fairy tale."

"It is no fairy tale, husband! We must heed this warning and move on from this place before we anger Nawabitsi Skanopi any further."

"What the hell is she talking about, Lieutenant?" one of the men yelled out from behind Joseph.

Clark shook his head. "It's not important. What is important is that we protect the remaining horses from whatever *animal* is out there. I want additional men placed on sentry duty each evening until we clear the mountains. We'll run the horse line closer to camp from now on and light fires along the camp perimeter after dark. Once we make it to the lowlands in a week or two, we should be fine. But until then, no one travels outside of camp alone. Understood?"

A wave of nods cascaded throughout the group. Clark glanced over at Lewis who simply continued gazing silently down at the dead horses. He took a deep breath and motioned for the men to disperse back to camp. As they slowly began to walk away, he gazed quietly into the dark forest beyond the moonlit clearing. He could feel something watching from beyond the trees, an unseen presence. *Was it studying him? Was it trying to determine how much of a threat he posed to it?* He stood silently for another minute, as if trying to show whatever was out there he wasn't afraid of it. But deep down he knew the truth of the matter was he had never been more scared in his life. Whatever this was, animal or otherwise, it was a threat to not just him, but every person in the expedition, and it was his duty to protect them.

The moon cast its glow upon the expedition's leader, his silhouette etched against the canvas of the forest. His eyes, thoughtful and focused, lingered on the shadows that clung to the edges of the trees. One thing was certain, they all now faced a chilling new reality—the unknown had claws, and it hunted the land they were now crossing.

FRONTIER

THIRTY

Excerpt from Lewis's Secret Journal

It has been several weeks since I last made an entry in this journal, and since then momentous things have occurred. On October 16, we finally reached the fabled Columbia River. Lieutenant Clark quickly ordered a fleet of canoes to be constructed to carry us down the mighty artery into the Oregon Country and eventually, to the Pacific.

On the 18th, we encountered the Nez Perce. A small group from the tribe made contact with us on a bluff overlooking the river and invited us to their village that evening. I readily agreed and with Lieutenant Clark and a group of thirteen others, made the four-mile overland journey to their camp. There, we met the Nez Perce chief, Twisted Hair, who provided us with food and other supplies, as well as a pair of guides who would help us traverse the mountains of the west and reach the great waters of the Pacific.

We have been on the river for almost four weeks now. I can feel the Pacific is close and I am eager to finally lay my eyes upon it. But as we continue what I pray is the final days of our long expedition, I cannot help but reflect on all that we have accomplished thus far. From the vast plains to the rugged mountains, we have faced countless challenges and overcome them together as a team. Now, with the Pacific within our grasp, I am filled with a sense of anticipation and wonder at what lies ahead. The completion of our expedition marks not only a historic achievement but also the beginning of a new chapter in our nation's history. I am confident that whatever the future holds, we will face it with the same courage, determination, and spirit of exploration that has brought us this far.

-Meriwether Lewis
November 14, 1805

THIRTY-ONE

"Rocks, plants, insects, and some arrowheads. I believe all of these will make the President very happy." Lewis gathered the items in front of him and stuffed them gently back into the large leather bag beside him. When he was finished, he looked up across the vast expanse of blue water before him. "Have you ever seen such a beautiful sight?"

Nearby, Clark smiled as he too gazed out across the waters of the Pacific Ocean. "Let's see how beautiful it is come January."

"Nonsense," Lewis snapped back. "I've always loved the ocean. You know, I nearly joined the Navy when I was younger. I wanted to sail the seven seas and explore the world."

"And instead, you joined the Army, and got to explore the dirt trails and mountain paths between here and St. Louis. Well done." Clark laughed as Lewis tossed a clump of sand at him.

The Pacific stretched out before them, vast and shimmering under the soft light of the late autumn evening. The cool breeze carried the salty scent of the sea, which mingled with the earthy aroma of the sandy beach beneath their feet. Waves gently lapped at the shoreline, their rhythmic motion creating a soothing melody that echoed in all directions. As the sun dipped below the horizon, painting the sky with hues of pink and orange, the water seemed to come alive with color. It glistened with golden reflections, while distant clouds tinged with purple drifted slowly across the darkening sky. Seagulls cried out overhead, their wings gliding gracefully as they soared on the ocean breeze. A few yards away, Seaman chased a pair of seagulls toward the water, his tail wagging frantically as he dove headfirst into the chilly waves. A few moments later, he emerged and shook himself off, before chasing after another seagull that landed close by. When the sun was almost completely below the horizon, Clark lit a fire and the two men huddled close to the flames as they finished cataloging the items from their journey that they planned to take back with them to Washington.

FRONTIER

"How long do you think it will take to reach St. Louis?" Clark asked as they finished counting a bag filled with specimen bottles.

"No more than six months, perhaps less if the weather is with us," Lewis replied. "The Columbia will take us back to the Rockies before summer and from there, if we can make it through the pass by late June, I expect us to reach upper Louisiana and the lands of the northern Sioux by August. Then it's just a month down the Missouri to St. Louis."

"If everything goes according to plan," Clark added, a flicker of concern splashing across his weathered face.

Lewis frowned. "Yes. Let's pray everything does."

As they listened to the crackling of the fire, their attention was suddenly drawn to the approaching figures of Silas Thornfield, the Field brothers, Willard, and a few others emerging from the shadows. The flickering flames of the fire danced across their faces, illuminating their expressions. As they drew nearer, the sound of their footsteps mingled with the gentle rhythm of the ocean waves. When the group reached the edge of the fire, Thornfield cleared his throat and began to speak.

"Cap'n Lewis, Lieutenant Clark, may we have a word?"

"Of course, Silas," Lewis replied with a smile, his curiosity piqued. "Please, join us." He motioned for the men to sit and join them by the fire. When they were settled, Thornfield took a moment to gather his thoughts before continuing. "We've all givin' a lot of thought to our return journey in the spring." He glanced over at Reubin Fields who nodded for him to continue. "And we have reservations about retracing our steps through the mountains."

"And why is that?" Lewis asked, exchanging a confused glance with Clark.

"The stuff that happened along the way. The howling, the smell, the horses…none of it seems right."

"I thought you didn't believe in superstitions?"

Thornfield paused and took a deep breath. "I tell you, Cap'n, I've journeyed across those mountains many times before, but I've never felt something…off during any of those times. Something wasn't right up there, and I don't think we should tempt fate by passin' through a second time."

Lewis sighed, the frustration evident in his expression. "What would you propose we do instead?"

Thornfield glanced over at Reubin Field and the others before settling his gaze back on Lewis. "We should head south. To California. We can hire a guide in San Francisco to get us across the great western desert back to St. Louis. It may take us longer to get back, but we all feel it's the right choice."

Reubin and his brother nodded in agreement. "We were lucky to make it through the first time, sir," Reubin said solemnly. "But who's to say we'll be as fortunate on the return journey?"

Clark leaned in, his expression contemplative. "But heading south along the coast presents its own risks, gentlemen. We'd be venturing into unfamiliar and potentially hostile territory, with no guarantee of safe passage. It's no secret the Spanish are exactly happy with the sale of Louisiana." He let out a sigh and turned to Thornfield. "I'm sorry, but we cannot risk this expedition being captured by the Spanish, or worse. We will return through the Lemhi Pass and across the Sioux lands to the north. There will be no further discussion on the matter."

"Then you condemn us all to death!" Joseph Field shouted, his voice rising with fear. "Something was watching us, Lieutenant. And don't tell me it was just some bear. I've hunted bears, and this was no bear, whatever it was. This was something…else."

Thornfield nodded in agreement. "Joseph's right. We cannot ignore the signs any longer. There was somethin' in those woods, something we couldn't see or understand. What it did to those horses…"

Clark's frustration simmered beneath the surface as he exchanged a troubled glance with Lewis. "This is madness," he muttered in a low, angry voice. "To let fear dictate our actions, to cower before some imagined threat. We're explorers, damn it! We face dangers head-on, we don't cower in the shadows like frightened children. There is nothing in those woods that cannot be explained through reason."

FRONTIER

Thornfield met Clark's gaze, his expression resolute. "I told you before, sir, back in St. Louis. I've seen things in those forests that can't be explained. I had heard the tales of creatures that stalked the shadows—that moved between the trees like ghosts. Back then, I dismissed them as stories meant to frighten children, but now…" He shook his head, his voice faltering. "Now I'm not so sure."

The fire crackled in the heavy silence that followed. The men sat motionless, their faces lit by the shifting glow of the flames. Lewis studied them carefully—the hardened lines of Thornfield's face, the nervous fidgeting of Reubin and Joseph Field, the unease in Willard's darting eyes. These were not men given to flights of fancy, yet their fear was palpable.

"Let's not lose our heads," Lewis said at last, his tone measured. "I don't deny that we encountered…strange things. But the wilderness is vast and full of mysteries. Unfamiliar sights, unfamiliar sounds—it's easy for the mind to conjure fears when it doesn't understand what it sees."

Thornfield's jaw seemed to tighten as he leaned forward. "With respect, Cap'n, this ain't just fear talking. This is survival. We've all heard the stories from the tribes—the creatures they warn about, the spirits that haunt the mountains. You can call them superstitions, but after what we've seen and felt, can you really dismiss it so easily?"

Clark shook his head, his frustration bubbling over. "Yes, I can, and I will. Every step of this journey has tested us, from the roaring rivers to the bitter cold, and we've endured because we've kept our wits about us. If we start running from shadows now, we might as well give up and go home."

Joseph Field rose to his feet abruptly, his hands clenched into fists. "We're not running from shadows, Lieutenant! We're running from *something*. Call it what you will, but it's out there, and it's watching us. You saw what it left behind. You heard the noises, the screams, the—"

"That's enough!" Clark snapped, his voice cutting through the tension like a blade. He stood and squared his shoulders, towering over the group. "I understand your concerns, but this expedition does not yield to fear. We will return by the route we know. That is my final word on the matter."

Lewis raised a hand, his expression calm but commanding. "Let's not let this divide us. Silas, I hear your concerns, and I don't dismiss them lightly. But Lieutenant Clark is right—we have a mission to complete, and we can't let uncertainty sway us from that path."

Thornfield looked at Lewis, his gaze steady but weary. "I just hope you're prepared for what might be waitin' for us out there, Cap'n."

Lewis said nothing, but his mind churned with unease. The men slowly dispersed, their muttered conversations fading into the night. As the fire burned lower, he gazed at the distant silhouette of the mountains with their dark ridges sharp against the starry sky. He took a deep breath, trying to quiet the creeping doubt that had wormed its way into his thoughts. His mind told him the men were being ridiculous, surrendering to unfounded fears and Indian superstitions. Yet, beneath his rationality, a faint but insistent doubt lingered. Something out there *had* unsettled the horses and sent waves of fear and doubt through seasoned men.

Shaking his head, he pushed the thoughts aside. They were explorers, driven by reason and the pursuit of knowledge. He wouldn't let fear cloud their judgment—or his. And yet, as he turned his gaze from the mountains to the embers of the fire, he couldn't quite shake the sensation that something in the darkness was watching them still. Deep down, he couldn't help but wonder: what if Thornfield was right?

FRONTIER

THIRTY-TWO

Excerpt from Lewis's Secret Journal

Winter continues to grip our camp with an icy vengeance. The biting cold gnaws at our bones, yet we find solace in the fact that this will be our final winter amongst the vast, untamed wilderness of the West. The winter snows have not been as formidable as we feared, but the cold continues to paralyze us, forcing us to remain largely in our small huts huddled together for warmth.

Our interactions with the Chinook and Nez Perce have proven invaluable during these trying times. They have welcomed us into their village, sharing their knowledge of the land and its resources with generosity that humbles the heart. They provide us with weekly rations, including meat, which we have consumed with immense gratitude. Life at this miserable winter camp is a delicate balance of survival and camaraderie. But there is something different about this winter than the winter last. The Corps seems to find itself at odds with one another. Silas Thornfield and about a dozen other men remain convinced that we should head south in the spring and take our chances with the Spanish in California. I tell them it's nonsense to presume the Spanish would agree to help us. We would lose all the specimens we gathered during our journey here and risk imprisonment in some California jail for God knows how long. Come spring, I pray they listen to reason and give up this insane notion of returning home via California.

But even as I curse those men for being fearful to return through the Lemhi Pass, I cannot help but find myself partially in agreement with them, though I would never admit as much to Lieutenant Clark. I must admit the strange things that happened to us last summer in the mountains continue to trouble me a great deal. I have tried to reveal this to Lieutenant Clark, but he will not hear any of it. I find it best to keep a separate journal to record what's been happening to us and record my feelings on the matter. This knowledge is unbeknownst to Lieutenant Clark, for I feel it is better to keep my thoughts on the matter of the Lemhi Pass confined to the pages of this journal.

For now, I must do my best to forge ahead through this unrelenting winter and begin preparing for the long-awaited journey home. Whatever peril may come on the road ahead, I have no doubt each man will fulfill their duty to themselves and to the country we all cherish. The men with me are courageous souls, and with the courage of our convictions we will make it home. We must press onward, and conquer whatever challenge awaits us, and emerge triumphantly on the other side.

-Meriwether Lewis
February 23, 1806

FRONTIER

THIRTY-THREE

It would take until mid-March for the weather to turn warm enough for the return trip to St. Louis, and by that point, the members of the Corps of Discovery, having been cooped up inside the walls of Fort Clatsop all winter, were eager to venture out and begin the long-awaited journey home. All, at least, save for a few, led by Thornfield. All winter, Clark had tried to convince Thornfield and the others that the safest and most efficient course of action would be going east across the Rockies back into upper Louisiana. But Thornfield had continued to stubbornly refuse to entertain any plan that brought the Corps back through the Lemhi Pass. By early March, as the temperature began to warm and the snows began to melt, signaling the start of an early spring, it was all becoming too much for Clark, who continually ranted to Lewis about the need to punish the men who continued to obstinately refuse his orders to prepare for the return journey across the Rockies. On March 10, he had finally had enough. That morning, he had sauntered into the tent of Thornfield and Alex Willard and informed them that if they were determined to fix themselves against traveling east across the mountains, they could leave the Corps and head south. But he had warned them, if they did, they would not be given any supplies or horses. They would be on their own. The threat had done the trick. The following day, both men agreed to follow the return path through the mountains.

That had been two weeks ago. Now, as Clark surveyed the fort one last time, he took a moment to take in the gray dawn. Down a small slope a few yards away, the waves of the Pacific crashed against the rugged coastline, their rhythmic roar a reminder of the vastness and power of the ocean. He took in a deep breath of salty air as he stood at the edge of the fort. In the dim light of dawn, the fort appeared silhouetted against the backdrop of the ocean, its weathered timbers bearing the scars of a long winter. He felt a pang of nostalgia as he reflected on the months they had spent there. The fort had been their home- their refuge in the wilderness-

and now it stood as a silent sentinel against the ever-changing tides of the Pacific.

"You look as if you have a lot on your mind, Lieutenant."

Clark's mind snapped back to the present. He looked over to see Sacagawea standing beside him. He nodded back at her with a smile.

"I'm just thinking about our journey here. The adventure's almost over. In a few months we'll be back in St. Louis, and all of this will eventually become just a distant memory."

"Will you ever return to these lands?"

He shook his head. "I don't think so. There's only enough time in a man's life for one great adventure."

"I would like to return here. It's peaceful."

"It's cold, windy, and dreary," he retorted back with a grin. Sacagawea simply shrugged. "Well, to each their own," he said with a wry smile. "Perhaps one day you'll have the chance to return and enjoy the peace and tranquility of these lands once more."

Sacagawea nodded thoughtfully, a hint of longing in her eyes. "Perhaps," she said quietly, her gaze drifting out toward the ocean. "But for now, I am content to savor the memories we've made here."

He paused, unsure of how to ask her what he wanted to ask. After a few moments of silence, he turned toward her, his expression earnest yet hesitant. "Sacagawea," he began, his voice soft but determined. "There is something I want to ask you."

She met his gaze with a mixture of curiosity and warmth, her dark eyes reflecting the gray dawn. "What is it, Lieutenant?"

Taking a deep breath, he forged ahead. "I have come to admire your courage and resilience more than I can express. And I cannot help but wonder…what are your plans for the future?"

Her brow furrowed slightly as she considered the question. "I…I have not given it much thought," she admitted. "My focus has been on helping you and Captain Lewis reach these waters." She paused, and with a slight tinge of resignation added, "but my place is with my husband, and my future leads down whatever path he chooses."

FRONTIER

He nodded in understanding. He felt slightly disappointed at her response, though he knew he had no right to feel that way. She had been an invaluable member of their expedition, and he respected her commitment to her family.

"I understand," he said softly. "Your loyalty is admirable. And whatever path you end up following, I have no doubt that you'll continue to inspire those around you."

She beamed at his words; her smile radiant in the early morning sunlight. "Thank you, Lieutenant. Your friendship has meant more to me than words can express."

"There is something else I'd like to know," he continued, looking back at her. She frowned and tilted her head slightly, curiosity flickering in her eyes. "What is it, Lieutenant?"

"Do you believe in Nawabitsi Skanopi?"

She turned her head back toward the ocean with a reticent gaze. "Nawabitsi Skanopi," she repeated softly, her gaze drifting out toward the vast expanse of the ocean before them. "I wasn't sure whether I believed it or not. But it is a belief held by some of my people that the Great Spirit, the Creator of all things, created Nawabitsi Skanopi to protect the lands chosen by the Great Spirit as the most beautiful lands in all of creation."

Clark nodded, his own gaze following hers out toward the horizon. "Do *you* believe he exists?" he pressed gently, his curiosity piqued.

Her lips curved into a smile while her eyes reflected the shimmering light of the morning sun. "I believe in the power of the natural world," she said quietly. "In the interconnectedness of all things, and the reverence we owe to the land and the spirits that dwell within it. When I was a young girl, I did not believe in his existence. But now, I am not so sure."

Clark nodded again. He pondered her words, though the rational part of his mind couldn't bring himself to even entertain such fantastical notions of spirit people walking the earth protecting lands for made-up God's. "I appreciate your honesty. But I must admit, I find it difficult to believe in the existence of such beings. I've seen a lot of this continent and never in my travels have I come across anything that cannot be explained rationally and scientifically."

She smiled. "This world is vast and filled with wonders, Lieutenant. Perhaps, you have not seen as much as you think you have."

"Perhaps," he conceded. "But I cannot believe the forests are stalked by tall, furry beasts, bent on punishing those who trespass onto their lands. The rational side of me refuses to believe it."

"There is no rationality when one is alone and lost within the depths of the forest," she replied in a solemn tone.

He let out a long sigh. "I hope, for our sake, your people are wrong."

"And I hope for my sake, and my baby's, that when the time comes, you will be ready to believe."

He frowned as he watched her quietly begin walking back toward the small tent she shared with Charbonneau and her baby. He wasn't sure what he believed anymore. His mind told him to push notions of mystical beasts out of his mind and focus on getting the Corps back to civilization. But Sacagawea's words lingered at the forefront of his mind. What if there was more to the world than he had ever imagined? Perhaps, there was more to the vast wilderness than science could explain, and perhaps there *were* forces at work in the world that defied explanation. Reason would only carry them so far. He now had to be ready to face the unknown and whatever awaited them within its depths.

FRONTIER

THIRTY-FOUR

The *crack* of rifle fire shattered the stillness of the night, jolting Clark from his sleep. Heart pounding, he scrambled out of his tent, his hand instinctively reaching for his pistol.

"What's happening?!" he cried out, adrenaline coursing through him.

John Colter, his face pale with fear, stepped forward, his rifle gripped tightly in his hands. "There's something out there!" he shouted back in a trembling voice.

Clark looked over and saw York and Sergeant Ordway approaching, each with their rifles clutched firmly in their hands. He glanced back at Colter. "What happened?"

Colter, trying to catch his breath, gripped his rifle harder as he gazed out into the pitch-black darkness of the forest. "I was on guard duty, sir. But I went to piss over by those rocks there." He pointed to a pile of rocks a few yards away near the tree line. "But while I was pissing, something threw a rock at me!" He pointed wildly into the forest. "It came from the trees, I swear it. Then I heard footsteps, and that foul stench, the same as last summer…" He aimed his rifle into the darkness. "I fired two shots at whatever it was. I don't smell the stench anymore."

Clark began to sniff the night air, but he couldn't smell anything except the pine trees and a small tinge of gunpowder. His mind raced as he processed Colter's story. The eerie familiarity of the situation sent shivers down his spine. "Indians?"

Colter shook his head, his eyes still wide with fear. "I couldn't see a thing, sir. But whatever it was, it meant to hit me. And I think it's still out there, watching us now…"

Clark furrowed his brow, unsure of what to make of the situation. "Why throw a rock if it meant to attack?"

Lewis appeared from the darkness, his pistol held out firmly in front of him and his jaw clenched with frustration. "What happened?"

"He says something threw a rock at him," Ordway replied, gesturing toward Colter.

"Indians?"

Clark shook his head. "I don't know. But there's no reason to believe the Shoshone, Nez Perce, or any other tribe we've met along the way would have any reason to do us harm. If they wanted us dead, they've certainly had ample opportunity."

Lewis glanced nervously at Clark. "We can't take any chances. I want every man to arm himself at all times and no one is to leave camp. Our strength is in our numbers. At first light we'll pack up and move along. I want us out of this pass and through the mountains as quickly as possible."

As the men hurried to grab their rifles, Clark's thoughts swirled with uncertainty. Whatever was lurking in the darkness beyond their campfire, it was a threat they couldn't afford to underestimate. And as the long dark night stretched on, he couldn't shake the familiar feeling of being watched. He hated that whatever foe they were dealing with continued to cling to the shadows. He preferred a straight fight with an opponent he could see and defend himself against. The fact that whatever was watching them remained elusive made him feel vulnerable and powerless—a feeling that made his stomach twist in knots. He anxiously awaited the daylight. It would give him a chance to finally pursue whatever this unknown enemy was and deal with it accordingly. But until then, he quietly settled his back against the base of a nearby tree, waiting for the dawn, and the answers that would hopefully follow with it.

FRONTIER

THIRTY-FIVE

The morning sun filtered through the dense canopy of trees as Clark and the others trampled through the forest searching for any sign of whatever had stalked them during the night. Shafts of golden light filtered through the leaves, casting shifting patterns on the forest floor as they moved deeper into the wilderness. To his right, York and Ordway moved along at a brisk pace, their rifles hung at the ready, while a few yards behind them, Joseph Field and Alex Willard skulked along quietly, their eyes darting nervously from tree to tree. To his left, Drouillard and Charbonneau moved in tandem, their steps measured and cautious as they navigated the thick undergrowth.

As the group emerged into a large field dotted with sunflowers, Clark took a moment to survey their surroundings. To the north, a dense pine forest loomed on the horizon, while to the south, a meandering stream wound its way through the field, its waters sparkling in the sunlight.

"We're journeying quite a way just to find a bear," York said with a tinge of sarcasm.

Clark smirked as he shielded his eyes from the bright sunlight. "If it's a bear, which it most likely is, we need to kill it. Otherwise, it'll keep stalking us the entire time we're in the pass."

"I've never known a bear to toss rocks at its prey."

Clark eyed him with a mixture of frustration and determination. "Whatever it is, we can't take any chances. We need to be prepared for anything."

"I don't think it's a bear, sir," Ordway said, approaching them. "We haven't found any tracks or anything else to indicate bear activity in this area."

"Then what else could it be, Sergeant?" Clark snapped back.

"I'm not sure. I just don't think it's a bear."

Clark let out a frustrated sigh. "There was bark ripped off a tree near the camp."

"That could have been anything."

"Lieutenant, we are wasting our time out here," Charbonneau groaned as he sat down on a nearby rock. "We've wasted almost half the day searching for this elusive bear or whatever it was that was at the camp last night, and we've found no signs of it. Can we *please* head back?"

Clark eyed him with contempt. He understood the men were growing impatient, but he couldn't shake the feeling that they were missing something crucial. "We can't afford to give up just yet," he replied firmly. "Whatever it was, it won't stop until we find it. We need to keep searching."

Charbonneau let out an exasperated sigh but nodded reluctantly.

"Maybe it's the Nez Perce," Drouillard offered, "or the Shoshone. We're probably back in their lands by now. Maybe they're watching us, making sure we leave."

"Maybe," Clark replied with a tinge of resignation in his voice. "But I've never seen Indians stalk like this. And why would they not make themselves known to us?"

"Maybe they're just stupid Indians," Willard suggested with a grin.

"If it is Indians, sir, we shouldn't venture much farther from camp," Ordway said in a cautious tone. "They could be watching us right now, trying to get us out in the open."

"Just like we are now," York replied in a worried voice. He stiffened up and began searching the field for any signs of movement in the grass or from the trees in the distance. Clark let out a resigned sigh. He knew Ordway was right. If it was an animal, it was likely long gone by now. But if it was Indians, they could be in danger at that very moment.

"All right. Let's get back to camp. Sergeant, you and Willard provide a rear guard, York and I will take point. The rest of you, spread out to the left and right and watch for any signs of movement on our flanks." Quickly, the group assembled into a diamond formation and began trudging their way through the underbrush back toward the camp. As they exited the field, Clark took one last look at the wide-open field before turning his gaze back to the forest. Whatever was out there, it had eluded him again. But he quietly resolved he would be ready for it if it decided to return.

THIRTY-SIX

They were left alone for two days.

On day three, whatever was stalking them returned. It started with the usual nighttime disturbances. Scraping against trees, distant howls in the night. But eventually, by day five, the terror increased. The men on guard duty were pelted with large rocks that sent them scurrying for cover while the howls drew closer, so close that Clark and the others could hear the bated breath of whatever it was that was hiding within the shadows of the forest around them. With each passing night, the men's sense of dread intensified, and their nerves were soon stretched to their breaking point. On the morning after each encounter, Clark, York, and a few others would venture out into the forest to search for whatever it was that continued to stalk them through the pass. But each day, they found nothing except piles of rocks neatly placed every fifty yards or so from the camp, along with trees where the bark along one side had been completely stripped off. Clark cursed himself in frustration at not being able to find whatever was responsible for the nighttime attacks. Sacagawea assured them it wasn't her people, nor was it likely the Nez Perce or any other tribe in the region. She told them most tribes avoided the pass, and for good reason. But he refused to entertain any notion that what was happening to them was supernatural. Whatever was doing this to them, he was determined to find it and kill it. It would not be until the sixth night, however, that their situation would grow from bad to deadly.

***

Clark shielded his eyes against the midday sun as he scanned the ridgeline below with growing urgency. For nearly a full day, he and eleven other men had combed the rugged terrain in search of Elias Winchester and Samuel Treadway. Despite strict orders to remain close to camp, the two men had ventured out to hunt and never returned. Now, every gust of wind through the pines and every distant echo off the canyon walls seemed to mock their efforts, whispering of unseen dangers lurking just out of reach.

The wilderness stretched endlessly before them, a vast expanse of towering cliffs and dense pine forests that seemed to close in tighter with each passing hour. The silence was oppressive, broken only by the occasional rustle of leaves or the forlorn cry of a bird. It was as though the land itself was holding its breath, waiting to reveal its secrets—or its horrors.

"Lieutenant!" A voice called out from Clark's right, cutting through the tense stillness. Clark's heart leapt as he turned, squinting against the sunlight. In the distance, a hand waved frantically. Without hesitation, he descended the sloping ridge, the dry pine needles crunching beneath his boots. The voice grew louder, guiding him through the maze of trees and underbrush until he emerged into a small clearing.

Reubin Field stood waiting, his expression grim. Beside him were his brother, Joseph, and Peter Harrington, their rifles held loosely at their sides. Clark's heart sank at the sight. There was no sign of Winchester or Treadway.

"I thought you'd found them," Clark said with a sigh of disappointment.

"We haven't, sir," Reubin admitted, his gaze lowering to the ground. "But Joseph found...this." He gestured to a spot on the ground.

Clark stepped closer and frowned, recoiling slightly. It was a small pile of what appeared to be feces. He turned to Reubin, his voice sharp. "You called me over because you found a pile of shit?"

"You told us to report anything unusual," Reubin said defensively. "Maybe it's from Sam or Elias."

Clark pinched the bridge of his nose, struggling to contain his frustration. "You fool, I don't care about a pile of bear shit in the middle of the woods! And what exactly do you expect me to do with this? What we need are tracks, articles of clothing, signs of a campfire—anything that tells us where they went!" He let out a heavy sigh, his anger giving way to weariness. "Let's get back to camp and report to Captain Lewis. Maybe the southern search teams had better luck."

The group exchanged resigned looked before turning back toward camp. The journey back felt longer and more grueling than before. The rustle of leaves and occasional crack of branches heightened Clark's unease. He couldn't shake the feeling that they were being watched, though the forest around them seemed lifeless and still.

When they finally reached camp and hour later, the sentries at the entrance greeted them with cautious expressions, their rifles at the ready.

"Find anything, Lieutenant?" one of the men, David Hooker, asked him as he passed by.

Clark shook his head. "Nothing. I only pray the other group had better luck."

Hooker simply shook his head. "They arrived back fifteen minutes ago, sir. They didn't find anything either."

Clark's heart sank. He scanned the camp and quickly spotted Lewis weaving through clusters of men, his stride brisk, his face lined with worry. He approached Clark with an urgency that matched his own. "Any sign of them?"

Clark shook his head. "Nothing. We searched every ravine, every thicket, but it's as if they vanished."

"Well, they couldn't have just disappeared, Will. They must be out there somewhere." Clark could sense the worry and frustration radiating off his friend, mirroring his own feelings of helplessness in the face of the unknown. "Is it possible something else got them out there?"

"Something else?" Clark eyed him with suspicion. "What else?"

"Will, a bear didn't drag off two fully grown and armed men. There's something else out there, and it's been stalking us since we left the Columbia."

Clark bristled. "Meri, you're letting fear get the better of you. They're lost or injured, nothing more. We'll find them."

"But what if they're not lost, Will?! We have to start thinking about all possibilities."

"To include mythical furry beasts? My God, Meri, have you gone mad?"

But before Lewis could respond, another voice interrupted. "He's right."

Clark turned to see Thornfield approaching, his face scratched and bloodied from the hours in the wilderness. His rifle was held tightly, as if he expected to use it at any moment. "Something's been following us," Thornfield said, his voice trembling with conviction. "The Shoshone warned us about these mountains. They said they were cursed. We didn't listen, and now we're paying for it."

"That's enough, Silas," York said sharply, stepping forward. "You're scaring the men with campfire stories."

Thornfield's eyes narrowed. "You've hard it, Yorkie. The cries in the night. You've smelled them. Don't stand there and tell me you haven't felt the same damn thing we all have."

"Them?! So now we're being stalked by an entire *tribe* of mythical beings, are we? You've let yourself become scared by a creature made up by the Shoshone as a bedtime story for their children." York shook his head in disbelief. "I never would have thought someone who's lived most of their life on the frontier would be frightened by a children's story."

Thornfield took a step forward, his eyes flashing daggers toward York and the others. "I ain't scared of no man. But what's out there, ain't no man. It's…something else. We should turn back now while we still can."

Lewis raised his hand, silencing the escalating argument. "I know you're scared, Silas. We all are to one degree or another. But turning back is not an option. We've committed to this course, and we must stick to it. There's no other way."

"We can go back to Oregon!" Joseph Field shouted. "The Nez Perce will help us get through the winter like before. And then, next Spring, we can head south, to California, like we wanted to do in the first place."

"You will not survive the journey to California!" Clark roared back in anger. "We barely made it through these mountains once, and that was with the help of the Shoshone. Heading to California now would be madness!"

Joseph bristled, his voice rising with defiance. "We've faced worse than this! We can do it again, with or without the Shoshone!"

Clark's expression hardened. "This isn't about facing challenges, Joseph. This is about survival. Heading to California would be a death sentence for all of us."

Joseph's shoulders slumped, his defiance fading into resignation. Lewis glanced back toward Thornfield. "We're not going back." He paused and took a deep breath. "And no man will be allowed to leave the Corps. Our strength is in our numbers, and I won't let anyone jeopardize that." Clark glanced over at him with a look of surprise. "Anyone who refuses to keep moving east through the mountains will be flogged. And any man who attempts to steal rations and supplies from the Corps and return to Oregon will be hanged as a deserter." He scanned the faces of the men assembled around him, his words hanging heavy in the air. Some exchanged uneasy glances, while others nodded solemnly, acknowledging the severity of Lewis's decree.

"We must all stand together as one against this threat," he continued, his voice steady and unwavering. "That is how we'll survive." The men exchanged reluctant nods as Lewis finished. Clark, standing off to the side, watched as York gathered some of the men up to return to the forest and continue the search, this time with Seaman at his side. Sacagawea appeared, baby Pompey slung tightly behind her back in his sling.

"I'd like to come along as well," she told York, who nodded and motioned for her to fall in behind Peter Harrington.

As he watched the new group of searchers assemble, he glanced over at Lewis, who stood nearby, deep in conversation with Drouillard and Ordway. Their voices were low, but their expressions were grave, reflecting the weight of the decisions they would soon face. The prospect of venturing deeper into the forest filled him with a sense of foreboding, but he knew they had no choice. They had to find the missing men before it was too late. With a determined resolve, he slowly made his way toward York and the others, ready to join them as they ventured once more into the unknown. But as they disappeared back into the dense foliage of the forest, he couldn't shake the feeling that they were on the brink of confronting something far more sinister than they had ever imagined.

FRONTIER

THIRTY-SEVEN

As the morning dawned, Clark, flanked by Ordway, John Colter, York, and Willard, resumed their search into the mist-laden forest. The sun, obscured by a blanket of low-hanging clouds, cast a subdued light upon the towering pines that loomed overhead. The air around them was cooler than it had been in recent days, carrying with it a delicate mist that clung to the landscape, transforming the familiar surroundings into a ghostly expanse bathed in gentle shades and softened edges.

As Clark walked out ahead of the men, his eyes scanned the weathered map in his hands, tracing the imagined paths of their two missing comrades. At intervals, the men would emerge from the embrace of the forest, greeted by small rock outcroppings that provided respite from the thick foliage and a view of the towering Rocky Mountain range around them. As the day wore on, muted sunlight continued to filter through the canopy above, casting an enchanting glow on the forest floor below. By late afternoon, they had traversed over six miles of forest and still found no trace of the missing men. Clark sighed as he knelt atop a small rocky ledge overlooking the north side of the Lemhi Pass. He removed his hat and peered down into the valley below, hoping beyond hope to see some signs of life—a fire, smoke, anything to indicate the men were down there. After a few minutes of searching, he closed his eyes and began rubbing at his temples. He heard footsteps approaching and turned to see York standing beside him, his eyes also scanning the valley below.

"We're not going to find them, sir," he said in a low voice. Clark simply nodded and stood up.

"No, I don't imagine we are."

"Do you believe what Silas said last night? That something out there got them?"

Clark sighed and replaced his hat atop his head. "I don't know. They were seasoned men used to this type of terrain. I find it hard to believe they simply fell down a rock face or got turned around a mile from camp. A bear seems more plausible, but even that seems perplexing. They were together, so even if a bear attacked one of them, the other should have been able to shoot and kill it." He sighed. "I admit, I have few answers and even more questions."

York frowned. His gaze lingered a moment on the valley below before drawing level with Clark's. "Do you think it could be true what the Indian's said? About giant man-like creatures living in these mountains that kill all trespassers?"

Clark eyed him harshly. "No, of course not. It's all just savage superstition."

"Why not? The President said we may encounter wooly mammoths out here. So why not these man-like creatures?"

Clark shook his head in frustration. "The President has access to the greatest scientific minds the nation has to offer to inform about these lands. And there was never any mention of ape-like creatures stalking trespassers through the mountains."

York nodded with a sigh and let the matter drop.

"We should get moving," Clark said as he picked up his rifle and slung it back over his shoulder. The two men slowly began trudging back to the others. They moved in silence as each pondered their conversation from earlier. Clark tried to shove the thoughts from his mind, but he was finding it increasingly difficult to find a scientific reason for what was happening to them. But he couldn't bring himself to give into the Indian superstitions—at least not yet. His mind still held out hope there was a rational explanation to all of this. He thought about what Sacagawea had said to him back in Oregon: *This world is vast and filled with wonders. There is no rationality when one is alone and lost within the depths of the forest.* He turned the words over and over in his mind as they continued walking, wondering if he had truly reached the edge of reason and was now treading on the fringes of reality, where the laws of nature bent and twisted in ways that defied rational explanation.

Suddenly, York stopped and turned, his eyes wide as he scanned the trees around them.

"What is it?" Clark whispered, looking around to identify the source of York's sudden unease.

"The smell," he replied in a hushed voice. He unslung his rifle and continued peering off into the trees.

FRONTIER

Clark stopped and sniffed the air around him and suddenly, it hit him. He nearly gagged as the smell quickly overcame him, causing him to close his eyes and struggle to maintain his balance. He urgently unslung his own rifle and scanned the area. A few yards away he spotted Ordway and the others resting against some trees. He waved his arms at them, motioning for them to hurry over to where he and York stood. They obeyed and within a few seconds they were kneeling beside him, their own rifles cocked and ready to fire. The smell continued to waft in the breeze around them, nearly stifling their senses.

"Whatever it is, it's close," York whispered. Clark took in a deep breath of the foul air and began scanning the trees again, searching for any sign of what was causing the foul odor—and what was hunting them. After a few minutes of silence, he repositioned the rifle butt against his shoulder and paused, peering down the barrel toward a small cluster of bushes fifty yards away. He noticed the branches stir slightly. He narrowed his gaze and slowly squeezed back on the trigger of the gun. He heard the hammer crash down hard against the steel, the resounding echo blending with the rustle of leaves in the quiet wilderness. The bullet *zipped* through the air, slicing a fleeting path toward its target with a faint whistle. Clark watched as it penetrated the small clump of bushes and then paused, waiting for some indication it hit something alive within the bushes. But no sound came. He quickly began reloading the rifle as York and the others turned to see what he had shot at.

"What did you see?" York asked, aiming his rifle in the direction of the bushes.

"I thought I saw something move over near those bushes," he replied as he reached into his leather pouch for a fresh paper cartridge. The aroma of gunpowder now wafted in the air around them, mingling with the pungent stench of the foul odor. He stopped when he heard what sounded like footsteps hurrying off in the distance. Above them, tree branches rustled violently as something leaped from one branch to the other, and then onto another tree entirely as it made its way north away from the men. Suddenly, Clark heard a low, guttural howl ring out across the forest. The first howl was answered by a second, and a third, and finally, a fourth howl that sounded more like a high-pitched wail. The howling created a chorus that sent shivers down his spine as he finished loading his rifle.

"Lieutenant, what the hell is that?" Ordway exclaimed, his voice cutting through the tension in the air as he squinted through the trees.

"We should move," York urged, "we're exposed in this position."

"Exposed? You make it sound like we're surrounded by an enemy force," John Colter replied in a shaky voice.

"I believe we are," York said grimly, his eyes now searching upwards into the leafy canopy above.

Clark pulled up his rifle and glanced around at the trees. The foul smell still lingered but it seemed to be dissipating some. "I think now is our chance. Let's move." Quickly, the men stood and began hurrying away with Clark and York forming a rear-guard. After traveling almost half a mile, Clark motioned for them to stop and regroup.

"We should keep moving, Lieutenant," Ordway said, his eyes still flickering with a nervous unease. "We need to regroup with Captain Lewis and the others."

Clark nodded agreeingly. "We will, Sergeant. But we must also ensure we aren't being followed." He peered up at the trees and then scanned the forest once again for any signs of movement. He saw nothing. He let out a sigh, and then took in a deep breath of forest air. The foul smell was gone, replaced with the earthy aroma of pine and moss. That was as good a sign as anything, he thought as he rechecked his rifle to make sure it was loaded. When he was certain it was, he motioned to Ordway and the others. "Let's move. We'll try and make it down into the valley by nightfall. We'll have to spend the night."

"I ain't spending a night out here with just the four of us and whatever those things are that made those howling sounds," John Colter exclaimed in a frantic voice.

Clark turned toward him, his eyes narrowing in frustration. "Captain Lewis and the others are too far away for us to regroup with them before nightfall. And we'd be walking in circles if we tried to travel through the forest at night. I'm afraid we don't have a choice."

York glanced at him, and then turned to face the path that would lead them down the jagged rocks into the valley. "This way," he said, motioning with his hand. Clark slung his rifle behind him and hurried after him along with the others.

***

That evening, Clark ordered the group to ignite large bonfires at fifty-foot intervals around their small camp. He stood by and watched as the fire's flame's cast a warm, dancing glow along the edge of the small clearing they were in, pushing back the encroaching shadows.

"Higher!" he yelled, pointing to one of the fires that was slowly shrinking in the cool evening breeze. York hurried over and began piling more sticks and logs onto it and slowly the flames grew larger and higher. Satisfied, at least for the moment, that they were safe, he turned and walked over to where York stood, his tall frame silhouetted against the bright dance of the flames in front of him.

"I don't think I'll get a wink of sleep tonight," he said as Clark approached.

"I don't think any of us will. We have to keep these flames as high as possible."

"How will we know it's working?"

Clark paused, and then drew in a gulp of fresh, mountain air. He slowly exhaled. "The smell. We'll know if they're nearby."

They both turned their heads as a howl emanated through the night air. It sounded far off but it still caused them to look at each other with a sense of unease. More howls echoed through the night, as if the unseen inhabitants of the night were engaging in a haunting conversation.

"What do you think it means?" York asked.

"It sounds like they're formulating a plan."

"A plan? For what?"

Clark sighed and tightened his grip on the leather strap of his rifle. "For what they're going to do to us."

THIRTY-EIGHT

As the first rays of sunlight began painting the mountain peaks, Clark and the others gathered their packs and broke camp. The fires, once blazing guardians against the unknown, now smoldered as embers as Clark took one last look around the small camp before departing toward the rising sun. Despite their lack of sleep and food, they moved with astonishing efficiency, eager to put the forest behind them and hopefully, rejoin the rest of the Corps somewhere near the entrance to the Lemhi Pass. As the group began trudging their way eastward, Clark took a moment to take in the sunrise. He looked around as the sun's rays cast a warm glow upon the rugged landscape, revealing the majestic contours of the towering peaks.

"Despite what's happened, I'll never get used to this," he said, glancing at York. The two men paused and took in the breathtaking beauty around them.

"Now I understand why they don't want us here," York said with a sigh. He glanced back at Clark. "Would you want to share this with anyone?"

The men moved along at a brisk pace throughout the morning. At midday, they stopped and broke out the few meager rations they still had. As Clark munched on a handful of wild berries scavenged by Ordway, he traced a line along the crinkled map of the Bitter Root Range provided to him by the Shoshone. A few minutes later, York and John Colter appeared, their eyes studying the map in his hand.

"How far are we from the pass?" Colter asked, hovering above him.

He slowly folded the map and placed it back inside his coat as he stood up. "Seven, maybe eight miles. We'll reach it by dark if we keep moving. We just have to hope the rest of the Corps is there waiting for us."

"Do you think they'd leave us behind?" Colter asked.

He thought of Lewis and shook his head. "No, they wouldn't leave us."

FRONTIER

A few hours later, the group found itself walking along a shimmering creek that snaked its way through the southern edge of the valley. The gurgling waters, crystal clear and inviting, reflected the dappling sunlight that filtered through the dense canopy above. Wildflowers adorned the banks, their colors a vibrant contrast to the green and brown of the trees around it. Occasionally, they paused and took a few minutes to drink from cupped hands, savoring the crisp, cool water that flowed from the mountains. Recharged by the water, they quickened their paces. They continued through the forest into the mid-afternoon, eager to catch up with Lewis and the others before nightfall. But the dense underbrush continued to slow their progress. By three o'clock, he guessed they were only about a mile or so from the rest of the Corps, which he expected had continued down the pass eastward ahead of them the previous day as instructed. At three thirty, he ordered the group to stop and rest. With sweat dripping from his forehead, he paused near a large rock and took a quick swig from his canteen. His gaze lingered for a moment on a tall pine tree with a cardinal resting gently on one of its branches. Above him, birds chirped merrily in the warm afternoon air as they flew from tree to tree, their melodic sounds mingling with the soft gurgle of the creek beside him. He looked to his left and saw York leaning up against the trunk of a tree as he took a swig of water from his own canteen. Ahead, Ordway and Colter crouched by the creek, splashing water over their faces to stave off the heat and fatigue. Clark leaned against a nearby tree, taking a moment to sip from his canteen before slinging it back over his shoulder. After a brief rest, he motioned for the men to move on.

"Let's keep going," he called, his voice cutting through the stillness.

York took the lead, moving steadily up a small knoll and into the thick forest beyond. Ordway followed close behind, with Willard and Colter trailing him. Clark lingered for a moment, his gaze sweeping the trees as they re-entered the woods. He tightened his grip on the stock of his rifle, an unease settling over him like a heavy fog.

The forest swallowed them in its cool embrace. The air felt heavier here, and each step was muffled by the thick carpet of pine needles underfoot. Clark's focus sharpened as his eyes darted between the trunks, scanning for anything out of place. He hadn't taken more than a few cautious steps when Ordway's voice rang out from ahead.

"Lieutenant! You need to come see this!"

The urgency in Ordway's voice sent a jolt through Clark. Without hesitation, he unslung his rifle, its weight reassuring in his hands, and hurried toward the sound. He found Ordway and Colter standing frozen, their faces pale, their wide eyes fixed on something beyond the thick underbrush.

Clark followed their gaze, his pulse quickening. "What is it?" he asked. Neither man answered. Clark turned his head, his eyes scanning the underbrush as he stepped forward. Then, through the tangled branches, he saw it. Fifty yards ahead, nestled beneath a small crest running through the forest, was what could only be described as some sort of village, only it was nothing like any village he had ever seen. The village, hidden within the forest, was a marvel of natural construction. It consisted of several interconnected structures woven from an assortment of materials found in the surrounding wilderness—large branches, vines, and leaves intricately layered to create sturdy and sheltered spaces that blended seamlessly with the natural surroundings. Inside each structure were what appeared to be nests of some kind, though they had clearly been constructed for a creature much larger than a bird. The woven structures cast long shadows in the waning light, the intricate patterns and symbols etched along the wood seeming to shift and dance in the fading daylight. Scattered around the periphery of the village were animal bones, picked clean of all flesh and bearing the unmistakable signs of gnawing by teeth of some kind. Massive nests loomed overhead as well, creating an awe-inspiring sight against the backdrop of the towering trees. The air within the village carried the same foul odor the men had grown accustomed to whenever the unknown creature came around, though within the village, the odor seemed more an amalgamation of musky scents, decaying foliage, and the lingering trace of the creatures' presence.

Slowly, he and the others moved into the center of the village, peering into each of the structures with their guns level, ready to shoot at anything that emerged from within them. But as far as he could tell, the village was empty.

"Look at this!" Ordway shouted. He turned and hurried over to the sergeant, who pointed down at a small tower of rocks, atop of which had been placed the skull of what appeared to be a bear. A long eagle feather had been forced through a small hole at the top of the skull.

"There's another one over here," Colter exclaimed from his right. As he began walking toward Colter, he noticed another larger rock tower near the far edge of the village. He turned and rushed toward it, but he stopped when he saw what was on top of it. It was another skull, only this one was clearly human. Two eagle feathers protruded from the top of it, just like the bear skull Ordway had found. York appeared beside him and took a deep breath.

"What is this place?"

Clark had no answer for him. He simply stared quietly at the tower of rocks with the human skull on top, searching his mind for some sort of explanation, but he had none. He had never seen anything like this, not even from the most savage Indian tribes he had met in his past. Nothing he had witnessed in his life resembled anything like what he was seeing now. And what concerned him more was the fact the village seemed to hold some sort of sophisticated arrangement, as if whatever had created it held some semblance of intelligent thought. But something else concerned him as well. There were nearly a dozen structures, each built to house what appeared to be creatures of immense size. He guessed each one, fully grown, stood at least eight feet tall, maybe more. He thought of the trees the day before and how whatever was watching them from above seemed to be able to leap easily from branch to branch. He scanned the village again, his heart pounding within his chest. *What the hell were they dealing with?*

"We should leave," Ordway said, approaching Clark and York with his rifle held out in front of him. "Those…things could come back at any time."

"Where do you think they are now?" York asked, his eyes scanning the trees above.

"Out there," Ordway replied, motioning ahead with his rifle. "Hunting us."

Clark turned and flashed Ordway an angry look. "No one's hunting us. We've clearly stumbled across a savage tribe living in these mountains that don't want us here."

"If these are Indians, why didn't the Shoshone tell us about them?" Ordway asked.

Clark shook his head. "I don't know, Sergeant. Maybe the Shoshone don't know they're out here."

"How could they not know? How could they not warn us—"

"I don't know!" Clark snapped back. Ordway fell silent as he watched Colter stumble back toward the group, his face bearing the clear signs of someone on the verge of breaking down.

"Lieutenant, what are these things?" he muttered in a weak voice.

"The Lieutenant thinks they're just Indians," Ordway sneered back.

Clark eyed him with a look of disdain, but he knew they didn't have time to quibble. They had to move fast before whatever lived in this village returned. He shouldered his rifle and motioned for the men to follow behind him. "We move as a group from here on out. Stay together in a tight formation until we get out of these woods. Make sure your rifles are primed and ready to fire. Indians or not, whatever made these nests are probably close by. Be ready to defend yourselves." He gulped and slowly began moving forward out of the village. A distant howl echoed through the trees, sending a chill down his spine. *They're not far*, he thought to himself as he moved, a primal fear starting to take hold of him. He did his best to remain focused and not let himself be seized by fear, but the images of what they had just seen continued to stir in his head. What did those creatures want? Were they driven by a primal urge to defend their land, or was it something much more sinister? He forged ahead into the wilderness, his senses heightened, ready to battle whatever emerged from within the trees, though deep within him, he sensed any encounter with these creatures would resemble a slaughter more than a battle. He forged ahead anyway. They had no choice. Lewis and the others were ahead of them, while the beasts, and certain death, lay behind.

THIRTY-NINE

The sight of Lewis made Clark cry out with elated jubilation. Relief flooded through him as he quickly rushed over to hug his friend and the rest of the Corps, camped out along the edge of a small lake. The rest of his party hurriedly emerged from the trees and sauntered over to the main group. When things had quieted down, he and Lewis walked along the edge of the water, which looked dark and ominous in the evening twilight. He recounted what had happened to them over the previous two days and about the evening howls, the foul smell, and of course, the village tucked away deep within the forest. When he was finished speaking, Lewis looked at him, his face twisted into a mixture of emotions. A few minutes passed silently between them before Lewis opened his mouth to respond to the incredible story he had just been told.

"Did you see any of the creatures while you were out there?"

"No, but they couldn't have been far, and they'll know we stumbled upon their village." He looked out over the darkening water and let out a short sigh. "There's no knowing how they'll respond to such an encroachment into their territory."

"With violence, I'd imagine," Lewis replied, his face turning grave. "We'll need to fortify the camp. Use the water to our advantage." He turned to look at the lake. "Unless they know how to swim."

Clark looked at him through the darkness. "I think we should be prepared for all possibilities. We cannot continue to underestimate whatever it is we're dealing with. As far I'm concerned, they are an enemy force, and they're hunting us."

"Hunting?" Lewis let out a surprised laugh. "My God, Will, they're animals. They're not smarter than us."

"We've already lost two men to those things," Clark snapped. "I don't intend to lose anyone else."

"Nor do I," Lewis replied, his voice firm. "But we must not let fear cloud our judgment. Yes, they've taken Elias and Samuel, but we cannot jump to conclusions about their nature or motives. We need more information before we can devise a plan of action."

Clark, trying to mask his frustration, acknowledged Lewis's statement. He knew they had to keep their wits about them if they stood any chance of making it out of this wilderness alive.

For the next hour, both men moved back and forth from one side of the camp to the other, inspecting rifles, helping to dig trenches, and ensuring the fires were as large and hot as they could be. At around ten o'clock, the moon began to rise above the jagged peaks of the mountains silhouetted against the dark, starry sky. Inside one of the tents erected at the center of the camp, Sacagawea sang softly to baby Pompey as she tried to rock him to sleep, the glow of the lantern beside her creating a cocoon of light and shadow. The camp seemed to hush in deference to the intimate moment. The men, who before had been ceaselessly throwing branches onto the bonfires, paused momentarily to listen to the soft lullaby echoing out across the stillness of the night. Clark stood mesmerized, just beyond the entrance of his tent, his silhouette outlined against the canvas in the lanterns glow. He let himself forget, at least for a moment, the weight of leadership and the terror that lurked in the stillness of the night around them. He closed his eyes and allowed himself to be taken in by the tranquil sounds of her soothing voice. When he opened his eyes, a canopy of twinkling stars greeted him. With a deep breath, he absorbed the beauty above, peering at the stars as if they were somehow offering him a silent reassurance that everything would be alright. He smiled as he lowered his gaze back toward the men who had resumed their tasks of fortifying the camp, realizing he knew better than to think he could find comfort or solace from earthly troubles in the stars. It was up to them to ward off the dangers that would soon come calling from the wilderness.

FRONTIER

FORTY

The howling began shortly after midnight.

Clark, half-asleep and leaning up against the side of a large log he had dragged to the middle of the camp, bolted upright, his eyes scanning the edge of the darkness for signs of whatever it was that had made the sound. He looked over and saw York and Private Bratton hurrying toward the edge of the camp, their rifles level in front of them. To his right, he saw Drouillard emerge from his tent, a knife clutched firmly in his right hand. Another howl cut through the darkness, this time closer and more high-pitched. Clark grabbed his rifle and slowly cocked back the hammer. He scanned the darkness beyond the flickering firelight, his senses heightened by the eerie howls coming from the trees.

More howls, closer and more guttural sounding, pierced the night. This time, the howling was followed-up by the sound of loud *thwaps* as something began striking the trunks of the spruce trees nearby. Suddenly, he heard a loud splash echo out across the dark waters of the lake. He turned and peered out across the water, trying to ascertain the cause of the splashing sound. *Could they actually swim?* He pushed the question from his mind and returned his gaze to the tree line. More men appeared now, their rifles at the ready. He watched as Willard and Thornfield raced across the camp and stood nervously between a pair of raging fires along the west side of the camp. To his left, the Field brothers emerged from their tent, the barrels of their rifles reaching out toward the darkness. Seaman, tied to a post near Sacagawea's tent and alert to the danger quickly surrounding the camp, barked and snarled toward the trees. The howls and *thwaps* continued around him like an unsettling duet that stirred the night air. And then, it hit him—the smell. His face contorted as he tried not to breathe in through his nose the foul odor enveloping him and the others as they continued to peer into the darkness.

"They're close!" York screamed from up ahead.

"Close ranks!" Clark called out as he hurried forward to join York and Bratton. He lowered his rifle toward the nearest tree and waited. The smell continued to suffocate them as they tried to keep their rifles level. "Steady!" He shouted, the pad of his finger gently touching the smooth surface of the rifle's trigger. The seconds dragged on, each one heavier than the last. The howling persisted, growing louder and more piercing by the moment. He could now hear rustling from the depths of the forest, as if something—or someone—was moving among the trees. Then more howling—more strikes against tree trunks. There was another splash from the lake, this time much closer than before. He turned his head slightly to look over at the water. *They're trying to confuse us,* he thought as he heard another loud splash.

"What is that?" York yelled, peering back at Clark.

"Rocks," Clark replied, his gaze refocused on the tree line. "They're throwing rocks into the water to distract us."

York gave him an incredulous stare. "Since when do animals use tactics like that?"

"These aren't animals," Clark responded icily as another high-pitched wail rang out from within the trees. More men began firing off rounds into the forest. The bullets ricocheted off the trunks of the trees sending tiny splinters of wood in all directions. Another volley erupted from the men positioned near the water's edge, their bullets whistling deep into the darkness of the forest beyond. The howling continued to grow louder and more high-pitched. Clark waved toward the men firing. "Stop! Hold your fire! We need to conserve our rounds."

But as the last word left his lips, the air erupted with chaos. A volley of rocks hurtled through the darkness around them, whistling ominously as they descended upon the camp. The first few thudded into the ground harmlessly, but soon larger stones found their marks. One struck York square in the shoulder, forcing a sharp cry of pain as he staggered back. Another slammed into Reubin Field's head with a sickening crack, sending him reeling backward into the dirt. Clark caught a glimpse of blood streaming down the man's left cheek, glinting darkly in the dim firelight as he struggled to get back on his feet.

"Take cover!" Clark shouted over the yells of the men around him. More rocks flew, their impacts accompanied by grunts and cries of pain. Thornfield's panicked shouts rang out the din.

FRONTIER

"They're attacking!" he yelled, firing his rifle blindly into the forest.

The barrage intensified, the rocks seeming to come from every direction. Men scrambled for cover, some firing wildly into the shadows while others fell to the ground, clutching at fresh wounds. Clark tried to dodge the projectiles, but at least four struck him—two in the arm, one in the chest, and another grazing his thigh. The blows sent him staggering to his knees, pain radiating through his body as he clutched his rifle tightly. A larger rock sailed past his head, so close he could feel the rush of air as it flew by.

Forcing himself to his feet, Clark dashed toward the north edge of the camp, narrowly avoiding another hail of stones. Reaching the remaining defenders, he dropped to one knee and barked, "Make ready!" The men, bruised and battered, knelt beside him and aimed their rifles toward the tree line. Clark leveled his own weapon as he shouted, "Fire!"

The crack of musket fire split the night as a dozen rounds screamed into the darkness, shredding leaves, and splintering bark. The sharp tang of gunpowder filled the air as Clark quickly reloaded, his hands trembling but efficient.

"Reload!" he shouted, his eyes never leaving the tree line. The men worked in unison, their movements hurried and desperate. Another volley tore into the forest, the gunfire momentarily drowning out the howling that seemed to circle the camp. Shards of bark exploded into the air, illuminated briefly by the flashes of musket fire. The attack faltered, the rocks ceasing their relentless assault, though the oppressive stench still lingered like a malevolent presence. The howling receded, distant now, but its eerie echoes crawled along Clark's nerves.

Amid the brief reprieve, Clark reloaded again, his movements automatic now. Around him, the camp had descended into frantic activity. Men darted between tents, dragging wounded to safety. To his left, he saw Lewis pulling the limp form of David Hooker into one of the shelters, his face taut with grim determination. To his right, Willard, Charbonneau, and several others crouched near one of the bonfires, their rifles trained on the forest, ready to fire at the first sign of movement.

But then a new sound sliced through the night—a scream, raw and filled with agony. It came from the south edge of the camp, unmistakable and chilling. Clark froze, his breath catching in his throat. The cry came again, jagged and desperate, sending a wave of dread crashing over him. His heart raced as he turned toward the sound, the urgency in the man's voice spurring him into motion. Every instinct screamed at him to stay with the men—to hold the line at the north edge—but the cries demanded his attention. Clark gripped his rifle tightly, his knuckles turning white, and began moving.

"Over there!" someone shouted. Clark turned sharply, his pulse quickening even more as he followed the sound of the cries. His boots pounded against the earth, the screams growing louder, sharper—each one a visceral stab of pain and terror that sent dread coursing through his veins. He pushed forward, branches clawing at his face and arms, until he stumbled into a small clearing at the south edge of the camp bathed in moonlight.

And then he froze.

The scene before him seemed torn from a nightmare. In the dim light, the silhouette of a massive figure loomed, its shadow stretching grotesquely across the ground. The creature, easily towering over eight feet, seemed to shimmer with an unnatural vitality, its glowing eyes cutting through the darkness and locking onto Clark. The air was heavy with the scent of blood and musk, a nauseating mix that made his stomach churn.

Clark staggered back a step. The creature, its form both hulking and disturbingly agile, moved with a terrible grace, each motion radiating raw power. It lashed out violently, its limbs striking like coiled whips, and the screams of its prey pierced the air once more.

"Lieutenant! Help me!"

Clark's eyes darted to the source of the desperate plea. Ambrose Cartwright, his broad frame dwarfed by the creature's monstrous bulk, thrashed wildly as the beast lifted him effortlessly off the ground. Moonlight glinted off Cartwright's pale, terror-stricken face, his cries a mix of panic and agony as he struggled against the creature's iron grip. The beast's roar reverberated through the clearing, a guttural sound so primal it seemed to shake the very ground beneath Clark's feet.

Clark raised his rifle, his hands trembling as he tried to find a clear shot. "Ambrose! Stand clear!" he shouted, desperation cracking his voice. But the man's struggles only seemed to enrage the beast further. In a horrifying blur of motion, the creature clamped its massive hand around Cartwright's arm and pulled. The sickening snap of bone and sinew breaking filled the air, followed by Cartwright's bloodcurdling scream. Clark watched, helpless, as the beast tore the arm free from its socket, blood spraying across the clearing in gruesome arcs. The severed limb dangled from the creature's hand, and it raised it high above its head, letting out a triumphant, guttural howl that echoed into the night.

Clark's vision narrowed, his fear replaced by a surge of cold, focused rage. With a steadying breath, he aimed his rifle, his sights trained on the beast's hulking form. "Ambrose, hold on!" he shouted, though the words felt hollow even as he said them. He squeezed the trigger, the musket's report shattering the air. The bullet struck the creature in the lower abdomen, the impact forcing it to stagger backward. Its howl of pain was deafening and feral sounding. The beast turned its glowing eyes toward Clark, its expression twisting with rage and something disturbingly intelligent. It dropped Cartwright's limp, bloodied body to the ground with a sickening thud and began advancing toward Clark. Each step it took sent tremors through the earth, its massive frame swaying as it clutched at its wounded side. Clark scrambled to reload, his fingers fumbling with the powder and shot as adrenaline coursed through his veins.

The creature let out another roar, its breath steaming in the cold night air as it closed the distance between them. Clark raised his rifle again, his hands steady despite the hammering of his heart. He had no room for fear now—only the cold certainty that either he or the beast would not leave the clearing alive.

The bullet struck the creature in the left arm. It let out another roar and began pounding its fists violently against its massive chest. It was now nearly on him, its yellow eyes like glowing orbs staring back at him through the darkness. Its nose was flattened and wide, while its mouth contorted into a snarl, revealing a set of cracked, yellow-stained teeth. The stench emanating from the creature was almost overwhelming as Clark struggled to step back and reload his rifle. He knew the creature would be on him before he had time to reload but he decided to try anyway. As the creature prepared to lunge at him, he gripped the stock of his rifle, preparing to wield it as a club against the giant beast as it attacked. But just before the beast was on him, the sound of rifle fire echoed out from somewhere behind him. Two bullets struck the creature, one in the arm and one in the chest, causing it to stumble backward in pain. It howled again as it began grabbing at the bloody wounds in its fur. Clark turned and saw York and Lewis approaching, the ends of their rifles billowing with smoke as they quickly began to reload. He stumbled back toward them and began grasping for his leather bag so he could finish reloading his rifle. More howls rang out from the forest as the creature began staggering away toward the trees, blood oozing from its wounds as it tried to remain standing. It let out another long, painful howl before disappearing into the darkness. Clark finished reloading and leveled his rifle toward the trees, but the creature had vanished. Nearby, Cartwright had finally passed out from the pain as Thornfield and Ordway pulled him back away from the trees into the center of the camp. The howling continued in the distance, though now it sounded as if the creatures were retreating farther into the forest away from the expedition's camp. Clark stood quietly as he tried to catch his breath and assess everything that had just happened. He glanced to his right and saw Sacagawea running across the camp, baby Pompey slung securely her, toward the injured form of Cartwright. She knelt beside him as she examined his wounds.

"We must stop the bleeding if he is going to survive," she declared, ripping a piece of cloth from a nearby blanket and wrapping it around the torn skin of Cartwright's shoulder. "We must keep pressure on the wound."

"Help her! Get her whatever she needs," Lewis shouted to Reubin Field and John Colter, who were huddled nearby gripping their rifles tightly. The two men nodded and hurried to

FRONTIER

Sacagawea's side as she began giving them instructions while Clark walked over to where Lewis and York stood. Seaman had been freed from the post and now sat anxiously at Lewis's feet. He scanned the faces of his companions. The campfire, casting its wavering glow, revealed a subtle transformation—a shift from stoic resolve to the subtle dance of panic that traced along their features.

"What are we going to do if those things come back?" Lewis asked pointedly. "Just one of those things tore off a man's arm. What if more attack next time? We can't defeat an army of those things."

"We're almost through the mountains," Clark replied, his voice steady but still containing a trace of fear and uncertainty. "They didn't bother us before we entered the mountains before, so we must assume they will leave us be once we cross back over into Shoshone lands."

"Maybe this time they intend to kill us before we make it to Shoshone land," Lewis snapped back. "We don't know what these things intend to do to us or if they are even intelligent enough to formulate such planning. All we know is that they're dangerous and capable of killing every man here, with little effort."

"Then maybe it's time we started treating them like the violent force they are," Clark whispered back. He glanced over at York. "Nobody sleeps tonight. I want an inventory of every weapon we have available and how many rounds of ammunition we have left."

Lewis stared back at him, his jaw clenched. "What do you intend to do?"

Clark took a deep breath and placed a hand on Lewis's shoulder. "We've been attacked, Meri. We must prepare ourselves for another."

"Why do they want to kill us?"

Clark shook his head. "I don't know. But I think they know we were at their village, and tonight was some sort of demonstration of their strength. Only one of them came out from the trees to attack us, the rest stayed back. I think if they meant to kill us, they would have." He looked around, his eyes scanning the weary faces of the men. "We can't afford to underestimate them," he continued. "I think they are testing us, seeing how we will respond. We need to show them we're not easy prey. We need to make a demonstration of our own." He peered back at Lewis, his expression resolute. "It's time we showed those things what warfare truly is. Tomorrow, we take the fight to them."

FRONTIER

FORTY-ONE

The first rays of sunlight that stretched out across the sparkling water of the lake made Clark's heart race with excitement. He finished checking his rifle before striding purposefully toward the southern edge of the camp. There, York and a group of ten men waited in quiet readiness, their rifles in hand and knives resting securely at their sides. Charbonneau and Joseph Field stood near York, exchanging uneasy glances as Clark approached. To their right, Drouillard adjusted the hammer of his rifle with practiced precision, his expression calm but guarded. The others—Willard, Colter, Ordway, Thomas Chandler, Peter Harrington, and Benjamin Holloway—stood in a loose semicircle. Their faces revealed a mix of emotions: anticipation, fear, and grim determination. The air was crisp with the promise of a new day, and the distant call of waking birds punctuated the silence, a reminder that the forest remained indifferent to their plight.

Clark joined them and could immediately feel the tension of the previous night pressing heavily on their collective mood. "York," he began, "is everyone ready?"

York gave a curt nod.

"Each man has at least five rounds?"

The group nodded in unison, their grips tightening on their rifles.

Clark exhaled deeply, steadying himself as the responsibility of leadership settled squarely on his shoulders. "Good. We move in pairs and keep a tight formation. No one strays from the group. We know what's out there, but we also know we can hurt it." He paused, eyeing each of them. "Don't be afraid, men. Stay sharp and be prepared for anything."

The men's eyes shifted uneasily to the dense forest ahead.

"Remember," Clark continued with a firm tone, "we're not just fighting for our survival. We're fighting for the success of this expedition. Those things may be stronger than us, but they're not smarter."

The men nodded, though Clark knew his words offered little solace. The fear of what lay ahead clung to them like the morning mist, but they were soldiers and frontiersmen—they would press on, fear or not. With a motion of his hand, he signaled them to move out. As the group began their cautious advance into the forest, Clark heard footsteps behind him. He turned to see Lewis approaching, his face etched with concern. Without a word, Lewis extended his hand. Clark took it, and for a brief moment, the two men shared a quiet embrace.

"Don't get yourself killed, Will," Lewis said, his voice low but filled with emotion. "We've come too far and faced too much. I won't let those beasts take you."

Clark met his gaze. "We'll return, Meri. All of us. Just make sure everyone here is safe. Have Reubin and Nathanial start digging the trench—"

Lewis held up a hand, cutting him off. "It will be taken care of. You focus on killing those bastards."

A small, wry smile tugged at Clark's lips. "I'll see you soon."

Without another word, he turned and strode away, hurrying to catch up with the others who were already melting into the shadowy embrace of the forest.

***

It took the group nearly three hours to reach the rocky edge of the valley and another hour to traverse the jagged outcroppings that took them high up into the elevated pine forest that overlooked the valley below. When they reached the edge of the denser forest they had traversed the day before, they stopped and eyed a small path that led back to the beast's village. Clark watched as Charbonneau and York knelt to examine a set of large footprints that led west. York looked up and nodded at him.

"They've been here recently." He pointed to a broken branch near the side of the trail. Clark could just make out the traces of red blood sticking to the branch's small leaves. He knew the blood had to have been from the injured creature. York knelt beside the branch, examining it closely.

"It's fresh," he murmured. "Something brushed against it in a hurry."

FRONTIER

Clark felt a chill run down his spine. "Stay close and keep your eyes peeled."

"That creature from last night is still alive?" Willard exclaimed.

"It could be one of the others," York replied as he stood up. "We shot several volleys into the forest last night, some were bound to have found their mark."

"We move silently from here on out," Clark directed. Each man gave a slight nod as they continued carefully through the underbrush. For the next two miles they moved cautiously, carefully surveying the space between the pines as they moved, their footsteps muffled by the carpet of fallen needles beneath. Sunlight filtered in through the towering trees, dappling the forest floor with patches of light and shadow. The trail of blood grew more pronounced, leading them deeper into the forest as the day dragged on. The silence was oppressive, broken only by the occasional rustle of leaves or the distant call of a bird. Every so often, he would halt the group, raising a hand to signal to the others to stop. They would listen intently for any sign of the creatures stalking them, but the forest remained eerily quiet.

At around two o'clock, they reached a small stream. Drouillard signaled for the group to halt. He knelt by the water's edge to examine another set of tracks in the mud. "The tracks are fresher here," he whispered. "They stopped to drink."

Clark nodded, his eyes scanning the surrounding trees. "They can't be far. Stay alert." They began moving again, the forest around them growing thicker and darker as they pressed on. The blood trail seemed to be leading them deeper into the heart of the wilderness. Clark glanced up and noticed the light was struggling to penetrate the dense canopy above. As they approached a small clearing, he raised a hand, signaling the group to halt. He scanned the area, his rifle at the ready.

"What now, Lieutenant?" Willard whispered, his eyes wide with fear. Clark made a sniffing gesture with his nose and suddenly, he understood. A few feet to his left, York stopped and turned to face Clark.

"The smell."

Clark nodded. York's grip tightened on his rifle, his eyes scanning the surrounding trees.

Within a few seconds, the foul smell had enveloped the group and they knew the beasts were close. Clark breathed in deeply through his mouth, trying to steady his nerves. Slowly, he began moving forward, his eyes continuing to scan the forest around him. He motioned to York with a subtle finger gesture, indicating for him to watch the trees above. York nodded and began searching the canopy for any sign of movement. The smell grew stronger as they pressed on, inching closer and closer to the beast's village. Faint but distinct *thuds* echoed periodically through the forest, adding to the tension in the air. As the smell worsened around them, the group could hear low, guttural growls, accompanied by intermittent grunts and the occasional snapping of large branches. The lumbering footsteps of the creatures created an eerie rhythm, synchronized with the cadence of their vocalizations.

When they reached a spot of trees overlooking the village a few feet below, they stopped. Clark gestured for York to come over and together they surveyed their surroundings.

"Distance is our only advantage," Clark whispered to the others. "We stick to the trees. After you fire off a round, move. Don't remain in one spot for too long. They're strong but their strength counts for nothing if they can't reach you. Make your shots count and reload as quickly as you can. We have to keep them contained to the village." He quickly surveyed the landscape surrounding the village. "I want three men on each side. York and I will stay here. Wait for our signal, then fire. Is everyone ready?"

The men nodded in silent acknowledgment. They checked their rifles one last time and then began spreading out across the perimeter of the beast's village, blending into the shadows of the surrounding trees.

Clark turned and peered back down at the village, watching each of the beasts as they lumbered about. He counted fourteen in all, each varying in size. He noticed a group of larger ones huddled near one of the woven structures. They seemed to be hovering over something. He narrowed his eyes, trying to discern what they were so focused on. Nearby, three smaller beasts, no more than six feet in height, sat in a line. The one behind the first beast seemed to be picking through the fur on the first beast's back while the third did

FRONTIER

the same to the second beast. He watched with fascination. They appeared to be females, but he couldn't be sure. He surmised the smaller ones were likely adolescents, but there was no telling their sex. The larger ones near the woven structure parted slightly and Clark saw what they had been hovering over. It was the beast from the night before, and it appeared to be deceased. Clark grinned with satisfaction. *Now you know death. How does it feel?* The other beasts continued to crowd around the dead body of the other. He noticed the dead beast seemed larger than the rest. He wondered if that could have been their leader—the alpha of the group. *Even better,* he thought to himself as he watched them place shrubs of some sort around the body. *Their leader is dead and they're scared and unsure of what to do.* He slowly cocked his rifle and peered down the sights toward the head of one of the beasts huddled around their fallen leader. As he continued to watch them, he noticed it wasn't shrubs they were placing around the beast's dead body, but *flowers*. He recognized the wildflowers as the ones they had seen the day before that dotted the shores of the creek. Suddenly, it dawned on him what he was witnessing. The creatures were holding a funeral for their fallen companion. A few of them let out long, wailing howls as the last of the flowers were placed along the side of the dead creature. The females sitting nearby responded with high-pitched wails of their own. He tightened the grip on his rifle as he observed the solemn scene. Despite everything that had happened, he couldn't help but feel a pang of empathy for the creatures. Perhaps, they weren't mindless monsters but beings capable of grief and mourning, much like humans.

"We can't attack them now," York whispered, his voice barely audible over the wailing cries of the female beasts below. "They're mourning their dead."

Clark watched as the rest of the beasts let out long, high pitched wails that resonated throughout the forest. A few of the smaller ones—the ones he surmised were adolescents—began pounding their fists against the trunks of nearby trees, wailing in pain as they did. The mournful cries of the creatures echoed through the forest, filling the air with a haunting melody of grief and sorrow.

"We have no choice," he replied to York as he refocused his gaze on the large beast closest to the woven structure. "We can't risk them attacking the camp again. They're mourning now, but how long until they come looking for us bent on revenge?"

York sighed and with a heavy nod, repositioned his rifle butt against his shoulder.

Clark took a deep breath. *This was it*. He slowly exhaled and steadied his aim. He could see the beast's mashed-in face staring off toward one of the structures, unaware of the fate that was about to befall him. He took one last breath and slowly, he squeezed the trigger.

FRONTIER

FORTY-TWO

The gunshot shattered the eerie silence, its sharp crack cutting through the air like a knife. The bullet struck its target—a hulking beast—squarely in the left shoulder. A loud roar of pain erupted from the creature as it staggered backward, clutching at the wound with its massive hands. Dark blood oozed from the torn flesh, dripping onto the ground.

Instantly, chaos erupted in the village below. The other creatures, startled by the sudden attack, scattered in all directions, their mournful cries giving way to panicked shrieks. Some fled into the dense undergrowth, while others rushed to the aid of their injured comrade, their movements frantic and disorganized. Clark's men opened fire, and the forest roared with the staccato of musket fire. Bullets tore through the air, striking beasts with brutal precision. One creature fell clutching its bleeding arm, while another staggered as a shot ripped through its torso. A single bullet found its mark under the eye of a beast closest to Clark. It lashed out blindly, its guttural howls a mix of rage and pain, before stumbling backward over the body of its fallen leader and tumbling into a shallow ditch.

Clark swiftly reloaded his rifle. He spotted a female beast scaling the hill toward him, her powerful limbs clawing at the earth. He fired. The shot struck her in the lower torso. She let out a piercing wail before darting behind one of the woven structures. He stood up and bounded toward one of the other trees off to his right. Beside him, York crouched behind a pine tree, his breath coming in ragged gasps. With practiced hands he retrieved another paper cartridge from his pouch and tore it open with his teeth, exposing the gunpowder within. As quickly as he could, he poured the powder down the barrel of the rifle and retrieved another bullet, which he rammed down the barrel with his ramrod. Once complete, he took aim at a beast trying to clamber toward York and fired, striking the beast just below the armpit. The beast roared and turned toward Clark, its menacing eyes searching for the cause of its pain. When it saw Clark, it roared again and began sprinting toward him. Clark retrieved his pistol and aimed it at the creature's head ready to fire but something stopped him. The creature had stopped and stared at him. Clark peered down at his pistol and then back at the creature. *You know what this does now, don't you?* he thought as he continued aiming the barrel of the gun directly at the beast's large head. The beast let out a low growl before turning and racing back down into the village. Clark followed it with his pistol until it was far enough away to no longer pose a threat. He holstered the pistol and retrieved his rifle. As he began to reload, he watched as the larger beasts began herding the smaller ones inside the woven structures. Once they were all inside, the larger beasts turned and began racing toward the sound of rifle fire. He finished reloading and took aim at a beast bearing down on Drouillard a few yards away. He squeezed the trigger and sent the bullet straight into the beast's left side. As the beast writhed in pain, Drouillard finished reloading and stepped out from behind the tree. The beast growled and tried to raise its arms up in defense, but it was a useless gesture. Drouillard fired and Clark watched as the bullet penetrated the creature's left eye and exploded out through the back of its skull. Blood spewed from the creature's mouth as it gave one last confused look toward Drouillard before tumbling lifelessly back down the slope into the village. Clark reloaded his rifle and realized he was down to his final round. He rammed the bullet down the barrel and stepped out from behind the tree. He watched as York fired off a round, striking one of the beasts he had hit earlier in the shoulder. He took aim and finished the beast off, striking it on the side of the head. The beast collapsed, its body twitching and jerking for a few seconds as it lay sprawled atop the leaves of the forest floor. More gunfire erupted from the other side of the village. He looked over and watched with horror as Alex Willard and Thomas Chandler attempted to reload as two beasts barely ten feet away charged toward them.

"Get out of there!" Clark shouted as the beasts lunged forward, their massive forms barreling toward the two men with terrifying speed. Suddenly, he heard a shot from somewhere to his left. He glanced over and saw Ordway hurrying to reload his rifle.

FRONTIER

"Sergeant!" Clark yelled frantically, pointing frantically in the direction of Willard and Chandler. Ordway looked up at him and then over to the spot where the two men stood trying to reload their rifles. He finished reloading and took aim at the two beasts, but it was too late. The first beast reached Willard and grabbed him by the neck, lifting him high up off the ground. Clark watched as the man struggled against the creature's grip, his face contorted in agony as he fought for his life. And then, in one violent motion, the beast then slammed Willard's head into the nearest tree, crushing it between its hands and the tree trunk. Clark watched as Willard's body twitched and then went limp. The other beast then lunged toward Chandler, who was running as fast as he could in the opposite direction. Ordway fired off a round, but it missed. Clark leveled his rifle and fired, striking the beast that had killed Willard in the jaw. The creature cried out and stumbled away as Ordway pushed forward to try and head off the beast chasing Chandler. Clark motioned for York to follow him as they raced after Ordway, but suddenly, he noticed a third beast racing toward Benjamin Holloway, who appeared to be out of bullets as he desperately searched his waistline for his knife. He stopped and watched as John Colter, noticing Holloway's predicament, raced over to try and help, but he wasn't fast enough. The beast snatched Holloway by the left arm and threw him against the closest tree. Holloway, the terror evident in his eyes, cried out in pain as he tried to scramble away, his arm hanging loosely by his side. Clark snatched his pistol from its holster and took aim, but the beast was too far away for an accurate shot. As the beast lunged at Holloway for a second time, Colter arrived and leapt onto the back of the creature, driving his blade deep into its shoulder. The beast howled in pain as it easily threw Colter off its back. It then let out an engaged howl and began stomping its feet down hard upon Colter's torso. Colter cried out in pain as the creature stomped down on him again and again, breaking his rib cage and sending spurts of blood flying out of his mouth. A shot rang out from somewhere behind the beast. The bullet struck it somewhere in the back, causing it to kneel to the ground in pain. Clark watched as Peter Harrington appeared, his face twisted in terror as he ran toward Colter to try and pull him away from the wounded beast. By this point, Drouillard had also arrived and began shouting at the beast while waving his long blade wildly through the air. The beast grunted and made a grab at him, but Drouillard was too quick.

"Get him out of here!" Drouillard yelled as he continued to keep the beast at bay with his knife. Clark raced toward the men and grabbed hold of Colter, and together they pulled him back a few yards to a spot behind a large hemlock tree. But the relief they felt at pulling Colter to safety was quickly shattered by the piercing screams of Holloway somewhere in the distance. Spurred by the screams, Clark began racing into the trees, his heart pounding in his chest as he stumbled through the underbrush with York scrambling behind him to keep up. As the screams grew louder, he could make out the image of one of the beasts through the trees. He watched as Holloway stumbled back and tried putting one of the trees between him and the beast as it lumbered toward him with its arms outstretched.

"Do you have any ammunition left?" he snapped frantically at York.

"No, sir."

He cursed as he reached for his pistol and began racing toward Holloway and the beast. He began to yell and wave his arms, trying to attract the creature's attention. "Hey! Over here! Over *here!*" The beast stopped and turned, its yellow eyes staring like daggers back at him. Clark gulped and raised his pistol. Suddenly, he heard York shouting behind him.

"Master, Look out!"

Clark turned in time to see one of the adolescents racing toward him, saliva spitting from its mouth as it snarled in anger. He quickly turned to face the charging beast and fired his pistol. The bullet shrieked through the air and struck the creature in the center of its skull. The adolescent beast cried out in pain as the bullet exploded out of the left side of its face. With a look of shock, it collapsed to the ground, its now lifeless eyes staring straight up at the darkening sky above. He then heard the beast near Holloway let out a primal scream as it began thumping its large hands against its broad chest. He watched as the beast stared back at him, pain forming in its eyes as it looked upon the body of the dead adolescent. Instinctively, he reached for his pouch, but then he remembered he was out of bullets. The beast continued to howl and thump its chest, its blood-curdling cries echoing out across the now bloody forest around them. It turned back toward Holloway who was trying to stumble away. The man cried out in terror as the beast raced toward him and snatched him up off the ground by his leg. Clark and York stepped forward, but they knew there was nothing they could do. The beast, still holding Holloway by one leg, twirled around and smashed the man's body into a nearby tree. Blood and bits of teeth spewed out from Holloway's mouth in every direction as he gargled something before the beast swirled around again and with even more force, sent his face back into the trunk of the tree. Clark watched with horror as Holloway's skull exploded, sending pieces of brain and bone scattering in a gruesome display of gore and violence. The howling from the other beasts began to intensify. He grabbed hold of York and together they began running through the trees toward the other side of the village. As they ran, he spotted Drouillard and Charbonneau running as well. He could see Charbonneau's face was caked with blood as he ran as fast as he could away from the beast that had just killed Holloway. A sudden scream echoed through the trees as they ran. With a sense of dread, he knew the beasts had found Chandler. After a few minutes, they arrived at the spot where they had left Colter and Harrington. Harrington was crying as he cradled Colter in his arms. Colter wheezed in pain, trying to suck whatever air he could into his smashed lungs. His eyes stared blankly ahead, knowing the breaths he was taking were going to be his last.

"We have to go," Charbonneau stammered, urging Drouillard and the others to follow. Drouillard looked over at Clark, who continued to stare down at Colter.

"He won't make it, Lieutenant," Drouillard said in a hushed voice. Clark's heart sank as he looked down at Colter's battered form. He knew Drouillard was right, but the thought of leaving a man behind, even in death, was almost unbearable. Swallowing hard, he nodded grimly. Colter reached over with his hand and clasped Clark's ankle. Through strained breaths, the dying man whispered, "Please...kill me...Lieutenant." Clark held back the surge of emotions he was feeling and slowly took out his knife. He glanced at York who nodded and looked away. Clark placed his hand down atop Colter's forehead and looked into his eyes. Colter gave him an approving nod as he sucked in one last gulp of air. Quickly, Clark placed his hand behind Colter's head and slashed the edge of the blade across Colter's throat. Colter's eyes rolled back as he slowly fell back onto the forest floor, blood oozing out through the new opening in his neck. Clark wiped off the blade and placed it back inside his waistband.

"Move with a purpose," he said urgently as he stood up.

"What about John?" Joseph Field stammered. He stood a few feet away from his brother Reubin, who stared silently at the lifeless corpse of John Colter.

"There's nothing we can do for him now," Clark whispered. "We have to get moving."

"We can't just—"

Ordway stepped forward and grabbed Joseph by the shirt with his large hands. "The man's dead, son. There's nothing any of us can do for him now."

Tears welled in Joseph's eyes as he looked away, but Ordway tightened his grip and pulled him closer. "Don't cry. Focus on staying alive. We have to get out of here, and none of us will make it if we aren't focused on that alone. Do you understand?"

A series of howls echoed out across the still evening twilight. Joseph glanced around, his eyes darting at shadows in the trees. After a few seconds, he peered back at Ordway and nodded. "Y—yes, I—I understand."

Ordway released him and turned to Clark. "Let's go, sir." He pushed past the others to take point as the group hurried off toward the east away from the village of the beasts as the creatures' raw, primal howls reverberated through the stillness of the night.

FORTY-THREE

The moon hung low in the sky, casting an eerie silver glow over the forest as Clark and the others pressed on through the tangled undergrowth. Clark paused for a moment, glancing briefly behind him before resuming his quickened pace through the trees. A few yards ahead of him, York and Drouillard stopped and waited for the others to catch up. Clark paused again, his breath coming in ragged gasps as he listened for any signs of movement from behind them. In the distance, a long guttural howl pierced the night. He knew the beasts were likely pursuing them, the only question was how long they had until they caught up.

Another howl rang out, this time much closer. His heart raced as he signaled for the group to pick up their pace. He pulled his knife from its sheath and hurried forward. Ahead, he could hear the labored breathing of Harrington and Charbonneau as the men tried their best to keep running. Clark didn't look back, even as the beast's enraged cries continued echoing out into the night. When the group reached a rock ledge that led down into the valley, York stopped and turned back to face the others.

"Who's still armed?"

"I am," Ordway announced, holding up his rifle.

"We all are except Joseph and Toussaint."

York reached into his bag and removed two large knives, which he then tossed to Charbonneau and Joseph Field. "We're going to have to defend ourselves. They're catching up too quickly."

"We don't have enough rounds left to stand and fight," Clark said with resignation. "Our only chance is the sagebrush." He reached into his own bag and removed what was left of the pungent plant and held it in front of him. "All of you, head down into the valley. I'll try and hold them off for as long as I can."

"Sir, they'll tear you to pieces in seconds," Harrington exclaimed in a shrill voice.

"If we stand and fight, we will most certainly be killed. This is our only option." He glanced at York. "Keep moving as fast as you can, no matter what happens. Find Captain Lewis and the others before the beasts catch up to you." Behind him, the creature's savage howls were growing louder. He knew they weren't far off. "Go!" he ordered.

York nodded and urged the others forward. He gave one last brief glance at Clark before turning and fleeing quickly down the rocky ledge into the valley. In the moonlight, Clarks hands trembled as he reached into his bag and fumbled with the flint and steel. He dropped down to the ground and began striking the steel against the flint, desperately trying to spark a flame from the dry sagebrush. Each strike sent sparks flying into the night air, but the tinder stubbornly refused to ignite. Behind him, the sounds of the pursuing beasts grew louder, their unearthly howls sending shivers down his spine. He could almost feel their hot breath on the back of his neck, their presence looming closer with each passing moment. He struck the flint again, but again the sagebrush refused to catch fire. He breathed in a dose of the night air and nearly gagged. *The smell.* They had found him.

"Come on, damn it!" he muttered under his breath, his heart racing as he frantically struck the flint once more. Finally, a small ember caught hold, igniting the sagebrush in a burst of flame. Suddenly, a bloodcurdling roar pierced the night, and he felt a surge of adrenaline course through his veins. Without warning, one of the beasts burst from the underbrush, its massive form looming over him like a specter of death, its primal howls reverberating through the night. The beast stood up tall, its muscles rippling beneath its fur as it beat its chest with its fists. His hands shook as he raised the lit sagebrush as high as he could in front of him, the small embers serving as the only light in the clearing aside from the moon. The beast took another step toward him, its face contorted into what could only be described as pure rage. Clark wafted the lit sagebrush back and forth in front of him in an arcing pattern as he slowly took a few steps backward, praying his plan would work. If not, he knew he would soon be torn apart limb from limb. Two other beasts suddenly emerged from the underbrush, smaller but just as intimidating and angry as the first. The smell of the three beasts made him gag as he tried to breathe through his mouth. The beasts roared with anger but remained where they were. He took another step backwards and began shouting as loud as he could toward the angry creatures. The largest beast stepped forward; its long, muscular arms extended out in front of it. He braced himself as he waited for the inevitable onslaught. But none came. And then, something unexpected happened. As the flames licked at the dry sagebrush, sending the plant's pungent smell wafting into the night breeze, the creatures began to recoil. One of the beasts began to gag and retch as if repulsed by the smell. It stumbled backward, its eyes watering from the acrid smoke. To his amazement, the other beasts beside it soon began to exhibit the same behavior. With a feeling of relief that his plan was actually working, he held the sagebrush higher and wafted it more aggressively through the air, sending more billowing smoke toward the creatures whose howls soon turned to whimpers as they continued to stumble back away from him. Within seconds, they began to retreat into the underbrush, their menacing presence fading into the darkness.

As they slinked away, Clark wasted no time in gathering his senses. Cautiously, he began making his way down the rocky ledge into the valley, still listening for any signs of his pursuers. He could still smell the beast's pungent aroma, so he knew they remained close by. But for the moment at least, they were not attacking. He looked down at the sagebrush as he hurried along after York and the others. His heart began to race even more as his eyes darted nervously between the jagged terrain and the dwindling flames of the sagebrush. The once vibrant orange glow had begun to wane, the small crackling flame now reducing itself to smoldering embers. A sense of urgency gripped him as he realized his makeshift defense was rapidly fading away. Soon, the protective barrier that had repelled the creatures and bought him precious moments of respite would succumb to the darkness, leaving him vulnerable once more.

A loud wailing howl echoed through the night behind him. He glanced up toward the top of the rocky ledge and could see the beasts moving along the top, silhouetted against the silver moonlight. With grim determination, he quickened his pace, his boots slipping on the loose rocks as he navigated the treacherous path. He knew every second counted, and he knew that he needed to regroup with the others before the beasts decided to renew their attack. But as he reached the bottom of the ledge, the oppressive darkness began to close in around him. The lingering scent of the beasts still hung heavy in the air around him as he ran hard through the darkened forest. He took one last glance down at the dying embers of the sagebrush. As the last flicker of flame flickered out, he squared his shoulders and set off into the night, praying he would find the others before the beasts returned to finish what they had started.

FRONTIER

FORTY-FOUR

The dense forest seemed to swallow him as he plunged deeper into the darkness. Somewhere behind him, the howls of the beasts echoed on, a constant reminder of the danger that lurked just beyond the trees. With every step, he strained to catch any sign of the others, but he heard nothing, aside from the cries of the beasts behind him. The beast's odor still lingered in the air, though the stench had eased somewhat, making him feel slightly more secure. *I'm at least gaining distance between them and me,* he thought to himself as he ran along. As he continued through the underbrush, a sense of urgency gripped him like a vice. He knew he had to find York and the others before the beasts closed in for the kill. He knew they still stood little chance of escaping the beast's clutches, but there was still that hope, and that small bit of hope was all he had.

Suddenly, he heard a wailing howl in the distance. He froze, his mind racing with the grim possibilities of what the howls meant. He heard another howl, this time much closer. His blood ran cold as he suddenly realized the creatures were closing in. Every instinct in him told him to flee, but he knew he couldn't outrun them forever. With each passing moment, the darkness seemed to grow deeper, swallowing him whole as he stumbled blindly through the shadows. Behind him, the beasts continued to gain on him. He could hear them beating their fists against the tree trunks, their angry howls reverberating through the night air like a sinister chorus of doom. Every fiber of his being urged him to keep running, but he knew it was no use. They were gaining on him, and they had likely figured out by that point he no longer had the sagebrush. With a sense of hopelessness rising within him, he slowed his pace, his breath coming in slow gasps as he prepared for what seemed like an inevitable end. Deep down, he knew standing to face them would be futile—a mere act of defiance against the darkest forces of nature. He tightened his grip on the knife in his hand, his knuckles white with tension as he prepared to make his last stand. In the darkness, he could hear them drawing closer, their savage cries growing louder with each passing minute. He braced himself as he awaited his fate. But then, as the feeling of helplessness began to take hold of him, he heard a sound in the distance. He strained his head in the direction of the noise, trying to ascertain its source. He listened again, and within a few seconds, he heard what sounded like a lone, plaintive bark echo through the darkness. His heart skipped a beat as he strained to hear it again, his senses tingling with anticipation. *Could it be?*

Driven by desperation, he sheathed his knife and broke into a run, his footsteps pounding against the forest floor as he followed the sound of the barking dog. With each step, his resolve grew stronger, his fear giving way to a newfound sense of purpose. As he ran, his heart pounding hard within his chest, he knew he would not go down without a fight—that he would do whatever it took to survive, no matter the cost.

FRONTIER

FORTY-FIVE

The sound of barking grew louder as Clark raced through the towering pine forest. He pushed himself harder than he ever had before, using the moon's light to guide him. Within minutes, the dog's barking was loud enough for him to pinpoint precisely where it was coming from. In a flash, he changed directions and leapt high above a fallen log, careful not to stumble as his feet hit the forest floor on the other side. More barks echoed out, closer still. He ran faster, tossing his leather pouch to the side. He was so close, only a few more yards. Then it hit him, the familiar pungent odor of the beasts. *I'm too late.*

As he emerged into a moonlit clearing, a black form darted out of the shadows. He stopped and braced himself for what was about to happen. He closed his eyes and bawled his fists as hard as he could, praying that his death would be quick. The darkened form launched itself at him. He turned his body away, ready for the violent impact. And then...the form began licking him. He opened his eyes and sputtered in amazement.

"Seaman!"

The dog's face continued licking his as he staggered forward trying to regain his bearing. A few seconds later, he saw light emerging from the tree line. More light. Torches. They grew brighter, filling the clearing with orange light.

"Will!" a voice cried out. Clark looked to his right and saw the face of Lewis approaching, a burning torch grasped firmly in his left hand.

"Over there! Hurry!" another voice shouted from the darkness. He watched as York and Drouillard emerged from the trees, both carrying torches that they quickly tossed onto the ground near the edge of the clearing. More men arrived and began tossing leaves, sticks, and anything else they could find to make the torch's flames grow larger and brighter. Within minutes, the entire clearing was ringed by raging fires. The crackling flames leapt high into the night sky, casting shadows that danced on the forest floor. Clark, his heart still racing from the adrenaline of his near encounter with the beasts, watched as the inferno consumed the dry sagebrush the men were tossing on it, sending tendrils of smoke spiraling upward into the darkness. All around, the men worked feverishly to stoke the flames, their faces illuminated by the flickering light. Soon, the air was thick was the acrid scent of the sage.

"The sage..." Clark began, still trying to catch his breath. "It worked...it repels them somehow."

Lewis nodded with a grin. "We know. When York and the others found us, they told us you were trying to hold the beasts off with the sage you had in your bag. Thankfully, Sacagawea knew just where to find more. We've been stockpiling the stuff for the last few hours hoping we'd find you in time."

Clark took a deep breath and staggered over toward Lewis. He placed his hand on Lewis's shoulder and looked intently into his eyes, his breath still coming in short, ragged gasps.

"Meri...you...saved my life. I..." Tears began to well in his eyes as he diverted his eyes. "...I thought I was going to die."

Lewis pulled him into an embrace, his strong arms offering comfort and reassurance amid the chaos surrounding them.

Beyond the flames, the beasts howled and snarled in frustration, their primal fury echoing through the darkened forest. The trees beyond the clearing began to shake as the beasts pounded hard against their trunks. But it mattered little to Clark and the others. They knew so long as the fires continued to rage, they were safe from the beasts and their fury.

FRONTIER

FORTY-SIX

The fires burned for six long days as the beasts continued to prowl the perimeter of the camp. As the Corps' meager rations continued to dwindle, the morale of the expedition's men began to spiral as the relentless howls of the beasts echoed ominously through the forest. Everyone knew they could not remain in the clearing much longer.

As the sun rose on the sixth day, Clark staggered out of his small lean-to and surveyed the camp. Smoke from the smoldering fires hung low in the air, adding to the oppressive atmosphere. Men moved slowly, their faces gaunt and eyes hollow with exhaustion. He noticed York tending to one of the fires, his usually strong frame showing signs of wear. A few feet away, Drouillard and Charbonneau were huddled together discussing something in hushed tones. He let out a sigh as his eyes settled on Sacagawea slumped beneath a large pine tree trying to get Pompey to nurse from her breast. Beside her, Seaman laid lazily in the early morning sun, his head resting comfortable against her left thigh. He rubbed his eyes, trying to clear the fog of fatigue from his mind. He knew they had to make a decision soon. Staying where they were was no longer an option; the beasts were getting bolder, their howls growing closer each night.

He walked over to where Lewis was sitting, staring blankly at the dwindling fire. "We can't stay here much longer," he stated, sitting down beside him. "We're running out of food, and those things are getting more aggressive."

Lewis looked up, his eyes filled with the same exhaustion Clark felt. "I know, Will. But where do we go? Those things have trapped us between them and the mountains. We can't go back the way we came, and we can't move forward without more supplies."

Clark took a deep breath, steeling himself for what he had to say. "I've been thinking about what to do, and I think our best chance is to make a run for it. If we can reach the Shoshone lands, we might find help."

"Those things would be on us before we made it out of the pass."

"We killed several of those things back at the village. Only three chased me down into the valley. Therefore, it's logical to assume there are only three still hunting us."

Lewis frowned. "Just one of those things equals four men. Even with just three out there, I still don't like our odds, especially with our short supply of ammunition. And don't forget, Sacagawea is carrying an infant on her back."

"I know that, but if we divide the men into smaller groups and send each off in different directions toward the main camp, it might confuse the beasts and give us a chance to slip past them."

"That's a risky plan," Lewis replied, his brow furrowed in concern. "But..." he added with resignation, "it may be our only option."

Clark nodded. "We'll have to move quickly. I'll send George Drouillard to go with Sacagawea, Toussaint, Monroe, and the Field brothers. When they go, I'll take Bratton, Ordway, and Hooker, and we'll make as much noise as we can to try and divert at least one of them away from Sacagawea's group. You'll take Silas, the Hardy brothers, and Nate Chapman, and head south. Everyone else will head to the northeast. They'll need more men to help with Ambrose."

Lewis nodded slowly, his expression still clouded with worry. "We're putting a lot of faith into their only being three of those things out there. What if there are more? What if they want us to split up like this? And there's another thing..." He glanced over toward the remaining fires that were slowly starting to smolder. "We're nearly out of sagebrush."

"All the more reason we need to get out of here. We're out of water, they won't let us hunt, fish, or scavenge more sagebrush. We'll be dead in hours if we remain."

He could tell Lewis was mulling over his words in his head, trying to determine the best course of action. Finally, he nodded in agreement. "All right. Let's tell the others." Clark rose and gathered the men around. He could see the exhaustion and fear they had endured over the previous days reflected in their faces as they peered back at him through weary eyes.

"Listen up," he began, his voice steady despite the tension. "We're moving out of here. We'll split into groups to increase our chances of making it through." He outlined his plan again, ensuring each man understood their role. "George, you'll go with Toussaint, Sacagawea, Jack, Joseph, and Reuben. Make as little noise as possible and move quickly. I'll take Will, Sergeant Ordway, and Joe Hooker. We'll try and divert their attention while you make your way northeast. The rest of you will go with Captain Lewis."

The men nodded, their expressions grim but resolute. Clark continued, "We don't know exactly how many more of those creatures are out there, but we do know they're dangerous. If you must engage, keep your distance. Don't let them get close enough to you to attack." He paused before letting out a long sigh of determination. "Stick together and move quickly and you'll be fine." He surveyed the group one final time before glancing toward Lewis. He offered a silent nod of affirmation. As the men dispersed to gather their things, he felt a hand on his shoulder. He turned to see Lewis, his face serious but with a glimmer of hope.

"We'll make it. We've come too far to fall now."

Clark nodded. "We'll make it." He turned back toward the group. "Prepare yourselves. It's time these beasts saw what violent men can do."

FORTY-SEVEN

Clark listened to the distant rumble of thunder off to the west as he and the others began their escape out of the clearing. As they began to move, the first drops of rain splattered onto the forest floor, the sound melding with the sound of their boots sloshing along the muddy trail. The scent of damp earth mixed with the lingering odor of the sagebrush, creating an unsettling but familiar atmosphere as Clark trudged his way through the dense underbrush. The canopy above offered little protection as the rain intensified, transforming the serene woodland into a veil of mist and shadows.

His eyes scanned the landscape ahead as he pressed forward. "Stay close and keep moving," he whispered, glancing back to ensure no one was falling behind. The group moved as quickly as they could, their breaths coming in ragged gasps. The rain began to fall more steadily as it morphed from a soft patter to a steady drizzle that hindered his visibility. The forest, usually full of life, seemed eerily quiet except for the rain and the occasional rumble of thunder.

The men hurried forward ahead of him, eventually breaking off into their prearranged groups while Lewis and a handful of others waded quickly off to the north hoping to draw the beasts toward them. Clark glanced to his right and saw Drouillard's group, led by Sacagawea, slicing their way through the obscured labyrinth of ancient trees. Behind him, the beasts roared violently, their cries echoing out through the veil of rain behind him. He glanced quickly over toward Thornfield, who stood nearby armed with a rifle in one hand and a knife in the other. The trees began to shake as the sound of the beasts' howls grew louder, their giant footsteps slamming hard onto the muddy forest floor. Clark unslung his rifle and motioned to the others.

"They're coming," he announced, his voice cutting through the rain-soaked air. The men swiftly shifted into defensive positions, rifles clutched tightly, and knives unsheathed. To his right, Ordway muttered something under his breath as he leaned up against a large tree. Behind Ordway, Thornfield, his eyes sharp and focused, nodded in acknowledgement. From the shadows emerged Charbonneau, Bratton, and Hooker, each armed and visibly nervous but resolute. As Clark turned back to face the approaching beasts, a loud banging reverberated through the woods, as if the trees themselves were under assault. The group tensed, their eyes scanning the rain-drenched surroundings. Suddenly, rocks flew through the air, slamming hard into the trees around them. One struck Charbonneau in the face, sending him crumpling to the ground in pain, while another struck Ordway in the neck. Ordway grimaced but remained standing as he tried to take shelter behind the tree. More rocks followed, battering their makeshift defensive positions, and sending splinters of wood flying.

"Stay down! Clark shouted, his voice barely audible over the clamor. He crouched low, peering through the rain, trying to spot their attackers. The downpour made it nearly impossible to see, but he could hear the guttural growls and snarls of the beasts drawing nearer.

York fired a shot into the darkness, the gun's flash illuminating the trees for a split second. Somewhere in the distance, one of the beasts roared, which was followed by an angry chorus of howls that sent chills down Clark's spine. The beasts were closing in, and their chances of survival were dwindling with each passing second.

"We need to move!" Ordway shouted, his voice urgent. "We can't hold this position!"

Clark knew he was right. Staying put would only lead to their deaths. "Fall back!" he commanded. "Head for the valley, now!" Another rock came hurtling through the air, forcing Clark to duck and cover his head and face. He looked up and squinted through the rain, trying to discern their location. The beasts' howls grew silent, yet their noxious stench lingered in the air like a malevolent ghost. He knew they were close. As he grimaced from the foul odor, he tightened his grip around the base of his rifle.

The men scrambled to their feet, grabbing Charbonneau and helping him up as they began to retreat. The rocks continued to rain down, and the howls grew louder and more frantic. Clark fired his rifle into the trees, buying them precious seconds as he covered the retreat. He saw York and Drouillard pulling Charbonneau, while Bratton and Hooker supported Ordway, who was bleeding from his neck wound. As they moved, he felt a sharp pain in his leg. A rock had struck him just below the knee, nearly knocking him down. He gritted his teeth and pushed through the pain, hobbling as fast as he could to keep up with the others.

A few minutes passed and they made it to a narrow ledge. Below, Clark could see the valley through the mist of rain. He paused to catch his breath as the men slowly began their descent down the ledge.

"Keep moving," he urged, his voice strained. "We can't let them trap us here." He watched as Charbonneau knelt near the edge of the ledge and took in a series of deep breaths. York stopped and looked back toward Clark.

"We need to hold-up, sir."

Clark glanced around at his exhausted men. The rain was relentless, and he could tell their energy was waning. But he also knew staying there was too dangerous. "Just for a moment," he conceded. "But we can't stay long."

York nodded and helped Charbonneau to a more stable position. Clark took the brief pause to assess their surroundings. The valley below offered some cover, with dense underbrush and rocky outcrops that could provide temporary refuge.

Suddenly, he saw Charbonneau gasp in horror and point to the edge of the forest. Clark followed his gaze and saw dark shapes moving through the trees. The beasts had found them.

"Everyone, up! Move now!" he shouted, adrenaline surging through him. He grabbed Charbonneau by the arm and pulled him to his feet. "We need to get to the valley floor. Now!" But even before he finished saying the words, he knew it was too late. He watched as one of the beasts emerged from the trees, its massive form looming menacingly and its hulking silhouette cutting through the rain-drenched shadows around them. A guttural growl emanated from its throat as its narrow face and yellow eyes focused on the group of men standing near the ledge.

FRONTIER

Charbonneau, panic in his eyes, hastily raised his rifle and fired off a shot that sliced through the air in the direction of the beast. The bullet grazed a small tree a foot from where the beast stood. The creature let out a ferocious roar, its anger evident as it bared its sharp teeth at them.

"Run!" Clark shouted as he spun his rifle around and took aim at the colossal creature. He let loose a shot that grazed the creature's right shoulder, prompting a roar of pain that reverberated through the forest. The wounded beast, fueled now by primal fury, lunged toward Charbonneau as the trader scrambled away frantically. As Clark quickly reloaded, he saw a second beast emerge, this one slightly smaller but just as menacing. Its yellow eyes darted from Charbonneau to Ordway.

"Move, Sergeant!" Clark yelled, raising his rifle. Ordway, transfixed by the sight of the massive creature before him, dove to his right just as the creature lunged, its massive arms narrowly missing their target. Hooker, standing a few yards from Ordway, took aim and fired off a round, striking the beast in the left leg. The injured creature stumbled but quickly regained its footing, its attention now divided between the men before it. Clark looked to his right as Bratton fired, striking the beast in the back. The beast moaned in pain, momentarily hobbled by the barrage of gunfire. Simultaneously, the first beast, having dodged Charbonneau's shot, sprinted toward Ordway with unbridled rage. Ordway, his rifle poised, fired off a shot that struck the beast in the stomach. Wounded and now even more enraged, the beast let out a loud howl and lunged forward, once again narrowly missing Charbonneau, who dove quickly behind a nearby tree. Clark, his rifle one again reloaded and primed, took aim and squeezed the trigger. He felt a small jolt against his shoulder as the rifle fired and the bullet whistled through the air and rain. It struck the beast just below the right breast, causing it to stumble backward toward the shelter of the trees. Charbonneau, regaining his senses, aimed his rifle and fired, striking the beast in the chest. The beast let out one last gurgled roar as it fell limply to the ground.

Behind him, the trees shook violently as the third beast broke through the underbrush, its massive form blocking out what little light Clark could see from above the forest canopy. It let loose a horrifying roar as it charged toward him. Reacting, Clark reached down and grabbed his knife just as the beast grabbed hold of him and swung him violently into a nearby tree. He cried out in pain as the beast brought its fist down hard toward his head. He jerked his head to the left just as the beast's fist flew past him, colliding hard against the trunk of the tree and sending splinters of bark flying in all directions. The beast turned back toward him, its yellow eyes glinting with rage as it advanced. With a surge of adrenaline, he grabbed his knife and drove it deep into the beast's side. The creature roared in agony, its grip on him momentarily loosening as it stumbled backward. Seizing the opportunity, he pushed himself off the tree and lunged forward, driving the blade even deeper into the creature's flesh. The beast howled as it staggered away from him, clutching frantically at its side as blood oozed from beneath the thin layer of fur covering its torso.

"Lieutenant!" Ordway shouted from a few yards away. He fired off a round from his rifle. The bullet struck the beast behind the left shoulder. The beast roared, momentarily distracted as Clark hurried away from its grasp. The first beast now charged toward Ordway, its mouth contorted into a twisted snarl. Two shots echoed out through the rain, each striking the beast in the back. The beast's body fell limply to the ground in front of Ordway, lifeless. The remaining beast cried out in rage as it watched its companion fall to the ground. It gazed toward Clark, its eyes lingering briefly on him as he stumbled up against a large rock, as if calculating its next move. Clark stared back at it, his breaths becoming heavy pants as he tried to fight through the throbbing pain in his shoulder. In the corner of his eye, he could see Ordway reloading his rifle. The beast's stare lingered a few seconds more. Clark could see the primal rage in the creature's eyes as it struggled to comprehend everything that had just happened. He surmised the beast had rarely seen such death it itself had not inflicted and now, it was unsure of how to proceed. It stood up straight, its massive frame taking up nearly all of Clark's vision. It then let out a low grunt before darting off quickly into the trees just as Ordway raised his rifle. Clark continued staring at the spot where the beast had disappeared, as if expecting it to emerge at any moment to finish them off, but it never did. Within minutes, the beast's foul smell was gone, and Clark lowered his head in weary relief. His shoulder throbbed and his head was bleeding, but he was alive. He turned to the others, a small grin forming on his face as he licked the blood from his lips. They had faced the untamed beasts of the wilderness and lived to tell the tale.

FORTY-EIGHT

Excerpt from Lewis's Secret Journal

It has been five days since our last encounter with the creatures. Our progress has been slowed considerably because of the injuries in our party, but we are now merely days away from leaving this hostile place.

In the days since our battles with the creatures, the forest has fallen silent, devoid of the menacing howls and threatening presence that has haunted us for so long. Lieutenant Clark is slowly recovering from his injuries, thanks to the diligent care of Sacagawea, whose skill as a healer has proven invaluable in these trying times.

As I sit here by the fire watching over the camp, my mind is consumed with thoughts of our next move. We have faced these creatures head-on and emerged victorious, but I cannot shake the feeling that our trials are far from over. The decision of whether to divulge the truth of our encounters to President Jefferson upon our return continues to weigh heavily upon me. The implications of such revelations are vast and uncertain, and I fear the repercussions they may bring.

For now, however, my focus remains on the safety and well-being of our expedition. We must press onward. Our destination lies in the east, where the lands of the Shoshone offer the promise of refuge from the dangers that lurk in these forests. I pray we can continue to outrun the shadows.

-Meriwether Lewis
June 3, 1806

FRONTIER

FORTY-NINE

It would take the Corps of Discovery two more weeks to emerge from the depths of the Lemhi Pass, their feet slogging slowly across the muddy ground day after day as they limped their way eastward out of the mountains. The journey had taken its toll on them, physically and mentally. But despite their exhaustion, they pressed on, driven by the promise of reaching the end of their long ordeal.

Clark, still nursing his injured shoulder, led the group with a determined stride, his face etched with lines of pain and exhaustion. Each day as they trudged along, they cast wary glances over their shoulders, half expecting to see the shadowy figures of the beasts lurking among the rocky crags. The pass itself seemed to stretch endlessly, the narrow trail winding its way through steep ravines and dense pine forests, wilderness upon wilderness. Each of them longed for the open plains and the familiar landscapes of home, where the threat of the beasts would be nothing but a distant memory. When they finally emerged from the pass and set foot on the open grasslands of the northern Louisiana Territory, a sense of relief washed over them. The vast expanse of prairie stretched out before them, a welcome sight after weeks of confinement among the rugged mountains.

Lewis ordered the men to halt and make camp a few miles beyond the mouth of the pass. As he watched the men begin setting up their tents and gathering wood for the evening's fires, Clark approached, his arm bound in a sling against his chest.

"I want to scout ahead a way, see if I can find water."

"Good idea," Lewis replied, reaching for his rifle. He quickly slung it behind him and motioned for Clark to follow him. "I'll go with you."

Clark let out a sigh. "So, you're my protector now?"

Lewis chuckled softly. "Just making sure you don't get yourself into any more trouble. Besides, we both know you're the better scout." He gave Clark a playful nudge with his elbow. "We should take York and George as well, just in case."

"You think they're still following us?" Clark asked softly.

Lewis sighed. "I don't know. It's been two weeks and no sign of them. But I don't want to take any chances." He glanced over his shoulder at the camp where York and Drouillard were finishing up their tasks. "Let's gather them and head out before it gets too dark." From behind York, Seaman emerged and barked loudly as he hurried to Lewis's side. Lewis glanced back at Clark and smiled. "We have nothing to fear now, Seaman will scare away the beasts."

Clark flashed a brief smile as he gathered his bag and rifle. He hated being seen as weak, but he also knew in his current condition there was little he could offer in ways of defense. So, he quietly swallowed his pride and let himself accept the indignity of being looked after. Fifteen minutes later, the small scouting party moved forward down the rocky trail until they were almost a full mile from the rest of the expedition. Seaman ran off ahead, barking at squirrels and other critters as his bushy tail wagging excitedly behind him. Clark, his wounded shoulder throbbing with each step, continued scanning the surrounding landscape for any signs of danger. Beside him, York walked briskly along, his rifle at the ready, ever vigilant for any threats that might emerge from the shadows. Drouillard followed closely behind, his eyes darting nervously from side to side as he kept watch over the group.

The trail stretched out before them, winding its way through the grassy hills and wide valleys. Tall pine trees towered overhead along certain stretches, their branches swaying gently in the warm summer breeze that swept down from the peaks of the Rockies behind them. Despite the natural beauty all around them, each man was acutely aware of the dangers that lurked in the shadows. Every rustle of leaves or snap of a twig sent a shiver down their spines, their senses heightened by the ever-present threat of the unknown. The air was crisp, with a hint of pine and damp earth. Clark felt a sense of relief being away from the camp and away from the prying eyes of the other men. Here, surrounded by nature's beauty, he could momentarily forget the hardships and dangers they faced. As they hiked, Lewis occasionally pointed out familiar landmarks from the previous summer's trip through the same landscape.

FRONTIER

Despite the pain in his shoulder, he found himself grateful for the company and the distraction from his own thoughts.

Suddenly, Seaman's barking ceased, replaced by a low growl. Clark's hand instinctively went to the hilt of his knife, his heart pounding in his chest as he prepared for whatever might lie ahead.

"Is it them?" York asked, his grip tightening on his rifle.

"I don't think so," Clark replied, slowly moving forward toward the underbrush where Seaman continued growling.

"How can you be so sure?"

"Because the air still smells like pine."

A few yards ahead, Lewis cocked the hammer back on his rifle and slowly stepped forward. With a silent hand signal, he directed Drouillard to flank to the right, while he stealthily advanced to the left, his eyes scanning the dense undergrowth for any hint of movement. Behind him, Clark and York maintained a vigilant watch, their gaze sweeping the trees for any sign of movement. As they advanced forward through the underbrush, the air was thick with an eerie silence, broken only by the occasional rustle of leaves in the wind. Quietly, they emerged into a large field and what appeared to be the remnants of a camp. Clark scanned the horizon, on guard for any sign of the beasts lurking in the shadows waiting to pounce, but all he saw were a pair of squirrels running playfully among the branches above. Taking a deep breath to steady his nerves, he turned his attention back to the grim scene before him. The once bustling site now lay in ruins, the remnants of tents torn and tattered, their fabric fluttering like ghostly banners in the breeze. Scattered around the grounds were the skeletal remains of soldiers, their bodies mangled and torn.

"Keep your eyes peeled, boys," Clark muttered under his breath, his voice barely audible above the rustle of the leaves. "We don't know what else might be lurking around here." York nodded solemnly beside him. Drouillard began to move cautiously through the camp, his rifle at the ready, scanning the underbrush for any sign of movement. Clark's gaze fell back upon the soldiers, who were now little more than desiccated husks scattered among the debris of the camp, their uniforms weathered and faded, their flesh picked clean by scavengers. Some lay twisted in unnatural positions, their limbs contorted in agony, while others appeared frozen in the final throes of battle, their faces etched with expressions of terror and disbelief.

"These look like Spanish uniforms," Lewis remarked as he knelt beside one of the mangled bodies. "It looks as if they've been here for months."

"What the hell are the Spanish doing this far north?" Clark queried in disbelief.

"They were probably sent to find us."

Clark cast another troubled glance at the mutilated bodies strewn across the ground. His jaw tightened as he considered the implications of Lewis's words. If the Spanish had been sent to intercept them, it meant their presence had been discovered. Would Spain send more soldiers to try and find them? Would they be captured and sent to California or Santa Fe as prisoners?

"Spain has been claiming the purchase of these lands was fraudulent," Lewis stated as he slowly stood back up, "They claim Louisiana was never rightfully owned by Napoleon, and therefore, wasn't his to sell."

"First giant beasts, and now the Spanish," Drouillard muttered quietly as he continued to peer around the deserted camp.

"We cannot afford to ignore this," Lewis said, looking at Clark. "If the Spanish are here, it means we're not alone, and our journey just got more complicated."

"It looks as if the beasts have taken care of that complication for us," Clark replied gravely. The men exchanged a somber glance. The sudden silence was quickly broken by a voice ringing out from the edge of the field.

"Over here!" It was York, his voice tinged with urgency. "I found something!"

Hearts pounding with anticipation, Clark and the others hurried over to where York stood, his figure outlined against the dim light filtering through the trees. As they approached, they saw him crouched beside a patch of disturbed earth, his gaze fixed intently on the ground.

"What is it?" Lewis asked, out of breath.

FRONTIER

York looked up, his expression grim. "Tracks," he replied, pointing to a series of large footprints imprinted into the soft mud. "Fresh ones."

The men exchanged worried glances.

"I thought those things were all behind us," Drouillard said, glancing nervously around as if one of the beasts was poised to lunge out from behind a tree at any moment.

"That group of them in the pass are," Clark replied soberly. "But there could be dozens, even hundreds of those things scattered across the mountains."

"Maybe they migrate in the summer," York offered, his eyes still fixed on the giant footprints in the mud below.

Lewis frowned. "It's possible," he admitted. "But it doesn't change the fact that they're out here and we need to be cautious."

"We should go back," York said with a glance toward Clark.

Clark nodded as he knelt beside one of the muddy footprints. "These tracks," he muttered, gesturing towards one of the large footprints, "they're fresh. The beasts may be closer than we think."

"Let's just pray they're heading south, *away* from us," Lewis said with concern.

"I hope that's the case," Clark replied, standing up. "I've had enough of those things for a lifetime." He glanced back at the Spanish encampment, a shiver running down his spine as he imagined the horrors the Spanish soldiers must have endured. The only problem was he didn't have to *imagine*, he knew exactly what they had gone through. The thought made him close his eyes and breathe in deeply as he tried to push away the images of violence and terror that haunted his mind. But no matter how hard he tried, he couldn't shake the feeling of dread that gripped his heart like a vice. "Let's get moving," he said with a sigh. "There's nothing left for us here."

NICHOLAS KANE

FIFTY

"July twenty-fifth."

Clark glanced over at Lewis, his mouth agape in surprise. "Are we really that late into the summer?"

Lewis nodded with a smile, his gaze lingering on the distant horizon. "We are. We'll be back in St. Louis by late August if we can keep up our current pace."

"Well," Clark began, his attention split between Lewis and a large rock he was carving into, "we're moving faster now that we've sent Ambrose ahead with Sacagawea and Charbonneau. But the sooner we're back on the Missouri, the better."

Lewis gave another nod, knowing the meaning behind Clark's words. Each member of the expedition felt the same way; each wanted to put the mountains, and what lurked within them, as far behind them as possible. In the distance, Lewis could still make out the snow-capped peaks of the Rocky Mountains, rising like jagged sentinels against the horizon. They marked a stark boundary between the fertile meadows and rolling fields of the upper Louisiana plains and the rugged, untamed expanse of Oregon's high desert and winding valleys. Below him, the wind teased the tall grasses, setting them into rhythmic motion and creating an emerald tide that rippled toward the horizon. A variety of flowers speckled the green expanse with bursts of color—golden sunflowers, deep blue lupines, and pale white yarrow—while a nearby creek traced a silver ribbon through the land, its gentle murmurs mingling with the sigh of the breeze. He glanced back over at Clark, who was still hunched over the large boulder near the edge of the windswept bluff they stood upon. The sounds of a chisel echoed off the surrounding cliffs as Clark carved into the boulder's weathered surface. When he finished, he stepped back, admiring his work.

"There," he proudly proclaimed with a satisfied grin. He motioned to the inscription. Lewis walked over and surveyed the inscription, which simply read:

W CLARK JULY 25 1806

FRONTIER

"I dub this rock *Pompey's Pillar!*" he said with a grin.

"Quite the honor for young Pompey," Lewis remarked, a wry grin of his own playing at the corners of his lips.

Clark's laughter echoed across the bluff, carried away by the late afternoon breeze. "Indeed! Sacagawea will surely appreciate the gesture."

They gathered up their things and slowly began making their way down the bluff toward camp, the wind tugging at their coats and tousling their hair. After a few minutes of silence, Lewis looked up and stared off toward the northwest, his eyes lingering on the prominent white peaks that loomed in the distance. "I used to always wonder what laid beyond those mountains—what mysteries the wilderness held there." He sighed and glanced back at Clark. "I've lost that…feeling of curiosity; of needing to know what was beyond each sloping horizon or over each mountain peak. I've lost what it means to be an explorer."

Clark gave a solemn nod, his own eyes now scanning the vast wilderness to the northwest. "There will always be that need to press onward, Meri. To press forward, into the unknown. It's the lure of discovery and the thrill of the journey itself that drives us onward. And I refuse to let those beasts take that from me." He glanced over at his friend, a thoughtful expression gracing his features. "Don't let them take it from you. Despite everything that's happened, there's no other place I'd rather be right now than here, in this place, with you and the others by my side. We must soak this in for as long as possible because it won't last. More people will come to this place and one day, it will lose the splendor that makes it appealing to men like you and me. It will lose the specialness it now holds."

Lewis nodded, his gaze fixed on the distant horizon where the sun was beginning to dip and cast long shadows across the windswept landscape. The sweeping plains seemed to stretch endlessly beneath the sun-kissed sky. He turned his attention back to Clark as the pair resumed their march back toward the camp. "You intend to tell the President about everything that's happened?"

"I feel we have little choice in the matter. The rest of the men will surely divulge everything upon our return to St. Louis, and we will have to account for Ambrose's injury as well as the deaths of Harrington and the others."

Lewis nodded in understanding. "I suppose we'll leave it to the President to decide what to do with the information."

"I reckon he will be more disappointed we did not find a wooly mammoth during our travels."

Lewis laughed and the two men once again fell into a comfortable silence, the only sound being the rustle of the wind through the grass and the distant murmur of the camp below. As they approached the flickering glow of the campfire, the men's faces illuminated by its warm light, each of them felt a sense of camaraderie and purpose wash over them. As they neared the fire's warmth, they exchanged contented looks with one another as they shared a silent understanding—a bond forged in the crucible of adversity—a bond they knew they would share for the rest of their lives.

FRONTIER

FIFTY-ONE

It was the last day of July, and the air was tinged with a hint of crispness, signaling the arrival of autumn, yet the late afternoon sun still carried the lingering warmth of summer. From where Clark stood, a vast meadow unfolded before him like a green carpet under the mid-summer sun. The grass, a vibrant green tinged with golden hues, swayed gently in the warm breeze, creating a mesmerizing dance of light and shadow. Wildflowers of every color dotted the landscape, their delicate petals swaying in the gentle currents of air. As he knelt beside the sparkling blue waters of the stream, he glanced over at Lewis who stood about thirty yards away stooped over one of the wildflowers. He watched as his fingers traced the delicate petals of the flower, his mind absorbing the intricate patterns of nature's design. Lewis stood up and jotted down something in the small journal he kept tucked in his pocket. As he completed his observations, he straightened up and cast a glance towards Clark, offering a brief wave before striding purposefully into the heart of the meadow. Clark acknowledged the gesture with a smile, his gaze lingering on his companion for a moment before returning to the swift-moving stream. He closed his eyes, finding solace in the soothing sounds of the flowing water. Slowly, he dipped his hands into the cool, crystal-clear currents, feeling the refreshing touch of water against his weathered skin. With each breath, he felt the tension of the journey melt away, replaced by a deep sense of peace and clarity. He knew moments such as these had been few and far between and soon, they would be replaced with the hustle and bustle of civilization once more. But for now—for this brief moment—everything seemed to be at peace.

He let out a long sigh as he arched his neck back, allowing the warm rays of the afternoon sun to bath gently across his weather-beaten face. He felt his muscles begin to relax under the sun's soothing touch of warmth, like an old friend greeting him in a gentle embrace. Below, the water continued to glisten as it flowed through the meadow, its melodious babble adding to the serene atmosphere of the moment. He savored the tranquil moment. With each breath, he drank in the crisp, clean wilderness air, filling his lungs with the invigorating scent of pine and wildflowers. The aroma was a symphony of earthy fragrances, carried on the breeze and mingling with the sweet perfume of sun-warmed grass. If Heaven existed, he was surely in it.

His breath caught in his throat as he leveled his head and opened his eyes, gazing out across the sparkling waters toward a clump of trees a dozen or so yards away. He blinked, momentarily questioning the image before him. He rubbed his eyes and stared again. His heart skipped a beat as a chill ran down his spine at the realization of what he was seeing. Slowly, the scent of decaying flesh filled his nostrils. The once vibrant air, alive with the sweet scents of nature, was now replaced and tainted by the unmistakable stench of death. His breath quickened as he stared intently at the clump of trees and the hulking figure standing amidst its shadowy foliage. Slowly, he propped himself up, ready to stand and flee. The beast stood motionless amidst the trees, its presence looming like a specter in the fading light. He felt a surge of primal fear grip his heart as it continued to stare back at him from across the grassy expanse of the meadow. It's tattered fur, matted and streaked with dirt and blood, hung in ragged strands around its massive frame. Long, bloody scars crisscrossed its shoulder and torso, remnants of the fierce battle it had waged against him and the others a month earlier.

But it was the creature's eyes that held Clark's gaze—a pair of gleaming orbs, burning with an otherworldly intensity, fixed upon him with a look of unyielding vengeance that held him captive. Its face, with its wide nose and mashed-in features, reflected the primal savagery of the wilderness. For a moment, they both stared at one another, man eying beast. Memories of their previous encounter flooded his mind as he sat, transfixed and unable to move. He shifted slightly, preparing his body to flee. His mind raced, trying to remember where he had left his rifle. *The rock.* He turned his head slightly to the right and saw a small pile of rocks a few yards down the stream. He knew the chances of reaching his rifle and firing off a shot before the creature was upon him were slim at best, but he had to try. In the meantime, he had to find another way to defend himself. His eyes began searching the ground frantically for anything that could help him. Across the meadow, the beast remained motionless, its eyes still gazing intently in his direction. His heart raced as he scanned the ground once more, his mind racing for a solution in the face of imminent danger. That's when he saw it. A large branch, weathered and worn by the elements, laying nestled amidst the tall grass. He took one last glance toward the beast as he willed his body to lunge for the branch. Finally, he took in a deep breath and bolted to his right, lunging for the branch in the grass. He felt his fingers close around its rough bark as he wrenched it free from the earth. The branch felt reassuringly solid in his hands as he brandished it like a makeshift weapon, his knuckles white with tension as he prepared to face the beast. It may not have been a rifle or a sword, but it was all he had, and he was determined to make the most of it.

Quietly, he steeled himself, his grip tightening against the bark of the branch. Every instinct screamed at him to run, to flee from the monstrous creature looming on the other side of the stream, but he forced himself to stand his ground. He summoned all his courage and resolve, ready to face whatever brutal fate awaited him.

FIFTY-TWO

Lewis finished jotting down the last of his notes and quickly tucked his journal back inside his coat. Around him, the late afternoon sun bathed the meadow in a warm golden hue, casting long shadows across the grassy expanse. The tranquility of the scene was almost palpable, and he couldn't help but feel a sense of peace wash over him as he took in the beauty of the wilderness surrounding him.

He noticed the sun was beginning to dip lower toward the western horizon. He let out a soft sigh, knowing their peaceful day would be ending soon. Clark had encouraged him to join him on this little side trip while the men prepared the boats for their final trip down the Missouri the following day. He knew that by reaching the river, their expedition was coming to an end. Days like these would become more infrequent, until eventually, they would find themselves back along the bustling wharfs of the St. Louis waterfront. He thought back to the countless trials they had all faced since leaving St. Louis over two years earlier—the things they had discovered, the men they had lost, and of course, the creatures they had encountered. The thought of the creatures made him shudder. It had been over a month since their last encounter with one of them, and nearly two weeks since they had discovered the Spanish camp. He prayed they were far behind them now.

He slowly trudged his way across the center of the meadow toward the stream where Clark had been filling his canteen. He anticipated that convincing Clark to depart from this beautiful place would take some persuasion, but the rapidly fading afternoon sunlight would have to be compelling reason enough to get moving. As he crested a small rise, he caught sight of the stream below. His gaze swept the water's edge until it settled on Clark, who was crouched down with a large branch held defensively before him. Perplexed, Lewis followed Clark's intense stare across the stream to a cluster of trees where a massive figure suddenly emerged, hurtling towards Clark at full speed.

"Oh my God..." Lewis croaked out as he broke into a run toward the stream.

FRONTIER

FIFTY-THREE

Clark gripped the branch tightly as he watched the beast begin charging across the empty meadow toward him. The large branch in his hands trembled slightly, the sharpened tip aimed outward as a desperate weapon against the oncoming force of nature before him. He tightened his grip, his muscles coiled with adrenaline, and forced himself to steady his breathing. The beast was coming. Fast. The tall grass parted in its wake, bowing under the sheer force of its charge. Clark's pulse quickened as the beast reached the stream, its momentum barely slowing as it plunged into the icy waters. The stream exploded in a spray of glistening droplets that caught the sunlight, but the beauty of the moment was lost in the terror of what followed.

The beast let out a feral howl as it powered through the current. When it emerged on Clark's side of the stream, it snarled at him, revealing an assortment of yellow, chipped teeth. Its fur, matted and soaked with water from the stream, clung to its muscular body, accentuating the raw power that propelled it forward. Its eyes burned with a primal rage; blazing orbs of fiery determination fixed squarely on its prey. With each thunderous footfall, the ground seemed to tremble, sending shivers of terror down Clark's spine.

The beast was now a mere ten yards away. It let out another deafening howl, causing him to squint his eyes as he braced himself for the creature's imminent assault. In that harrowing moment, he felt the crushing weight of terror bearing down on him as he gazed one final time into the beast's eyes, its massive frame now towering over him in a grotesque display of raw power and savagery. In that moment, he was reminded of humanity's fragile place in the unforgiving natural world. He locked eyes with the beast, its fierce gaze piercing his skull. It was almost on top of him now, its massive frame blotting out the fading light of the late afternoon sun. He braced himself one last time, ready to thrust the branch into the beast's chest. But before he could make his move, a shot rang out from behind him. Startled, he glanced up to see

Lewis, his rifle still smoking, standing several yards away. The shot had missed its mark, but it had caught the beast's attention. With a menacing glare, the creature turned its gaze toward Lewis.

Seizing the opportunity, Clark plunged the tip of the branch toward the beast's stomach. But the creature's thick, leathery hide proved too resilient, and the branch barely pierced its skin. Enraged, the beast swatted the branch away with a powerful swipe of its massive arm.

Clark lurched sideways just as the beast's arm came crashing down onto the spot where he had been kneeling. He tumbled back toward the stream as the beast lunged after him. Another shot rang out, this time hitting the beast somewhere in the back. It turned and howled in pain as its long arms searched futilely for the wound on its back. He glanced over in the direction of Lewis who hurried toward him.

"Will!" Lewis shouted as he tossed an object down onto the sand near the edge of the stream. He glanced over and saw it was his knife. As the beast staggered toward Lewis, he dove headfirst and seized the knife with his fingers. He turned and watched as the beast grabbed a large log off the ground and began swinging it wildly in Lewis's direction. Lewis, caught off-guard by the log being suddenly swung in his direction, tossed his rifle aside as he dove for his life. The beast snorted with anger as it continued swinging the log with savage fury, unleashing its relentless assault on Lewis. Clark's heart pounded in his chest as he watched in horror, his mind racing for a way to help his friend. Lewis rolled again, narrowly escaping the blow from the log as the beast swung it down hard again upon the ground. Clark, the knife gripped tightly in his hand, lunged forward, and charged toward the beast with ferocity. With a primal roar of his own, he leapt onto the beast's back and plunged the knife down into the creature's exposed flank with all his might. The beast howled with a mix of pain and fury as his blade ripped through its skin and muscle. With lightning speed, the creature turned and easily swung him loose from its back. He landed with a hard *thud* a few feet away. He scrambled to move as the beast stomped its way toward him, but he wasn't fast enough. He felt the beast's hand clasp around his ankle and pulled him hard back toward it. Twisting in mid-air, Clark brought his left arm up to protect himself from the beast's arm as it swung its fist down toward his skull. The beast's fist crashed into his forearm with bone-crushing force, sending a searing pain shooting up his arm. He gritted his teeth against the agony, refusing to let it slow him down. With a surge of adrenaline, he pushed through the pain and struck back with all his might. Using his right hand, he jabbed the knife toward the beast's face, aiming for its eyes. The creature recoiled, its roar turning into a guttural growl of pain and fury. Another shot rang out as a bullet pierced the beast's left side. The beast howled in pain once more. Clark knew that was his chance. As the beast grabbed hold of him and prepared to swing him down violently into the ground, he lunged forward and let out another guttural roar as he drove his knife down hard into the beast's neck. The beast let out a deafening howl and staggered backward, dropping Clark in the process.

Clark wasted no time. With every ounce of strength he had left, he scrambled to his feet and sprinted toward Lewis, who was struggling to rise from the ground. Without hesitation, he grabbed his friend by the arm and pulled him away from the injured creature. As they stumbled away, he cast a quick glance over his shoulder. The beast was staggering, blood pouring from its wounds, but it still glared at them with primal fury. Clark had to pause a moment to take in the look of rage emanating from the creature. He had never seen anything like it before in any living thing. He understood now that the beast would never stop hunting them; would never allow them to leave its domain. It would follow them to the edge of the known world and back, searching for and seeking its revenge upon them. It was a primal, unrelenting rage that would not cease until they were dead. He thought back to the beast's village and the funeral ceremony the creatures seemed to have been conducting. He now understood these things weren't just animals or creatures with no sense of purpose to their lives. They were intelligent creatures capable of feeling emotions like love and hate, and revenge. That was what Clark now saw in the creature's eyes as it started racing toward them once more. He was certain now that only one being would be leaving the grassy meadow.

The beast grabbed a hole of two large rocks as it charged toward them. It quickly hurled one toward Clark, forcing him to drop Lewis and tumble hard onto the ground. The beast hurled the second rock, which struck Lewis in the side. Lewis screamed in pain as he collapsed onto the ground, clutching his injured side. Clark's mind continued to race as he watched the beast closing in. He knew he had to act fast before the creature reached them. Ignoring the searing pain in his own body, he lunged toward the injured Lewis and pulled him behind the nearest cover—a fallen tree trunk. The beast's roars echoed through the meadow as it ran. It was now less than twenty yards from them.

"Stay here," he said to Lewis as he stood. "I'll draw its attention."

"No, Will, you'll never make it—"

"You have to trust me, Meri."

Lewis sighed and with a grim nod watched as Clark darted back out from behind the log. He waved his arms wildly at the charging beast, trying to gain its attention. The beast roared with fury as it weaved its way through the meadow, its eyes fixed on Clark. As it drew to within a few feet of him, he braced himself, readying for the inevitable clash. The beast roared and lunged at him, its massive hands outstretched to scoop him up in a violent embrace. Clark let out a guttural roar of his own and leapt forward. As he did, he pulled his right arm around in a wide arc, bringing the rock he had clutched in his hand down hard into the beast's wounded shoulder. The creature howled as the rock contacted its flesh, but it was still able to grab ahold of him and throw him down hard into the ground. He winced in pain as the creature rubbed furiously at its shoulder, as if trying to rub away the searing pain it now felt. Clark, sensing an opportunity, hurled himself upwards and grabbed ahold of the creature. The creature roared and tried to grab hold of him to swing him off, but as its hands latched onto his neck, he reached his hand forward and grabbed the knife that was still lodged in the creature's neck. He pulled hard and extracted the blade from the flesh. With a loud yell, he began raining down a barrage of strikes upon the creature, each blow fueled by determination and desperation. The beast stumbled backward, its massive form swaying as it struggled to maintain its balance under the relentless assault. Clark's heart pounded in his chest as he fought with all his might, every muscle in his body straining against the weight of the beast. With a final surge of strength, he delivered one final thrust of his knife into the beast's chest, its tough skin giving way beneath the sharp, bloody blade. The beast staggered back and finally collapsed to the ground in a heap. Gasping for air, Clark stood over the fallen creature and watched as it took its final breaths, the last flicker of rage dwindling from its yellow eyes. A sense of relief washed over him as he dropped to the ground, his eyes still lingering on the lifeless form of the beast in front of him. It was over. Nature had thrown her fiercest, most violent predator at him. And he had won.

NICHOLAS KANE

FIFTY-FOUR

The late summer sun cast a warm glow over the Hidatsa village, its lodges bustling with activity as members of the tribe went about their daily routines. Smoke rose lazily from cooking fires, mingling with the scent of wildflowers that carpeted the nearby meadows. The sound of laughter and conversation filled the air as children played games in the dusty lanes between the lodges, their voices echoing off the wooden walls. Near the edge of the village, members of the Corps of Discovery had set up a small camp, their tents arranged in neat rows along the riverbank. Some men were busy tending their horses, while others engaged in lively trade with the Hidatsa, exchanging goods for fresh food and supplies. A few men had wandered down to the river's edge and were tossing a stick into the water for Seaman to fetch. The dog bounded eagerly into the water, his tail wagging furiously as he paddled after the stick each time it was thrown. His tongue lolled out of his mouth in a canine grin as he splashed through the shallows, his brown coat glistening in the sunlight. The men laughed and cheered him on from the riverbank, their voices mingling with the gentle rustle of the breeze through the nearby trees.

Side by side, Lewis and Clark made their way through the village, their eyes scanning the faces of the Hidatsa people. As they approached a cluster of Hidatsa huts, they spotted Sacagawea and Charbonneau standing together, their figures framed against the backdrop of the village. Swaddled in her arms was Pompey, whose eyes were wide with curiosity as he took in the sights and sounds of the bustling village around him.

"Sacagawea," Clark called out, his voice carrying across the distance. The duo turned to face them, their expressions filled with a mixture of joy and sadness at the sight of their companions. "We've come to say farewell."

Charbonneau nodded curtly, his gaze flickering briefly to Pompey in Sacagawea's arms. "It has been an interesting journey," he remarked, his tone lacking any warmth as he turned to walk away. He paused when Sacagawea turned and handed

FRONTIER

Pompey to him. He let out an annoyed sigh as he positioned the infant in his arms. "Don't linger here long, Sacagawea," he grumbled before turning on his heel and striding away. Sacagawea lingered a moment longer, her eyes meeting those of Lewis and Clark. They betrayed a mixture of sadness and affection.

"Thank you," she said softly.

"It is we who should be thanking you," Lewis replied with a grin. "You and your husband have been invaluable to us on this journey. Without your guidance, we might never have made it."

She flashed a brief smile of gratitude before reaching out and embracing the two of them. She held them tightly for a long moment before slowly releasing them. "Safe travels," she whispered, her voice thick with emotion. "May the Great Spirit watch over you on your journey."

She turned to leave, her deerskin dress swaying gently behind her with each step. But suddenly, she stopped, and in a swift motion, turned back around to face them. She reached into a small leather pouch clasped to her belt and retrieved a handful of dry, brittle leaves tinged with a pale green hue. Clark frowned, unsure of what she had in her hand. But finally, he realized it was sagebrush and his lips curled into a broad smile. She approached him and dropped the tiny pale-green leaves into his outstretched hand.

"Just in case," she murmured softly, her voice carrying a weight of unspoken meaning. For the last time, she turned away, her figure slowly disappearing into the shadows of the village. Clark watched her go, a sense of unease settling over him like a heavy shroud. As they turned to leave, he noticed the last rays of sunshine casting long shadows across the village, hinting at the darkness to come. He tightened his grip around the sagebrush, now serving as a tangible reminder of the ominous presence that still lurked somewhere in the wilderness beyond.

FIFTY-FIVE

The narrow streets of St. Louis teemed with life as Clark wandered through the bustling crowd, his boots striking the cobblestones with a rhythmic echo. The pathways wound unevenly between rows of timber and brick buildings, their facades painted in the warm, amber hues of the setting sun. Shadows stretched long across the streets as twilight descended, casting a soft, golden light that bathed the city in a fleeting glow. Vendors at makeshift market stalls shouted their final calls of the day, their voices rising above the clatter of wagon wheels. The scents of roasting meats and freshly baked bread wafted through the air, mingling with the faint tang of wood smoke and the earthy musk of cobblestones still warm from the day's heat. Children darted between adults making their way home, their laughter a brief reprieve from the hum of commerce and conversation.

It had been a month since the Corps of Discovery had returned to St. Louis, their mission complete and their lives irrevocably changed. Yet, as Clark moved through the familiar streets, he felt strangely disconnected. The city, once so vibrant and full of promise, now seemed smaller, its concerns trivial compared to the vast wilderness he had traversed. The monumental discoveries, the towering mountains, and the unyielding rivers they had conquered felt a world away from this place of walls and narrow streets.

A passing wagon jolted him from his thoughts, its iron-rimmed wheels rattling against the stones. He stepped aside, brushing against a man leading a mule laden with sacks of grain. The man tipped his hat in polite acknowledgement, but Clark barely noticed. His gaze drifted upward to the church steeple silhouetted against the fading sky, a stark reminder of how far he had traveled and how different this world seemed now.

He kept his head down as he walked, his footsteps echoing on the uneven cobblestones of Market Street. The stares of the city's residents followed him, their gazes a mixture of curiosity and reverence. He could feel their eyes on him, hear the whispered voices carrying his name and the names of the other men of the

FRONTIER

Corps of Discovery. Since their triumphant return, they had become local legends, their journey immortalized in the awestruck stories shared in taverns and around family tables. But despite the accolades and newfound fame, a deep unease gnawed at him. The memories of their harrowing expedition clung to him like a shadow. The trials they had endured, the vast wilderness they had conquered, and the battles they had fought—both against the elements and the nightmarish beasts—were etched in his mind. The familiar sights of the city no longer offered comfort. Instead, the narrow streets and tightly packed buildings felt stifling. The air, thick with the mingled scents of roasting meat and river mud, seemed stale compared to the crisp mountain winds of the Rockies. He longed for the wide-open plains and the unbridled freedom that had come with venturing beyond the edge of the known world.

Shaking the thoughts from his mind, he glanced up as dusk settled over the city. Shadows stretched across the streets, swallowing the warm glow of the day. His mind drifted to the final days of their journey, and to Cartwright, who had succumbed to sepsis just four days before they reached St. Louis. He pictured the small hillside overlooking the Missouri River where they had laid him to rest, a simple wooden cross marking his grave. He remembered standing there as the first light of dawn spilled across the water, thinking how fitting a resting place it was for a man who had braved the unknown frontier. The image lingered, bittersweet and heavy.

Their return to St. Louis had been met with both relief and melancholy. There was joy in finally coming home, but also a deep sadness in leaving behind the wilderness that had shaped them. Beyond the mountains lay a world of both breathtaking beauty and unimaginable horror. The journey had exacted its toll, carving into them physically and emotionally. He knew it would take years— if ever—for them to fully return from the darkness they had endured.

Within weeks of their return, most of the men had scattered, each seeking to reclaim the lives they had left behind. Some found solace in the familiar embrace of family and friends, while others ventured off into new pursuits, changed forever by the trials they had faced. Few dared to speak of the beasts. The mere thought of those monstrous creatures seemed to carry the risk of summoning them into this fragile, civilized world. For most, silence was a refuge—a way to bury the terror they had faced and the memories they wished to leave behind. The scars on their bodies could be hidden beneath clothing, but the scars on their minds were harder to conceal. They feared not only the haunting memories but also the judgment of those who could never understand. To speak of the beasts was to risk ridicule, to be dismissed as liars or lunatics. What civilized man could believe in creatures that belonged in nightmares?

And so, most chose to forget—or at least to pretend they had. But there were some for whom forgetting was impossible, the horrors too deeply etched into their minds. For them, the wilderness was not just a place they had left behind, it was a shadow that followed them, lingering in every dark corner and quiet moment of their existence.

But for him, there was no forgetting. Each night since their return, sleep had become a battlefield. Despite the comfort of a soft mattress and warm blankets, his mind refused to rest. When sleep did come, it brought nightmares that dragged him back to the forests of the Lemhi Pass. In his dreams, he was lost once more in the wilderness, the guttural howls of the beasts echoing in the recesses of his mind. He could feel the foul stench of rot and decay filling his nostrils, hear the snap of branches as unseen horrors closed in around him. He would awaken drenched in sweat, his heart pounding, his hand instinctively reaching for the pistol by his bedside. Each night brought the same relentless torment, a cycle of fear that stretched into the small hours of the morning. The more he fought to stay awake, the more the memories clawed at him, until finally, long past midnight, exhaustion claimed him. But it was never a true reprieve—only a descent into the terror-filled depths of his mind where the beasts still roamed, waiting for him.

Now, as he walked the streets of St. Louis, the city seemed to blur around him. The world he had returned to felt distant and

FRONTIER

hollow, its concerns trivial compared to the vastness of the wilderness he had left behind. He wondered if he could ever truly return—or if part of him would forever remain lost in those dark, wild forests.

As he rounded a corner, his gaze settled upon the familiar sight of The Buckhorn Tavern, its weathered wooden sign swinging lazily in the evening breeze. Despite the allure of warmth and company within, he hesitated. He knew what he would find inside, or rather, *who* he would find. With a heavy sigh, he steeled himself and crossed the dusty street toward the tavern's front door. A few moments later, he stepped inside, the creaking wood announcing his arrival. The air was thick with the scent of tobacco and the raucous laughter of frontiersmen. His eyes scanned the dimly lit interior, searching for any sign of the man he was looking for amidst the crowd of rugged faces. At a table near the back, he spotted him, his silhouette illuminated by the flickering glow of the oil lamps. Relief washed over him as he made his way toward his long-lost friend. Lewis sat slouched over, his gaze fixed on the half-empty glass of ale before him. As he approached, Clark tried to muster a smile, but his efforts were futile. He stopped beside the table and looked down at his friend and companion with a mixture of sympathy and frustration.

"Meri," he said, announcing his arrival.

Lewis glanced up, his eyes clouded with the haze of alcohol. "Ah, William," he slurred, "my dear friend. What burdens we share and can never relieve ourselves of."

Clark sighed as he pulled out a chair and seated himself opposite Lewis, his concern deepening. He could see the deep lines of exhaustion etched into Lewis's face. "I thought we could share each other's company this evening. I spoke with York earlier, he said I might find you here."

Lewis scoffed and took a sip of his ale.

Undeterred, Clark persisted. "What's wrong?"

A flicker of something akin to amusement crossed Lewis's face, and he raised his glass in a half-hearted toast. "Why, William," he replied with a crooked smile, "I dare say I am doing quite fine now." He took another sip of his ale.

Clark studied his friend's face, recognizing the pain that lurked behind the façade of bravado. He sighed with impatience. "We must finish cataloging our specimens. Those, along with the maps I created during the expedition, will serve as nice presentations to the President in Washington."

Lewis nodded, but said nothing,

"It would be nice if you could assist me. We leave for Washington in a few days."

Still, silence.

Clark slammed his fist on the table, the impact sending Lewis's glass clattering, its contents spilling across the rough-hewn surface. The sharp noise cut through the low hum of the tavern, drawing the attention of every patron. Heads turned, and conversations faltered as the room fell into a tense hush. Lewis's startled eyes darted up to meet Clark's, the sudden outburst breaking through his haze.

The air between them grew heavy, thick with unspoken words. Slowly, Lewis's gaze steadied, meeting Clark's with a mixture of defiance and resignation.

"Meri..." Clark began, his voice carrying through the uneasy quiet of the room. "This path you're on—this self-destruction—it leads nowhere. We have obligations, responsibilities we can't just ignore."

Lewis's jaw clenched, his fists tightening until his knuckles turned white. "And what would you have me do, Will?" he snapped, his voice raw with emotion. "Gallop off to Washington as if nothing's changed? Pretend the horrors we witnessed never happened?" His voice cracked as he let out a bitter laugh, then raised his hand to the barkeep. "Another!" he barked, the word sharp enough to make the man hesitate.

The barkeep glanced nervously at Clark, who shot him a glare before the man reluctantly began pouring another drink. Clark leaned in closer, his frustration and worry etched into every line of his face.

"No, Meri..." Clark said, his voice quieter but no less intense. "I'd never ask you to pretend. We've both seen things that will haunt us forever. But drowning yourself in ale won't change what happened out there. We have a duty to the men who followed us—to Holloway, Chandler, and Cartwright. They deserve to have their stories told—to be remembered."

Lewis's eyes, now clouded with both alcohol and anguish, softened briefly at the mention of their fallen comrades. He slumped further into his seat, his defiance giving way to a deep, bone-weary sorrow. "Do you think I don't know that?" he muttered, his voice barely above a whisper. "Every night when I close my eyes I see their faces. I hear their voices. The beasts…the wilderness…it's all there, waiting for me in the darkness."

Clark reached across the table, placing a firm but gentle hand on Lewis's arm. "And that's why we must keep going. We can't let those memories destroy us."

Lewis stared back at him through tired eyes. For a moment, silence hung thick between them, broken only by the distant sounds of revelry echoing through the tavern. Then, slowly, Lewis's shoulders sagged, the fight draining from him like water from a punctured canteen. "I don't sleep anymore," he whispered hoarsely.

"Nor do I," Clark replied softly. "And when I do, I have these awful night terrors. Even in sleep I cannot escape the memory of those things."

"The way they killed…the way they looked at you with those yellow eyes…" He leaned back in his chair as the barkeep placed a fresh glass of ale in front of him on the table. Clark watched as he snatched it up and began gulping down the brown liquid. When he finished, he took in a deep breath and exhaled slowly. "What will the President think?" When Clark didn't respond immediately, Lewis stared back at him incredulously. "You don't want to tell him, do you?"

Clark sighed, his gaze steady as he met Lewis's troubled expression. "I don't know."

"He's the President, he must be told that those beasts exist. He'll need to deploy the army, notify General Wilkinson."

"And then what?" Clark retorted. "Assuming they even believe us."

Lewis hesitated, his eyes flickering with uncertainty as he considered the question. "I don't know," he admitted quietly, a sense of unease settling over him. "But something must be done. We cannot keep this hidden forever."

Clark's jaw tightened, a flicker of frustration flashing across his features. "If we tell the President—if we alert the army...it could spark a panic. It will ruin any hopes we had of settling the region before the British or the Spanish do. We cannot risk that. But there's also our reputations to consider. Everything we saw—what we had to do—who would believe us?"

"But what happens when more settlers begin journeying to Oregon? What if those beasts attack them and they are unprepared?"

"And what if President Jefferson does send the army west? We would become embroiled in a conflict not only with those things, but the Indian tribes as well—the same tribes we just gave assurances to that the United States means them no harm. And what about the British? You know sending the army west means the nation would have inadequate defenses against any potential British assault from Canada. And then there's the Spanish who will seize Louisiana at the first opportunity. And if the people knew the truth about what lies within the mountains, none will venture west. We must consider the implications of that. If Americans don't occupy those lands, Spain or England will. Our nation will be confined to the eastern half of the continent."

The silence that followed was heavy with unspoken fears, the weight of their shared uncertainty pressing down upon them like a suffocating blanket. For a moment, they sat in silence, grappling with the enormity of the decision that lay before them. Finally, Clark sagged his shoulders in resignation. "I don't have the answers, Meri," he admitted quietly. "But we can't let fear dictate our actions. We have to find a way to live with what we've seen and move forward."

Lewis let out a sigh, his gaze steady as he met Clark's troubled expression. "He'll understand, Will. The President is a wise man. He'll know what to do."

Clark's expression softened slightly. Yet, he still harbored a lingering sense of doubt that gnawed at his gut. "And if he doesn't?"

"Then we'll find a way forward," Lewis replied through slurred words. Clark could tell the brief moment of lucidity he had enjoyed with his friend was coming to an end. He watched as Lewis reached down and gulped down the last of his ale. Another silence settled between them. For a moment, they sat in quiet contemplation, grappling with the enormity of the decision that lay before them. And as they sat in the dimly lit tavern, surrounded by the murmurs of the evening crowd, a sense of uncertainty lingered in Clark's mind. But amidst the doubt, there was a sense of relief in knowing he still had Lewis to confide in. It offered him at least a small morsel of hope that one day his friend would be alright with everything that had happened. And as they exchanged a silent nod of understanding, the weight of his burden seemed just a little lighter, knowing that they would face whatever lay ahead together, come what may.

NICHOLAS KANE

FIFTY-SIX

It was three days before Christmas, and a gentle snowfall blanketed the grounds of the Executive Mansion in Washington, muffling the world in a serene, wintry hush. Outside, the scene was tranquil, as if nature itself had paused to admire the season's quiet beauty. Snow fell softly from the branches of the trees, landing in delicate heaps atop fences and pathways. Lanterns along the walkways flickered faintly, their golden light casting a warm glow against the icy stillness. The faint crunch of boots against packed snow echoed now and then, but otherwise, the world seemed at peace beneath its frosty shroud. Inside, the warmth of the season filled the air, the scent of evergreen boughs mingling with the faint aroma of burning wood from the fireplace. Candles placed in sconces along the walls illuminated the hallways, their soft light dancing over garlands of pine and cedar draped over doorways and windows.

Within the confines of the President's study, Lewis and Clark, dressed in their finest attire, stood beside one another as they faced the President and Secretary of War Henry Dearborn, to relay their report on the expedition. Around them, the room was adorned with simple yet elegant decorations. Evergreen wreaths hung on the walls, each fastened with red ribbons and clusters of holly berries, while garlands of pine and cedar framed the doorways and windows.

President Jefferson sat on a small couch along one side of the room, his tailored velvet suit lending him an air of composed authority. His expression, however, betrayed his unease. His normally animated features were drawn taut as he processed the grim report delivered by the two explorers. Beside him, Dearborn stood quietly doing his best to muffle his shocked expression. As the weight of the report settled upon the room, a heavy silence took hold. The President's usually animated features were drawn tight with concern as his mind grappled with the implications of the expedition's horrendous discovery. Dearborn's shock was palpable, his rigid posture betraying the urgency of his thoughts.

FRONTIER

"Mr. President, we cannot ignore the threat these creatures pose," Dearborn declared, his voice cutting sharply through the heavy silence. "We must mobilize the army at once. If word reaches the public that such...things exist, it will destroy any hope of settling the territory. The fear alone will keep Americans from venturing west, and that will leave the land open to exploitation by the British and Spanish."

Jefferson's gaze shifted to Clark, who stood silently for a moment, his brow furrowed in thought. Finally, he nodded, his voice measured but cautious. "I agree with the Secretary, sir, but we must proceed carefully. Mobilizing the army and moving with force could provoke unintended consequences with the Indian tribes of the region. A hasty response could destabilize an already precarious balance."

Deaborn scoffed, a sneer curling his lips. "Lieutenant," he said, his tone biting, "weren't you the one who described the Sioux as 'the most damned rascals to ever inhabit the earth?'"

Clark's expression darkened, but he gave a reluctant nod, his discomfort evident. Dearborn dismissed him with a wave of his hand. "I care little for the Indians or their alliances. Our priority must be the safety and security of American citizens. If these creatures pose a threat to our people, they must be eradicated swiftly and decisively."

Jefferson remained silent, his expression troubled, his hands clasped tightly in his lap as he considered the arguments. The flicker of the firelight reflected in his eyes, highlighting the lines of worry on his face. Finally, he spoke, his tone calm but resolute. "Gentlemen, I understand the urgency of the situation, but we must consider the broader implications of our actions. Mobilizing the army against these creatures is not a decision to be made lightly, nor is it one I can make unilaterally.

Dearborn's face flushed with frustration. "Mr. President, every moment we delay risks our control over the territory. The Spanish and British will not hesitate to exploit any sign of weakness. If settlers refuse to move west out of fear, we lose not just the land but a strategic advantage over our rivals."

"Henry," Jefferson began in a calming tone, "it is unlikely Great Britain or Spain intends to invade Louisiana tomorrow or next week. The matter requires careful thought, not rash decisions driven by panic."

Dearborn groaned in exasperation, but before he could respond, Clark interjected, his voice steady but conciliatory. "Perhaps and more measured approach would be best, sir. A reconnaissance mission could allow us to gather intelligence and assess the true extent of the threat. That way, we can respond with precision and avoid unnecessary escalation or conflict with the tribes."

Jefferson nodded thoughtfully. "A reconnaissance mission seems prudent. We need to know what we are up against before we commit our forces."

This seemed to perk Deaborn up. He straightened, a renewed interest in his eyes. "I can notify the governors of Kentucky, Ohio, and Tennessee to begin raising their militias," he announced with bravado, seemingly ignoring Jefferson's statement. "I will order General Wilkinson to march his men north from New Orleans to St. Louis. The army can be staged there and move north into the Rockies by spring." He peered back over at Lewis and Clark. "Captain Lewis, you will be given command of five hundred men. I want you to scour the mountains for those things and kill every last one of them."

"Sir," Clark shot back, "you cannot simply invade Louisiana with a thousand men. The region is dangerous enough without having to move a large army through it. And the presence of such a large force will only antagonize the Sioux and the Shoshone." He let out a sigh and glanced toward Jefferson. "This situation calls for a more precise and deliberate approach than simply sending a bunch of untrained men into the wilderness."

"You believe one thousand army regulars are not capable of killing off a few hundred giant apes, Lieutenant?" Deaborn snapped back.

"We cannot know for sure how many of those things are out there. But I can tell you they fight with a savagery I have never witnessed before nor wish to again. You cannot simply treat them as mere animals. They have an intelligence to them, we saw it. And you will be fighting in *their* territory."

"Forgive me, Lieutenant, but I am confident my army commanders will deal with those creatures quickly and decisively and have them cleared out of the mountains by the end of the year." He turned to Jefferson, his expression resolute. "Sir, with your permission, I will make the necessary arrangements to deal with this...problem."

Jefferson let out a long sigh as he ran his fingers through his graying hair. "Henry, I understand your urgency, but I am not quite ready to dispatch the nation's army at this juncture. Besides, what excuse would I give the Federalists in Congress? Am I to tell them I wish to raise an army of over a thousand men supplemented by the militia of the western states so I can send them west for reasons I am not willing or unable to share? They would label me a despot and overthrow me on the spot." He gestured toward Clark. "Lieutenant Clark is correct. This problem requires a more delicate solution."

Dearborn's jaw tightened with frustration, but he nodded reluctantly in deference to the President's words. "Of course, Mr. President," he replied in a strained voice.

Jefferson's eyes settled on Lewis. "Captain, you've been awfully quiet during this discourse. Tell me, what are your thoughts on the matter?"

Lewis, who had been standing quietly by Clark's side, stepped forward. He glanced at Clark briefly, as if unsure of what to say. After a pause, he turned back toward Jefferson. "Mr. President, I recommend we send a small, well-armed party back to the region to observe and report on these creatures. This will allow us to devise a strategy based on solid information rather than speculation." Dearborn's eyes narrowed, but he said nothing. Jefferson opened his mouth to speak, but Lewis cut him off.

"And I believe we should warn the people, sir."

The room fell silent. Clark turned to stare at Lewis, his brow furrowed in surprise. But Lewis kept his gaze fixed ahead, his posture steady despite the ripple of tension his words had caused.

"You want to disclose what you encountered on your journey to the public, Captain?" Jefferson asked, his tone cautious, his eyebrows raised in disbelief.

"Yes, sir. It is their right to know. The existence of these creatures is too dangerous to be kept secret."

Jefferson's expression darkened, his concern evident as he leaned back, steepling his fingers. "Do you understand what you're suggesting, Captain?" he asked carefully. "Revealing this information would incite panic. Westward expansion would grind to a halt, crippling the nation's economy. I did not authorize the purchase of Louisiana for fifteen million dollars just to see it lie barren and unoccupied."

"I understand, sir. But secrecy carries its own risks. If settlers venture west without knowing what they might face, we'll be sending them into peril blindly. That would be a betrayal of the trust they place in us as their leaders. They deserve the truth."

Before Jefferson could respond, Dearborn interjected, his tone sharp and dismissive. "And what then, Captain? Should we arm every farmer and settler with muskets and expect them to hold the frontier against beasts they can scarcely comprehend?"

Lewis turned toward Deaborn with an unwavering gaze. "I think the people are stronger than you give them credit for, Mr. Secretary. They've braved the wilderness before, and they'll do it again. But they need to be prepared—armed with knowledge as much as weapons."

Jefferson raised a hand, silencing the exchange. His voice, though calm, carried the weight of finality. "Captain Lewis, your loyalty to the people is commendable, but your reasoning is flawed. Panic and fear would do far more damage to this nation than the creatures themselves. If word of their existence spreads, it won't just be settlers fleeing—it will be investors pulling out, supply lines disrupted, and foreign rivals seizing the opportunity to settle the region themselves. Do you understand the implications?"

Lewis's jaw tightened, his frustration evident. "And what of the dead men, sir?"

"What of them, Captain?"

"Elias Winchester, Samuel Treadway," Lewis began, his voice hardening as he listed the names. "Alexander Willard, John Colter, Benjamin Holloway, Ambrose Cartwright. Men who followed us—who trusted us—and who gave their lives to this expedition. Do their sacrifices mean nothing?"

Jefferson's gaze did not waver. "Their sacrifices mean everything, Captain. That is precisely why we must ensure their deaths were not in vain. If we allow fear to consume the nation, if we allow settlers to abandon their westward ambitions, then those men will have died for nothing. I will not let that happen." He paused, his voice softening slightly but retaining its authoritative tone. "This nation is in its infancy, Captain. Its strength lies in the promise of its future. The Louisiana Territory represents that promise. If we lose the trust of the people—if we stoke fear instead of confidence, then the foundations we've built will crumble. That is a risk we cannot afford."

Lewis's hands clenched into fists at his sides. "And what about the risks we're taking by staying silent? More men will die, Mr. President. Settlers will wander into those territories blind to the dangers. How will we justify their deaths?"

Jefferson's expression tightened. "We justify it by ensuring that when settlers do move west, they do so with strength, with numbers, and with the knowledge that their government stands behind them."

Lewis opened his mouth to retort, but Jefferson raised a hand, cutting him off. "This is not up for debate. You will not speak of these creatures to anyone outside this room. This matter remains classified until I determine the appropriate course of action. Am I clear?"

Lewis stood rigid, his jaw tightening as he struggled with the command. His eyes darted briefly to Clark, who met his gaze with quiet concern. Finally, with visible reluctance, Lewis gave a short nod. "Yes, sir," he said, his voice barely above a whisper.

"Good," Jefferson said, rising from the couch with deliberate calm. "Gentlemen, you have done your nation a great service. The information you have gathered from the western lands over these last several years will undoubtedly prove invaluable." He frowned, pausing briefly to glance at Dearborn. "The sacrifice of your men will not be forgotten, Captain. But the narrative must be managed carefully."

Lewis shook his head in frustration. "You would not even mention the names of the men we lost."

"It is important to prevent the spread of panic, Captain," Dearborn interjected, his tone curt and dismissive.

Lewis tried to restrain his fury. "So, we lie?" he shot back, his voice beginning to rise once more. "We hide the truth for the sake of *convenience?*"

"It's not a lie, Captain," Jefferson responded, his hand raised. "It's a strategic omission. The truth is a powerful weapon, yes—but it is also a source of fear and chaos if wielded recklessly. Our goal is to secure this nation's future, not to jeopardize it by inciting panic."

Lewis let out a bitter laugh, his shoulders trembling with frustration. "Strategic omission," he muttered, shaking his head. "That's what we call it now?"

Clark, standing beside him, placed a steadying hand on his shoulder. "Meri," he said quietly, his voice imploring. "Let's trust the President's judgment on this. He's thinking of the bigger picture."

Lewis's gaze darted to Clark, his anger softening for a brief moment, replaced by a flash of hurt. He exhaled sharply, his shoulders sagging under the weight of his frustration. Finally, he looked back at Jefferson, his voice quiet but no less intense. "Very well, Mr. President."

Jefferson nodded. "Good," he said, motioning toward the study door. "And now, we must celebrate your successful journey. The nation awaits eagerly to hear tales from your adventures on the frontier." He stepped toward the door, followed closely by Dearborn, who threw a quick, disdainful glance in Lewis's direction. From the next room, the low hum of conversation drifted through—polite laughter, murmured voices—as Washington's elite, along with members of Congress, began to arrive at the mansion to bask in the glow of the expedition's success.

Clark turned toward Lewis, his eyes searching his friend's face. "Meri—"

But Lewis had already turned away, his expression a mask of simmering anger and resignation. He moved toward the door without a word, his shoulders rigid. Clark stepped forward, intending to stop him, but his path was immediately blocked by Dearborn.

"I plan to raise an army to combat those beasts, Lieutenant," he said in a hushed tone while placing his large hand on Clark's chest. "And I'll need you and Captain Lewis on my side." He paused as his eyes darted toward Jefferson in the next room. "The President intends to name you Superintendent of Indian Affairs for Louisiana Territory, as well as a brigadier general in the militia. He also intends to appoint Captain Lewis as Governor of the territory. When that happens, I will send word. Can I count on you, Lieutenant?"

Clark hesitated, a shadow of doubt crossing his face as he weighed the implications of Dearborn's statement. His sense of duty warred with his reservations about the proper measures to take toward the beasts. But he knew in his current situation, with the Secretary of War cornering him demanding his support, there was little he could do. He sighed softly. "I still have my concerns, sir," he admitted, his voice betraying the sense of uncertainty he still felt. "But I will do whatever the President requires of me." Dearborn scoffed and moved past him without another word. Clark took one last look around the room before turning and continuing into the next room where the President's guests awaited. As he walked, he felt the weight of the future pressing down on him. He knew future missions would carry with them the fate of not only the West, but the nation as well. He thought of Dearborn's message—that the President intended to name him Superintendent of Indian Affairs in Louisiana Territory. He would certainly take the position if asked to, but he worried what actions such a position would require on his part. Would Dearborn truly raise an army to invade the Rocky Mountains and exterminate the beasts? Would he task him and Lewis with leading that army? He felt torn about what to do. He wanted to do his duty, but he also feared what doing his duty might cost him. He paused as he reached the doorway to the study. Was it fear he felt? Fear of possibly wading back into the vast unknown frontier? He cursed himself for allowing such emotions to enter his mind. He had never feared anything before and thought nothing could ever make him reluctant to return to the frontier. Yet, here he was, standing within the President's Mansion in Washington worried that he might be asked to go to war with the beasts he had only narrowly escaped. Was he truly prepared to confront them once more? The very thought sent shivers down his spine. He thought of the President's words from earlier: *We must accept the impossible.* Was that what he would have to do now? Accept whatever fate the President thrust upon him in the coming months and years? He had grappled with worse things before, far worse things. But he knew one thing for sure—he would mind where he walked the next time he found himself traversing the periphery of civilization—the next time he grazed the edge of man's knowledge of the natural world around him. Because, when one ventures too far off the beaten part, they find themselves in unknown territory—in *their* territory. For in the heart of the wilderness, amidst the untamed landscapes and primal forces, lay a mirror reflecting the essence of humanity itself. It was a realm where the boundaries between civilization and savagery blurred—where the primal instincts that dwelled within Man emerged from the shadows. It was a confrontation with the fundamental questions of existence, of life and death, of order…and chaos.

For the rest of his life, he would catch himself, from time to time, looking beyond the trees, into the empty expanse of shadows beyond, always wondering what was looking back at him from within the darkness.

FRONTIER

EPILOGUE

August 1883
Yellowstone National Park, Wyoming

The mid-afternoon sun cast elongated shadows across the rugged landscape of Yellowstone National Park as President Chester A. Arthur and Secretary of the Interior Henry M. Teller stood atop a large rocky outcrop overlooking a vast valley. Arthur, a distinguished man in his early fifties, cut a striking figure against the backdrop of the bright blue sky. His tailored overcoat, adorned with gold buttons, complemented the crisp, mountain air that swirled around the two men. Well-groomed mutton chops framed his face, their graying edges highlighting the wisdom in his sharp, intelligent eyes. His hair, meticulously styled and streaked with silver, lent him an air of dignified authority. In one hand, he held a finely crafted cane—more an accessory than a necessity—and in the other, a cigar, its smoke curling lazily into the air.

Below them, the sprawling expanse of Yellowstone stretched out in all its glory, a pristine wilderness untouched by the hand of man. Towering peaks loomed in the distance, their snow-capped summits glistening in the sunlight, while verdant forests carpeted the valley below. It was a scene of unparalleled beauty and a testament to the raw power and majesty of nature.

To the west, the sun cast a warm, golden glow over the towering geysers that intermittently shot steam and boiling water into the sky, creating a mesmerizing dance of nature's raw power. The Yellowstone River meandered gracefully through the landscape, its waters glistening like liquid silver under the afternoon light. In the distance, the rugged peaks of the Rocky Mountains loomed, their snow-capped summits standing in stark contrast to the green forests and grassy meadows below.

Beside Arthur, Teller stood quietly, taking in the view of the valley below. A broad-brimmed straw hat shielded his face, its brim catching the light of the sinking sun. Like Arthur, he too grasped a cigar in one hand which he occasionally brought to his lips, exhaling plumes of smoke that blended with the mountain air.

"Yellowstone is truly a marvel," Arthur mused, his voice carrying a note of awe. "It's no wonder we have to preserve it."

"Indeed, Mr. President," Teller replied, his voice reflecting a similar sense of wonder. He took another puff of his cigar, the smoke curling lazily above him as he fixed his gaze on a herd of buffalo grazing peacefully in the distance. "But as you're aware, sir, the real reason behind these parks extends beyond preserving natural beauty."

Arthur sighed, knowing all too well what Teller was alluding to. The mysterious beasts that stalked the wilderness of the Rockies and the Pacific Northwest had long been a quiet concern for American presidents, tracing back to the days of Thomas Jefferson. Their existence, whispered about in the reports of explorers and traders, was often dismissed as folklore or the delusions of frightened men. As the years passed and more settlers pushed westward, these encounters grew more frequent—and far more deadly. For a time, the remote and untamed expanses of the frontier served as a natural shield, relegating these encounters to the fringes of credibility. Reports of monstrous creatures lurking within the forests of Oregon, Utah, and Montana Territory were buried beneath tales of Indian skirmishes, treacherous mountain passes, and harsh winters. To the public, they were nothing more than the fabrications of drunkards or the embellishments of wild-eyed frontiersmen. But even the vast wilderness could not keep such secrets forever. As the settlements expanded and trails carved deeper into the wilderness, the isolation that had hidden the creatures began to erode. Wagon trains vanished without a trace and hunters and trappers disappeared, leaving only signs of violent struggles behind. Survivors spoke in hushed tones of shadowy figures lurking in the trees and of guttural howls that echoed in the dead of night. And they spoke of eyes—glowing and predatory—watching from the darkness.

The growing number of such stories alarmed officials, who recognized the threat the creatures posed to westward expansion and the fragile stability of the frontier. By the 1870s, those concerns had reached the desk of President Ulysses S. Grant. Quietly, Grant had acted. While the public was told that the creation of large parks and forest preserves across the western territories was to preserve the nation's natural beauty, the true purpose was far more calculated. These protected lands were placed under federal control not only to preserve wilderness but to monitor and contain the mysterious creatures that stalked the frontier. Within these remote, federally managed regions, rangers and soldiers alike were tasked with keeping a watchful eye. Official reports spoke only of wildlife management and land conservation, but among those who patrolled these vast tracts of land, the truth was whispered: these parks were as much prisons as they were preserves. The creatures that had haunted the dreams of settlers now had boundaries, but the question loomed—how long could they truly be contained?

"Nawabitsi Skanopi," Arthur muttered, almost to himself, remembering the name given to the creatures by the Shoshone. "Do you think they'll ever truly be controlled?"

Teller took a long draw from his cigar. "We can only hope to manage their numbers and keep them isolated. The army killed most of them off years ago. What's left of their numbers have been driven west into Washington Territory and Oregon, but there are a few still lingering within the Lemhi Pass and even portions of Montana Territory. But the army will have those beasts relocated here to the park soon enough. I heard Congress is already preparing legislation for three additional parks in Washington Territory and Oregon. God willing, we can herd those things onto those parks by the end of the decade and be done with them."

"Done with them?" Arthur grinned. "I doubt this problem will ever truly be solved. Even if we confine them to parks, we cannot completely avoid their interactions with our people. But we can, at the very least, minimize the risks and provide a semblance of safety for those who venture into the wilderness." He paused, his gaze drifting over the serene landscape. "And who knows, perhaps one day, these creatures will become nothing more than legends only spoken of around campfires in hushed tones."

Teller nodded. "Very few believe the stories of their existence anyways. We can be grateful for that."

Arthur's face hardened. "We must keep it that way."

Teller nodded in silent agreement as he took another puff from his cigar. As the sun dipped lower on the horizon, the two men knew their brief respite from the day's activities was coming to an end, but neither man was quite ready to depart. Arthur watched as an eagle soared gracefully overhead, its wings outstretched against the purple evening sky. He stood in quiet reflection, knowing his actions would shape the future of the American West and the legacy of those mysterious creatures that roamed its wild expanses. Finally, he let out a restless sigh and motioned for Teller to follow him back down the rocky outcrop toward their cabin where an evening meal of baked salmon and smoked elk awaited them. Despite his lingering doubts, he held onto a glimmer of hope for the future. He knew that the legacy of the West would endure, shaped by the courage and determination of those who dared venture into its uncharted territories. And though the beasts would remain a constant threat, he remained steadfast in his belief that one day, the wilderness would be a place of beauty and wonder, untainted by the shadows of fear. As the evening twilight enveloped him and the stars began to twinkle overhead, he found solace in the quietude of the night. Surrounded by the rugged beauty of Yellowstone, he knew that the spirit of the West would endure, unbroken and unconquered.

In the distance, a howl echoed out into the evening twilight. Arthur stopped and gazed out in the direction of the howl. He wondered what creature had made it. Perhaps, it was just a wolf or some other predator in the night calling out to its kind. But within the deep recesses of his mind, he knew better. And as he approached his cabin with its warm, welcoming fire glowing in the fireplace, he had never been so relieved to escape the encroaching darkness of the night.